Natalie Normann grew up in a small shipping town in Norway. She wanted to be a writer as soon as she realised that books were written by real people. She is a prolific short story and serial writer, and has written romance stories for women's magazines for years.

Since 2007 she has written historical romance series in Norwegian and recently published her 56th book.

Summer Island is her first book in English.

Growing up she lived in a hotel for two years, sailed to Jamaica on banana boats with her captain father and lived for three years in Spain surrounded by almond and orange trees in the garden.

Natalie took typewriting in high school, so she could write faster, and later got a degree in history and literature. Like many Norwegian writers she worked as a translator while writing. She published her first short story in 1994 and first novel in 1995 – and never looked back.

In her free time, Natalie enjoys avoiding winter and trying to bake the perfect bread.

Also by Natalie Normann

Christmas Island

Summer Island

Natalie Normann

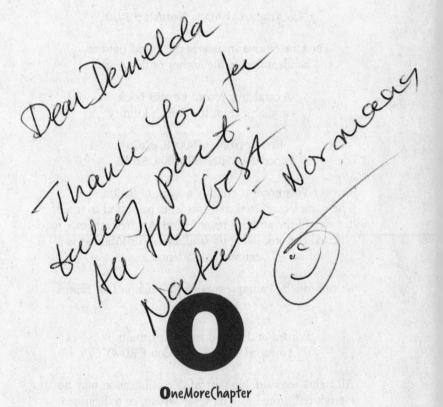

Dear Demelda
Thank you for
takes part.
All the best
Natalie Normann

O

OneMoreChapter

One More Chapter
a division of HarperCollins*Publishers*
The News Building
1 London Bridge Street
London SE1 9GF

www.harpercollins.co.uk

This paperback edition 2020

First published in Great Britain in ebook format by
HarperCollins*Publishers* 2020

Copyright © Natalie Normann 2020

Natalie Normann asserts the moral right to
be identified as the author of this work

A catalogue record for this book
is available from the British Library

Ebook ISBN: 9780008362676
Paperback ISBN: 9780008362683

This novel is entirely a work of fiction.
The names, characters and incidents portrayed in it are
the work of the author's imagination. Any resemblance to
actual persons, living or dead, events or localities is
entirely coincidental.

Set in Birka by Palimpsest Book Production Ltd, Falkirk
Stirlingshire

Printed and bound in Great Britain by
CPI Group (UK) Ltd, Croydon CR0 4YY

All rights reserved. No part of this publication may be
reproduced, stored in a retrieval system, or transmitted,
in any form or by any means, electronic, mechanical,
photocopying, recording or otherwise, without the prior
permission of the publishers.

For Maria — for always having my back and for telling me sternly to get in the coffee line

Chapter 1

'Karl, stop it. I don't want to hear it. You're such a liar.'

The wind swooshed past Ninni's ears as the bike crossed the Puddefjord Bridge and entered Bergen, making it hard to hear him through the earphones. Next to the bike, Frikk panted and grinned, having no problem keeping up the pace.

'I know the truth now, you bastard.'

The wind eased as Ninni lowered the speed through the narrow streets. Karl kept talking and the more he said, the angrier she got. She approached the roundabout leading to the bus station and slowed down even more.

'Shut up, shut up, shut up,' she finally yelled. 'You have been lying to me for two years, and you're still lying to me. Now, go to hell and have a miserable life.'

Ninni clicked off the phone and slowed down to manage the turn. She didn't even feel a bit relieved after yelling at Karl. The whole morning had been a nightmare. All she wanted to do was escape to the island, her only safe haven.

When the phone rang again she decided to ignore it and pulled at the earphones. Turning into the roundabout, she didn't pay attention for a second.

The screeching from car brakes and Frikk suddenly barking woke her up.

Ninni lost control of the bike. She tried to avoid hitting Frikk and fell headfirst into the flowerbed in the middle of the roundabout.

For a moment she was so stunned she couldn't breathe. Frikk put his wet nose on her face and she felt a rush of relief.

She sat up and shook her head. Before checking herself, she ran her hands over the dog to make sure he was okay. He licked her face. The wagging tail showed her everything was fine.

'Good boy, Frikk,' she muttered.

The car stood partly on the pavement, with the motor running. There was damage in the front where it had hit a fence on the other side of the road.

The driver didn't come out of the car. She could see the airbag hadn't deployed. Was he hurt?

Ninni tried to get up but her knee hurt, as did her elbow.

She finally managed to get on her feet and limped over to the car. She knocked on the window.

'*Er du skadet?*' she asked in Norwegian.

She fumbled with the earphones, pulling them out, while she knocked again. Perhaps he needed an ambulance. She could barely see him through the tinted windows.

Finally the door opened and the driver stepped out. He had a look of stunned horror on his face.

'*Er du skadet?*' Ninni tried to see if he had any injuries but, lucky for him, he looked fine.

'Sorry, I don't understand,' he said, looking confused and dazed.

Ninni repeated the question in English.

'What? No, I'm not hurt. That's what seat belts are for. What about you?'

'I'm fine.' Ninni looked properly at him for the first time.

He was driving a shiny car and wearing a fancy suit. No wonder he thought the road belonged to him. Idiot, she thought, relieved now.

He looked down and discovered Frikk, who bared his teeth for a second. 'Is the dog okay?'

'He's unharmed, and no thanks to your driving,' she said.

The driver looked surprised. 'This wasn't on me. Are you insane, coming into the road like that?'

Ninni's anger flared up. 'Are *you* insane? You could have killed us! Damned idiot,' she added for emphasis. She held onto Frikk. He didn't look terrifying, but his bite was sharp.

The driver pointed at the bike. 'You came flying out of nowhere. Why on earth would you ride across a roundabout like that?'

'I did not come flying out of nowhere. I was following basic traffic rules, which you clearly haven't mastered. Oh, and if you haven't already noticed, you were driving the wrong way through the roundabout!' Ninni waved her hand in his face. 'You shouldn't be allowed in a car.'

That shut him up. He turned around and looked at the road with a deep frown.

She knew all about his type. Driving a powerful car, blasting music and not caring about anyone but himself.

Frikk was right beside her, staring at the stranger with his ears perked. A quick look in her backpack and she breathed a sigh of relief when she saw the computer wasn't damaged.

Ninni then picked up the bike and examined it. Everything worked. She scowled at the driver again.

'You're lucky there's no damage. This is an antique bike.'

'I didn't see you,' he said again.

'And that's why you shouldn't drive,' Ninni said.

'Listen, I'm sorry. Are you sure you're all right?'

'You are really lucky,' she said when she limped back to the bike. 'If you had hurt my dog I would have reported you to the police in a second.'

'You're limping.' He finally looked worried.

'It's just a scratch. I'll live. But you should return that

car to the rental company and walk to wherever you are going.' She refused to show him that it hurt. 'Idiot,' she said again.

'I'm sorry,' he said.

'You should be. Learn to drive on the right side of the road and the correct way through a roundabout!' she said.

Ninni pushed the bike across the street and locked it in the stand by the entrance to Bystasjonen, the main bus terminal. Her father would pick it up later and take it to the bookshop. It would be safe there.

She looked across the street. The driver was standing next to the car, talking on his mobile. Should she have offered to help him contact the car rental company? She thought about it, then decided no. He was unhurt and more than capable of handling it on his own.

The bus that would take her and Frikk south along the coast already waited outside the station. Cigarette smoke wafted towards them. Ninni spotted the driver, leaning against the side of the bus. He frowned at Frikk, who was shaking himself.

'He's filthy,' he said, shielding the cigarette with his other hand. 'And so are you. What did you do? Roll in the mud before you got here?'

Ninni touched Frikk's head. 'I have a ticket for him. He'll be no bother.'

The driver shrugged. 'You're the only passengers. Hop in.'

5

Ninni found a seat for them at the back. Frikk crawled under the seat and promptly fell asleep. The trip to Haugesund, the only place where they could take the ferry to the island, would take at least three hours, more if the roads were busy.

Ninni rubbed her eyes and leaned back. As soon as the bus left the station, she fell asleep and dreamed of Karl.

It was midday when they finally arrived on the island. Ninni grabbed the end of a hawser from the deckhand and jumped down onto the pier. She fastened the thick rope like an expert and grinned at the man.

'You're putting me out of work,' he said.

'Just protecting my island from pirates,' she said, laughing at him now.

'Have a good stay,' the deckhand said.

'Thank you. I will.'

Ninni looked around, breathing in the cool, fresh air. The rain had stopped on the way over and the skies parted to let in a bit of sun.

This was the best place on earth. Her grandparents' old house was the safe harbour she always returned to. The only place to nurse a broken heart.

In a few weeks the small harbour would teem with boats of all sorts, from sailing boats and fancy yachts to fishing boats and rowing boats. Now the only other boat moored at the pier was a rickety old wooden rowing boat.

Ninni released Frikk from the lead. He shook himself again, sending droplets of water all over her. That was what happened after spending an hour outside on the deck. She had no patience for sitting in the salon. She needed to be outside, to scream against the wind.

Frikk looked at her and whined.

Ninni grinned. 'Run along then, you silly dog. Tell Alma I'm coming.'

Frikk shot off like a cannonball.

Ninni followed at a slower pace. The island corner shop, the *landhandel*, was located a short walk up from the pier. The house was small and white, as were most of the houses on the island.

Frikk burst inside the open door and a few seconds later Alma came out, scolding him and petting him at the same time. She smiled when she spotted Ninni.

'You're early this year. I thought you would celebrate 17th of May with your dad,' she said when Ninni approached her.

She opened her arms and Ninni walked into the hug. 'I just needed to get away,' she said.

'It's lovely to see you, my sweet.' Alma let her go. 'Is your dad coming too?'

'He's busy with the bookshop, as always. And he has his duties tomorrow.' Her father played trombone in one of the marching bands and always joined the parade on 17th of May.

Alma was tall and wiry, and looked a lot younger than her seventy-six years. 'I know, I know. He's married to his books, isn't he?'

'I'm afraid so,' Ninni said.

'Well, we'd love to see more of him. I remember when he was a schoolboy and used to steal toffees from the jars. Little rascal. So adorable in his dungarees and wellingtons.'

Ninni thought of her tall, burly father and smiled. 'I'll be sure to tell him exactly that.'

Alma pulled her into the shop. It smelled of fresh coffee and pastry. 'I wasn't expecting you until June. Any particular reason?'

'No, not really. I've just been working really hard for the last few weeks and I felt like a change. You know, I've had lots of translation work lately, deadlines and such,' Ninni said, hoping she sounded normal.

'You look pale and thin.' Alma tilted Ninni's chin towards her and looked her in the eyes. 'Man trouble?'

Ninni snorted. 'You should be a detective.'

'So it's a man. I can't tell you how pleased I am that I don't have to worry about that any more. You want to talk about it?' Alma let go of Ninni's flushed face.

'No, thank you. It's over and done with.'

Alma filled a mug of coffee from an old filter machine in the corner and put it in front of Ninni. 'Here. I'll bring you something to go with that.'

Ninni lifted the mug and sipped from it. 'You make the best coffee,' she said, avoiding any more discussion on the topic. She didn't even want to think about Karl.

'Here, eat something. You look like you haven't eaten in days.' Alma put a plate in front of her.

Ninni looked at the bun. Sticky coconut icing and a yellow custard centre covering a golden wheat bun. It smelled of home and everything cosy. 'My favourite. Thank you.'

Alma didn't ask any further questions. She understood. 'Fresh from the oven this morning. We have been baking for the last three days to be ready for tomorrow. Do you need any groceries?'

Ninni hesitated, but Alma lifted her eyebrows. 'I bet there's no food in the house. Neither you nor your dad have been here since Agnar's funeral in January. I'm guessing the only things to eat in the house are stale Christmas biscuits and perhaps a marzipan pig or two.'

'I can guarantee you there are absolutely no sweets. I made sure of that. For now, I just need the basics, fresh food to last me a few days while I settle in.'

While Ninni was enjoying the pastry, Alma went quickly round the shop, filling a basket with the essentials.

'Do you need any shampoo, stuff like that?' she called out from behind one of the aisles.

'No, just bread and milk, butter and cheese. And some apples. Everything else is there. You know Pappa, he fills up the house like the Russians are invading or something. Loads of fish and meat in the freezer and plenty of canned and dry food in the pantry.'

Alma set down two heavy carrier bags on the floor next to the door. 'I'll put it on your dad's bill.'

'Sure,' Ninni said. She'd pay him back. 'Has anything new happened this winter?'

'Not much. Sigrid and Olav's barn finally fell over in one of the storms. It's been rotting away for years, so it was a matter of time. They are planning to rebuild it. God knows how those hippies plan to pay for it. Do you know Sigrid told me that she's determined to clean all their clothes in the stream and not in a washing machine, because it's too modern?'

'Sounds exhausting,' Ninni said.

'God, when I think back to how we used to boil clothes with that ugly pine soap until the skin on our hands cracked. I cried with happiness the first time I got a washing machine in my house. They are weird.'

The hippies owned a smallholding on the south side of the island, where they grew organic food to sell in town.

'Then there's a new problem with Agnar's farm,' Alma continued. 'Turns out he had a will.'

'A will? I didn't know he had any relatives.' Ninni was curious. Agnar had been their only neighbour on the north side of the island.

'Nobody knows who's in the will except the lawyers

Agnar used to set it up. They're not talking to us, only to say they are looking for relatives. Which is a lot of malarkey. Agnar didn't have any family left. I told them that but they still need to earn their fees, of course. Leeches, the lot of them.'

Agnar was the cranky farmer who had died just after the New Year. He'd also been the largest landowner on the island. He'd owned the ground that most of their houses were built on.

'I knew he wasn't well,' Alma said, shaking her head. 'He refused any help. He just became more and more of a recluse. I tried to get him to see a doctor. He looked so frail towards the end. But you know how they are, these men, stubborn as mules and half as good-looking.'

'I remember him being so sweet to me when I was little, before he started isolating himself. I thought he was related to you?'

'No, not at all. We moved here after the war when I was four years old. Agnar was born in 1952 and such a surprise to his parents.' Alma laughed a little. 'I think they had given up hope of getting any children by then. And what makes it so sad is that Agnar was the last one in his family. We all wonder what will happen to the farm and the land when those lawyers give up this futile search for a relative. That bastard Haldorsen called in just a few days after the funeral, wanted us to support him in buying Agnar's land. He thinks he can just waltz in and get his dirty hands on our island.'

'Pappa said no.' Ninni knew her father had received the same offer.

Alma pulled a face. 'We all said no, of course. Again.'

'What will happen if they don't find any family?' Ninni knew Haldorsen. He had tried more than once to buy their property. Her father always turned him down.

'If that happens, the farm goes to the state and they will sell it on the open market, with no regard to the rest of us. Nobody wants Haldorsen getting his greedy claws into the island. Jens is looking through the old church records to see if we can find a relative. I wish Agnar was related to me or to Jens. We could have made a claim,' Alma said.

'I'll ask Pappa. Maybe we are related to him. You never know. Our family has been here for a very long time,' Ninni said before stuffing the last piece of bun in her mouth.

'I hope that's true. Haldorsen would have to give up then. Your dad would never sell,' Alma said and laughed.

'Neither would I.' Ninni got up from the chair. 'I have to go. Frikk hasn't been fed properly all day. He'll eat me if he has to wait much longer.'

'Before you go, I could use your help tomorrow. We are one short, unfortunately. Britt is taking the trip to visit her mother in Haugesund after the parade.'

'Where do you need me?' Ninni was happy for the distraction.

'The ice cream stand and probably a lot of other places. And then there's clean-up duty later. You know how it works.'

'Yes, I do. And you're lucky, you know. My *bunad* is here on the island.' She smiled and picked up the bags of groceries. 'These weigh a ton.'

'You need to eat.' Alma patted her cheek. 'My door is always open. You can tell me all about your broken heart when you're ready.'

'I will.' And her heart was broken. But Ninni couldn't handle kindness. Not now.

She walked slowly up the narrow hill, eager to get home. Frikk was running in circles around her, thrilled to be back.

Inside the house it was dark and dusty. Ninni opened a few windows and hung the bedding over the window-sill to let it air out. She found food for Frikk, who wolfed it down in warp speed and then settled down on the outside doormat with a happy and heavy sigh.

She put on the kettle and made herself an instant coffee, not bothering with the coffee machine. It took ages, and then the coffee always got cold before she remembered to drink it.

With the warm mug in her hand, she went outside and sat down on the step to enjoy the silence and the wind – the smell of the island, she thought, and took a deep breath. Salty seawater and freshly cut grass, the sweet scent from the early blossoms on the old apple tree and the sharper scent from the juniper bushes by the road made her close her eyes for a moment. It was so good to be here, so safe. Perhaps she would never leave. Perhaps that would make her feel like herself again.

Then her thoughts turned to Karl and she burst into tears.

Chapter 2

The sound of a marching band woke Jack up. A really bad, out-of-tune band with more enthusiasm than talent. More than one band by the sound of it, and all of them playing different melodies.

For a second he tried to remember if he had drunk anything last night – some strange Norwegian brew that gave hallucinations and amnesia? The drive from Bergen to Haugesund had taken a lot more than the three hours the car rental firm had said and since he had a later start than expected, thanks to that crazy woman at the roundabout, he had missed the last boat to the island.

The rental firm in Bergen had exchanged the car for him and made him fill out a report on the incident, before informing him that he was lucky he had bought the extended insurance package. He didn't feel lucky, he felt stupid after telling them that he had driven on the wrong side of the road.

On the bright side, the road trip from Bergen had

lifted his spirits, as had the trip on the car ferry. The countryside was not like any countryside he had seen, all mountains and ragged coastline. When he'd arrived in Haugesund he was promptly told by the hotel that there were no cars on that island. No cars? It was ridiculous.

Jack hoped it was a bad dream, but the music continued after he opened his eyes. Sound hallucinations were a symptom of brain cancer, weren't they? He pulled a hand slowly through his hair. It wasn't a hallucination from a really bad hangover either.

Reluctantly, he got out of bed and walked over to the window. He pulled the curtains aside and peered outside, not quite sure what he was looking at.

'This is weird,' he said.

The hotel window had a view over a small square and two streets. Further down he spotted a bridge. When he had arrived the night before, he hadn't really got much of an impression. It was just empty streets with lots of white houses.

Now the streets were filled with people. It looked as if there was a huge fancy dress party for the entire town. 'Weird,' he said again.

Lots of women dressed in long skirts with embroidery everywhere, others in summer dresses and colourful summer coats. Most of the men he saw wore suits and ties, but some of them had costumes as well, reminding him of Morris dancers.

There were Norwegian flags absolutely everywhere. Along the street stood flagpoles, outside every shop smaller flags decorated the shop fronts, and there were flags on the front and back of taxis and buses passing by on the upper street. There were small flags on people's bicycles and babies' prams, even flags fluttering from dogs' collars. Children and teenagers had flags painted on their cheeks or forehead, some on their whole face.

And so much noise. There were the marching bands he couldn't see, only hear. Then there were whistles and horns blaring, and yelling from hordes of children running around with plastic trumpets in their hands.

Jack rubbed his head and stretched. One thing he knew for sure, it had nothing to do with him. All he had to do was find the boat to the island and get on board. The sooner he got a good look at the property, the sooner he could sell the place and head back home to London, to his proper life. With money in the bank, he hoped.

After a quick shower, he packed the suitcase and took the lift to the reception. Someone had put a flag on the wall inside the lift.

The receptionist wore a long, pleated dark blue skirt, a white puffy shirt, a red vest with sequins on and, for some reason, a pin made of red, white and blue ribbons. She was blonde and good-looking, almost as tall as him. And she looked at his outfit with a slight frown, before putting on a professional smile.

'I'll have your bill ready for you in a second, Mr Greene. Have you had breakfast? The restaurant is open all day today. The breakfast on 17th of May is always special. If you're lucky there might even be Champagne and strawberries left,' she said in the singsong accent he had noticed most people had when they spoke English.

Champagne for breakfast? Weird brew, he thought. But he had had enough of restaurants for a while. 'No, thank you. I'm fine. I'm sorry to be so blunt, but what are you wearing?'

'Oh, this is a *bunad*,' she said, blushing when she smiled.

'Is that like a work uniform? Because I didn't see anyone wearing a costume like that when I arrived last night. And now it's everywhere,' Jack said.

She laughed. 'Today is 17th of May.' She seemed a bit taken aback that she had to explain the obvious to him.

'Yes, I know that, but why all the ruckus?' Jack noticed that there were flags inside the reception as well. Even the flower decorations had flags, and the flowers were red, white and blue.

He was distracted by a group of people entering from the street. They were dressed for a party, all suits and dresses. Almost all of them had red, white and blue ribbons attached to their jackets or coat collars.

'Constitution Day,' the receptionist said with a huge smile now.

Jack smiled back. She was cute. 'I know that too, but I have no idea what it means.'

'It's the day we celebrate our constitution. It's a really big deal in Norway. Everybody dresses up, eats and drinks, has fun, gives congratulations to each other. There are parades of school children all over the country. It's one of the best days of the year, especially if you're a kid. You'll see when you go outside.'

'Right. So all this is normal?' he said and pointed to the chaos outside.

'Only today. Tomorrow we all get back to our boring selves. With massive hangovers for some of us, of course.' She was laughing at him now. 'Would you like a ribbon? If you don't mind me saying so, you look a little under-dressed.'

Jack looked at the ribbon she held out to him and shook his head. He didn't think it would improve much on his jeans and sweater. Probably should have taken the suit, he thought. 'Thank you, but I don't think so.'

He gave her his credit card and paid for the room.

'I'm supposed to take a boat from here to this island.' Jack pushed a note towards her. 'I'm sorry. I can't pronounce it properly.'

'You can get the boat from Risøy. Walk straight down here, cross Haraldsgaten and Strandgaten, go across the bridge and go right until you come to the jetty. It's easy to find and should take you about ten minutes to walk.'

Jack thanked her. He pointed to the left. 'Just go that way, right?'

'Of course. You can't miss the bridge even if you try.'

She handed him back his credit card and a receipt. 'I hope you have a pleasant stay, Mr Greene.'

'Thank you.' Jack looked outside. More people. It looked confusing. 'Just across the two first streets, yes?'

'Yes, but you'd better hurry. The parade will pass by any minute on Haraldsgaten. When that happens, it may take you some time to cross. Every school in town is there. That's a lot of children.'

A parade, Jack thought as he made his way outside, pulling the suitcase behind him.

It took him a minute to realise that there was purpose in the chaos he had observed from the hotel room. People walked downhill, lining up on either side of the lower street. A sign on one of the buildings caught his eye. "Haraldsgaten" it said. Okay, so this was the first street.

The marching band music was getting louder. Jack followed the stream of people. He was tall, so he could see banners and flags coming towards them.

He looked at his watch. Not that it mattered what time it was. He had no appointments, no job to go to any more, no stress. He was free to do whatever pleased him. Plenty of time to cross a couple of streets and get into a boat to a godforsaken island.

He threaded between prams and hordes of small children clutching plastic trumpets and small, bright coloured windmills for some reason. Even the little ones wore *bunads*.

It was massive and it looked like people had fun. He envied them a little, the way everyone seemed to belong. He stopped in front of a barrier, like the ones used at concerts. The only opening was by a stern-looking policeman.

Jack walked over to him. The policeman looked him over.

'Excuse me, but I'd like to cross. I have a boat to catch on the other side of that bridge,' Jack said and pointed.

The policeman frowned. 'Today?'

'Yes, that would be nice. I'm told the boat leaves on the hour.' Jack pulled out the envelope again. He held it up, feeling rather foolish.

'Why are you going to the island today?' The policeman looked him over with growing suspicion. It made Jack wonder about what kind of island he was going to.

'Apparently I've inherited a farm there,' Jack said. 'It sounds absurd, I know. When the first email arrived, I thought it was one of those scams, you know? From Nigeria or Russia, only this was from Norway. So I deleted it. And then I deleted the next one. Then a letter came in the post from a British law firm, and I knew it was real. At least I think so. I'm going to the island today to check it out.'

What am I doing? he thought. Babbling on like a maniac.

Not that it mattered much. The policeman was clearly not listening to him any more. Instead he was staring over his shoulder and grinning from ear to ear.

'Hang on. See the girl carrying the school standard? That's my kid.'

He pointed and Jack looked. A girl of about twelve was using both hands to hold onto a school standard that looked far too heavy for her.

Her face lit up when her father waved at her. She had one of those *bunads* on. Behind her followed lines of children, all dressed to the hilt, waving flags, singing and yelling.

'Looks great,' Jack said.

'You bet she does. Strong too. Those standards are bloody heavy and she has to carry it all the way through town. Okay, stay close to me; I'll get you across.'

Jack followed him as he held up a hand like a traffic constable. The band stopped walking, creating a bit of a ruckus behind them as some children walked into the ones in front. Jack ran across. He turned to wave at the policeman, but he was already lost in the crowds.

Jack pulled his suitcase behind him. The noise from the parade faded. He thought about what had happened the day before. He'd been on his way from the airport to the lawyer's office when he'd hit that girl. God, he could have killed her. That would have been something for the papers, he thought. *Sacked Chef At One Of London's Hippest Restaurants Kills Norwegian Woman.*

At the lawyer's office everything had been very clinical. An hour later, he'd stood outside again with a large brown envelope in his hand – the papers that proved he was the rightful owner of Agnar Berget's farm. He couldn't bring himself to think of Agnar as his father. It was too odd.

Jack put his hand in his pocket and felt the key. One key for a whole farm. It was ... weird.

Perhaps he could call his dad from the boat. He knew the trip would take about thirty minutes.

He stopped on top of the bridge to have a look around. The harbour was filled with all sorts of boats, everything from small motorboats to large ferries, even a few rowing boats. Not one without a flag or two, he noticed.

Along the pier there were restaurants, already filled with people. So not everyone was taking part in the parade, he thought, and started walking again.

Someone pointed out the ferry for him and he found a place outside. The weather was sunny and windy. He was surprised. In Bergen he'd been told that in Haugesund it was always raining.

Not today, he thought, feeling the sweat on his back.

He stayed on deck until it got too windy. There were a few people on board. They looked at him, but no one talked to him.

Jack rang his dad, who answered at once.

'What's that noise?' Paul asked.

'Boat engines, I think. I don't really know.'

Paul laughed. 'How are you liking it so far? Did you meet the lawyer?'

'Yesterday. He gave me an envelope and a key. One key for a whole farm. I'm guessing it's filled with rotten outbuildings and a house the wind blew upside down.'

'Well, yes, but is it an adventure?'

Jack looked out of the window. It had salt water stripes from the seawater constantly showering the glass. 'It's okay, I guess. Bergen was a proper town. This town, Haugesund, is a lot smaller. They don't even have cars on this island, Dad.'

Paul chuckled. 'The fresh air will do you a world of good. Do some fishing, enjoy the sun and get your head straight. You need to learn to relax, Jack. You need an adventure.'

'I'm pretty sure I'll be bored out of my mind after a few days,' Jack said.

'Oh, by the way, that Fedra called again. Are you really not taking her calls?'

The last thing Jack wanted was to discuss Fedra. 'What did you tell her?'

'I told her the same thing I told her last time she called, that I have no idea where you have gone, how long you will be gone and that she should stop harassing me. She didn't like that,' Paul said.

I bet she didn't, Jack thought. 'Just block her, Dad. I'll talk to her in a few days.'

Jack didn't feel very encouraged when he put the phone back in his pocket. Not even a tiny bit. He knew all too well how persistent Fedra could be. She wouldn't give up.

Chapter 3

Ninni handed a strawberry ice lolly to a five-year-old boy, who took it with both hands. His eyes were bigger than the lolly.

'Are you sure you can eat that? I think it's your third one,' she said.

He carefully released the grip of one hand and held it up, spreading his fingers out. 'This many. That's more than anyone else has eaten,' he said, beaming with pride.

'Good luck,' Ninni said.

I wouldn't like to be your parents later tonight when the belly-ache starts, she thought. But on 17th of May the tradition was unlimited ice lollies and hot dogs for kids, or at least as many as they could eat.

She was manning the ice cream and hot dog stand outside the shop. Alma was inside, handing out soda and coffee to the adults. The island's small children's parade was over, and now there was ice lollies and sweets until the dance on the pier later. Even though it was technically a school night, most children would stay up, enjoying the party.

'Excuse me?'

She looked up and saw a man towering over her. He wasn't wearing the expensive suit, so it took her a few seconds to recognise him.

'You!'

He was standing there, like a tourist. How strange was that? It made her wonder if he had followed her after the accident. But why on earth would he follow her and then wait to approach her until the next day? It didn't make sense. 'Oh, God, are you stalking me?'

He frowned. 'Excuse me?'

Ninni raised her eyebrows. 'Excuse you? I'm not excusing you for anything. You're obviously a crazy person.'

He lifted his hands in defeat. 'I'm sorry. I have no idea who you are.'

Ninni was outraged. 'You ran me down with that stupid driving of yours yesterday. You shouldn't even be walking into revolving doors. Are you stalking me or something?'

He looked horrified for a moment. 'No, are you mad? I had no idea you were here. How would I know that? I'm just visiting. I'm sorry, but I didn't recognise you in your *bunad*.'

'Who are you visiting?' She couldn't believe it.

'I've always wanted to see a proper Norwegian island,' he said and then he smiled.

28

Ninni didn't like the jolt in her stomach. She glared at him. Dressed in jeans and a grey sweatshirt, he stuck out among all the people in their party clothes. He was pulling a suitcase behind him. Perhaps he really was a tourist. And he was so out of sync with everyone because of the way he dressed it was ridiculous.

'I'm a bit lost, I'm afraid,' he said. 'This is a bit overwhelming. I've never been to a Constitution Day before.'

She frowned. 'We don't bite.'

He smiled back at her. 'Do you promise?'

Was he flirting with her? She hoped not. That would be too weird. And for some absurd reason it made her feel guilty. For what, she had no idea. As if she was cheating on Karl, and that made her mad.

He really was a complete idiot if he thought flirting would get him into her good graces. What a prat, she thought.

'Ice cream or hot dog?' she said quickly, to avoid confusion. Whether for him or for herself, she didn't care to know.

'Excuse me?' He was staring at her with an intense look in his eyes.

'You look hungry. A hot dog is probably better for you.' Ninni took a bun from the grill and put a steaming, slightly burned hot dog in it. Then she pointed at the sauces. 'Ketchup or mustard, mayo or shrimp cocktail, onions or red beets?'

'That sounds a bit too much, to be honest. I don't really like frankfurters,' he said, looking at the hot dog.

'Then you're in luck. This is not a frankfurter; it's a grilled sausage wrapped in bacon. A Norwegian speciality.'

He looked baffled for a moment, then laughed. 'That doesn't sound half bad, actually.'

His smile was lovely, she thought. 'Try it. It's good, I promise.'

'I haven't had any breakfast.' He took a bite of the hot dog and chewed carefully. 'Good,' he said and took a bigger bite.

'Are you visiting anyone on the island? Perhaps I can find them for you. I know everyone here.'

He shook his head. 'I'm just passing through. I needed a holiday and Norway sounded interesting.'

'Okay. Are you camping? I'm asking because you don't look like an ordinary camper. No backpack or tent, or anything like that.' He was a strange man, she thought.

He smiled at her. 'I have accommodation, thank you.'

Ninni frowned. That sounded odd, she thought. 'So, you are staying at the B&B, then? I didn't know Britt had opened for the season,' she said.

Those blue eyes bore down on her. 'Do you live here on the island?'

'I live in Bergen, but my family have a house here. I usually stay during the odd weekend and most holidays.'

She held out her hand, determined to get more information about him. 'I'm Ninni Toft.'

He took her hand in a warm, firm grip. 'Jack Greene,' he said and let go of her hand. 'Nice to meet you.'

Direct approach usually worked best, in her experience. 'Why have you really come to our island, Jack?'

'For a short holiday,' he said, serious now.

She looked over her shoulder to see if Alma could come, but there was a long queue of customers inside and outside the shop. 'There's a dance here on the pier later. Lots of food. You are welcome to join us, of course. I'm sure Britt will bring you.'

He looked at her properly, then. His eyes shifted colours suddenly, more like the sea in the morning, and he looked oddly familiar. 'Maybe I will,' he said with a smile. 'Can I have more of that food, to take with me?'

She thought it an odd request, but still. He was English.

'You know, in case I don't make it to the pier dance? I would go to the shop, but it looks closed.'

'It opens again at ten tomorrow morning.' Ninni pointed at the grill with burgers and more bacon sausages. 'The fish burgers are highly recommended. The fish was caught this morning.'

He looked interested. 'Two, please.'

Ninni found a Styrofoam container and made up a couple of fish burgers for him, adding the relish and remoulade without asking, then she put it all carefully into a carrier bag.

When he held out his hand to take it from her, she shook her head. 'Money in the tin first,' she said, nodding at a tin on the desk, filled with banknotes and coins.

Jack smiled. 'Of course. How much do I owe you?'

'Twenty kroner per burger, and ten for the hot dog.'

He handed her a hundred kroner note and got the burgers.

'Thank you. Want something to drink with the food? I only have Solo and still water left, I'm afraid.'

'What's Solo?'

Ninni showed him the bottle of bright orange fizzy drink.

'You don't have any wine?' He looked at the bottle with a frown.

'No, this is a hot dog stand, not a restaurant, I'm afraid. Do you want it?'

'Sure. Thank you.' Jack put it in the bag.

Ninni counted the change and handed it to him. 'Here you go.'

'Thank you. Perhaps I will see you later,' he said.

A group of children ran towards her, screaming for ice lollies, and Ninni was distracted. When she looked up again, he was gone.

Alma will want to know, she thought. An Englishman who didn't want to say why he was on the island and seemed confused.

We'll see if he comes to the dance; I'll introduce him to Alma. She can use her mind-reading abilities on him, she thought, before concentrating on the children.

'Line up, little monsters. There's plenty of goodies for all of you.'

It took a fair bit longer than ten minutes to get to the farm. The road Jack followed wasn't much of a road. No wonder he missed the fork and had to walk back. The lawyer's map wasn't much help.

But here he was, standing in the farmyard, eyeing his new property.

Jack looked around. It wasn't like any farm he had ever seen. Not that he knew much about farms. Born and raised in London, most of his farming knowledge came from TV shows. And this was far from anything he could have imagined. Everything was built with timber, for one thing.

The house itself wasn't much to look at – a two-storey building with a narrow entrance door, built on a stone or brick foundation, he had no idea. The house was painted white, although the paint had peeled in some places.

On the other side of the farmyard was a small barn or stable.

'God, I hope there are no dead cows in there,' he said out loud to himself.

The farmyard also had other buildings, mostly sheds of some sort. The barn was red and sagging a bit, and

for some reason it had a lawn on the roof. A bit behind
stood a house built on four cairns. How odd, he thought.
Why would anyone want a house built on cairns?

The phone pinged and he read the message. Holly,
of course.

Dad says you're in shock. Is it a huge farm? Will you
make millions from growing strange Norwegian
vegetables and become too good for the rest of us?

Jack grinned. He put the bag with food on top of
the suitcase before answering.

I'm already too good for you lot. You should know
that by now.

He sent the text and hoped she'd be satisfied. Knowing
his little sister, he would get a barrage of texts if she
was bored. But the text brightened his mood.

Jack walked around the side of the main house. 'Wow,'
he said.

The views were stunning. A huge fence surrounded
the house, and on the other side was a large field with
rows of what he assumed were constructions of dry
hay. A small path through a fence led down a garden
to a snug beach with what looked like a couple of
boathouses, jutting out over the water. After that, open
sea as far as the eye could see.

'Wow,' he said again.

He took pictures with his phone, of both the view and the buildings, and sent them to his dad.

Finally he ran out of things to do. He had to go inside.

He brought the suitcase and the bag with him to the front door, pulled the key from his pocket and unlocked the door. He hesitated with his hand on the door handle. For a moment he remembered every horror movie he had ever seen.

'This is stupid,' he said and stepped into the empty hallway.

He walked inside, leaving the door open behind him and the suitcase nearby, just in case. Inside he turned on the light. A single light bulb dangled from the ceiling. Agnar wasn't much of an interior decorator, Jack thought.

Along the wall were pegs, loaded with clothes – jackets of all sorts, some older than him, Jack reckoned. On the floor were wellingtons and clogs, slippers and sailing shoes. All worn out, all in a heap. Not a tidy man either, he thought.

The rug on the floor was worn thin and faded. Jack frowned. The house smelled of dust and something else he couldn't identify. He sincerely hoped they had buried the body and hadn't just left the poor man in the house. He did not want to meet his biological father like that.

He walked further in. The hallway had three doors,

all closed. The first was to a drawing room filled with heavy, dark furniture that reminded him of old black-and-white movies. It looked like no one had been in there for ages. The dust was thick on every surface. And on the floor were stacks of newspapers and magazines.

One of the walls was covered in old photographs. Jack looked at them, one by one. Family photos, some so old they were black and white. His biological family, all of them, and he had no idea who any of them were. It was unsettling to see his own features on some of them. He had always been the odd one out with his blue eyes and blond hair in a family dominated by brown hair and brown eyes. But here, in these photographs, people looked like him. It gave him the creeps, so he backed out of there and decided to explore the rest of the house.

The second door led to the kitchen, a wobbly Formica table by the window and two metal chairs with spindly legs. The kitchen was clean, apart from the dust here too, but there was still cutlery on the counter by the sink.

The fridge was empty. Someone had cleaned out whatever food had been there. He wouldn't survive on a couple of fish burgers for long. Perhaps he could ask the brown-haired girl, Ninni, where he could buy proper food. And, if he was honest, he wouldn't mind seeing her again.

He put the food and the bottle of fizzy drink in the fridge and went to see the rest of the house.

The third door led to a combined bedroom/TV room. The TV was old and small, with something he guessed was an aerial protruding from the back of it. Probably black and white as well. He wasn't optimistic about a Wi-Fi connection out here. More stacks of newspapers and magazines, alongside wobbly stacks of paperback books.

He looked at the sofa bed. 'I hope he didn't die on that.'

On one of the old side tables there were more photographs. He picked up one and almost dropped it.

It was his mother with a man he assumed was Agnar. He could see the likeness to himself. Same colouring, same nose and jaw line.

He put it down again.

'I can't stay here,' he said aloud, as if someone could hear him.

Jack turned around and walked outside, closing the door behind him.

For a moment he just stood there, trying to breathe and not run. There was nowhere to run to, even if he tried.

He thrust his hands in his pockets and walked round to the garden. There was a wooden bench under a small tree. He sat down and closed his eyes.

This was all wrong. He shouldn't be here. What was

he doing, inheriting a farm from a man who'd been nothing more than a sperm donor? He had no connection to this past, this house or this island at all, and especially not to the stranger who had died and left him this white elephant.

You could have told me something about him, Mum, he thought. Something that I could have connected to. Perhaps she'd meant to, when he got older. 'Too late, Mum. Too late.'

Jack groaned. He should be in London right now, working in the restaurant, prepping food and doing what he loved. Instead he was sitting like an idiot on a bench under a tree, talking to his dead mother.

He looked up at the leafy branches. He didn't even know the name of the tree.

All of a sudden the absurdity of the situation caught up with him and he burst out laughing.

Ninni flipped over another burger. Around her, music filled the night air. Alma's husband, Jens, had brought his accordion and Olav and Sigrid played flutes. It had been a hot day, and the heat still lingered in the air.

She sighed with contentment, feeling her shoulders sinking. All the fuss earlier in the day, all the speeches about the constitution, the wreath at the memorial for the fallen soldiers, the children's parade and all the rest were over. It was time to simply enjoy the evening.

Everyone had gathered on the pier and for once it

wasn't raining. The wind was mild and filled with the promise of summer. It would be bathing weather any time now. Not many 17th of May's came with sunshine and clear skies. On the island, May usually was a wet and windy month. This year it was so warm everything had turned green three weeks ahead of schedule. It would be unsettling if they didn't enjoy it so much.

Ninni handed out burgers to anyone passing by. There was no need to take money; people put it in the tin by the table and somehow that always covered the costs.

Alma found her through the crowd. 'Why isn't anyone helping you?'

'When I'm fed up I'll just leave and someone else will take over. It's a miracle,' Ninni said, smiling at her.

'Have you seen him?' Alma stretched her neck towards the north path.

'No, not yet. He might not come.' Ninni put buns next to a couple of burgers and wafted away the smoke.

'It's so strange.' Alma wrung her hands. 'Who is he? And he spoke English? Are you sure?'

Ninni flipped the burger. 'Oh, yes. He is English, Alma. I'm able to hear the difference between English and Norwegian. It's all in the ear, you know.'

'Yes, yes, but I don't understand what he's doing here. Britt says nobody has booked with her. So where's he staying? And why would he lie about it? It's so annoying.'

Alma took the plate Ninni handed her and looked at it. 'I'm not hungry.'

'Jens told me you haven't eaten all day. Eat. It's good.' Ninni gave her a stern look. 'Why is this man bothering you?'

Alma picked at the bun. 'I don't know. I just have a bad feeling. What if he's a bad man, come to murder us all? Perhaps he heard that we never lock our doors and plans to rob every house.'

Ninni thought of Jack. 'I hardly think so. Did you see him through the shop window?'

'Yes, I did. And there was something about him,' Alma said.

Ninni thought about his eyes. She hadn't thought much about anything else since he'd talked to her. 'I'm sure he will tell us all about himself sooner or later. And, if not, he'll be gone in a few days' time, he said so himself.'

'Hmm,' Alma said before taking a bite of the burger. 'This is good.'

'Of course it is. Making great burgers is my special talent.' Ninni handed her another plate. 'Here, take this to Jens and enjoy the evening. Dance. Let Olav and Sigrid do the music for a while.'

Alma looked amused. 'Dance? I'd most likely break my hip.'

'I doubt that. I'm not sure if the flautists can do Chuck Berry.'

'They wouldn't know who that is, would they? They play weird meditation music or depressing folk music. It's just sad.' Alma shook her head.

'Go and eat. I'll be here for another thirty minutes, then I'll come over.'

Alma nodded. 'Okay. But let me know immediately if that man turns up. I want to talk to him. I can't relax until I know what's going on,' she muttered to herself and turned to join Jens and the others.

Ninni flipped another burger. She didn't worry about Jack Greene. Her thoughts went to Karl. If he was here, she would push him in the sea. Simply for being a mean bastard.

Chapter 4

An insistent bird was singing outside. Ninni opened her eyes and looked at the familiar ceiling. This had been her father's room when he was a boy. Model aeroplanes were hanging from the rafters and boyhood books from the fifties and sixties, even some from before the war, on the shelves mingled with her own collection from her childhood, including handwritten manuscripts from when she thought she'd be a writer.

It was too early to get up, but she knew she wouldn't be able to sleep any more. She was surprised she had slept at all. All day yesterday she had kept so busy she'd hardly had any time to think of Karl. There had just been fleeting moments, and then she'd found something new to distract her.

The Englishman was one such distraction. Alma hadn't stopped going on about him. The others had got involved and he'd become the topic for the rest of the night. Nobody knew where he was staying and nobody had seen him since he'd left the harbour.

Ninni had tried to stay out of it. Speculations seldom led to any real answers. It was a waste of time, considering he was only passing through.

When she'd come up to the attic the night before she was overtired and sad. Now she felt more relaxed, more like herself.

The magic of the island, she thought, and sat up so abruptly Frikk almost fell out of bed. He jumped down and went over to the door. He barked a few times, wagged his tail and finally pressed his nose against the door.

'I'm coming, I'm coming. You're the nuttiest dog I have ever met. And I've met a few.'

Ninni went downstairs and let him out, leaving the door ajar, then had a shower and made coffee.

Frikk came bouncing back after doing his business. Tongue lolling and tail wagging, he flopped down next to her. Ninni filled his water bowl and rubbed his ears.

'We have to inspect the island today,' she said. 'A lot has been going on since we left.'

Frikk lapped the water, making noises and splashing the floor.

Ninni looked at the computer on the kitchen table. Next to it lay the stack of reference books she needed for the next assignment. But today translating contracts for an oil company didn't tempt her. She needed a day off.

The phone pinged and she looked at it. Karl. She deleted the message at once, then blocked his number.

Ninni filled a thermos with more coffee, putting a spoon of chocolate powder in it and shaking it well.

'I'm bringing some salami for you and a sandwich for me. Think you can handle that?'

Frikk was looking at her as if he understood every word.

I'm talking to the dog as if he will turn around and quote Ibsen back at me one day, she thought, rolling her eyes.

Before she changed her mind, she grabbed a bright green sweater, put on a pair of jeans and red trainers, and headed out.

She always did the "grand tour" on the first day on the island. Even if it was only a weekend trip or midwinter. The tour always made her feel better.

Ninni looked down towards the sea. Waves were lapping in with the tide. She spotted litter among the pebbles and sighed. Why would people just throw their rubbish overboard? It made no sense.

Downhill from their house, she caught a glimpse of Agnar's farm. The house was snuggled on the high ground in a cove. He had access to one of the best beaches on the island and yet, at some point, he had put a tall fence around the entire property.

'It's to keep the landlubbers out,' he had said once

when she'd asked him. For a long time she had looked out of her window every morning to see if the giants had invaded his garden.

Frikk leaned against her leg. Ninni stroked his soft head.

'You know, if Haldorsen gets the land he'll build a huge marina down there. With loads of boats and cabins and building work for who knows how long. We don't want that, do we?'

Frikk just wagged his tail, not in the least worried.

Ninni sighed. It would ruin the island. She loved everything here, every tree and bush, stone and beach. She didn't want anything to change, at least not for the worse.

They continued on the path. Ninni noticed that the birds were busy and noisy. Frikk noticed too and made it his mission to scare them all out. Ninni kept walking. Her head felt clearer by the second.

After a half-hour walk, they arrived at the foot of the island's only mountain.

'It's not much of a mountain, is it?' she said to Frikk. But it had the best view and she always climbed to the top.

Frikk had run halfway up before she caught up with him. Twenty minutes of hiking brought them to the top.

A cairn rose above them. Ninni sat down on the ground, facing the sea. She leaned against the base of the cairn and didn't mind the stones poking at her back. To sit like this was more than enough right now. There would be bad days ahead, but she would be fine in the end. She hoped.

Frikk put his head on her leg and grinned.

'You never took to Karl, did you? You're so much smarter than me. I wish I could have sussed him out the way you did. It would have saved me a lot of misery.' She scratched him behind the ear. 'Thank God it's over. I'll never see him again. Not ever.'

She sipped coffee from the thermos and shared a sandwich with Frikk. Perhaps she would survive this after all.

'There's more to life than a broken heart, Frikk,' she said, feeding him the last piece of salami. 'It's hardly the end of the world.'

Frikk snorted and shook his head. Ninni laughed.

A moment later, she jumped to her feet. 'Let's take the boat out.'

The dog was happy to do whatever she wanted and followed her down the path that snaked past Agnar's house. It looked lost, with dark windows. She shivered and hurried by. There was something unsettling about the empty house.

Their boathouse was on one side of the path, Agnar's boathouse on the other side. It was rundown and the wood was silvery from the rain and the wind. But it was solid. Her grandfather had built it with his own hands. There was a small living space in the loft, as in most of the boathouses on the island.

The boathouse had a pier with a homemade diving board jutting out into the water. In the summer they would jump from the board and climb up the ladder on the side. Her mother hated staying on the island. She was convinced there were eels hiding in the flowing seaweed, waiting to attack her, and refused to swim. At most, she would sit on the beach and let the waves lap over her feet. Mostly she complained about the bad weather and how boring it was.

Ninni grinned at the memories. Her mother now lived the beach life in Spain. No seaweed, no eels, not even crabs, she had said before moving there for good. Just plenty of people living the good life and playing lots of bridge.

And she was right. The beaches in Spain were wonderful, but this was better.

Ninni bent down at the corner of the boathouse and pulled out the key from under the stone where they always hid it.

Inside the boathouse the familiar smell of old tar and dried seaweed wafted out. She inhaled it all. Over her head, her grandmother's old fishing nets still hung over the rafters.

Her boat was a small plastic one with an outboard engine. The family boat was larger and made of wood by her grandfather and her father. As always, she stroked her hand over the wood. It felt like silk. There were so many memories connected to that boat. She smiled at the thought of them. First time she caught a fish by herself; at four in the morning when the ocean surface was quiet like glass; first time she fell out of a boat and her grandmother laughed so hard she fell after her; first time she got bitten by a crab. And the picnics on the smaller beaches, with all of them going, filling the boat with fishing gear and blankets and enough food to outlive Robinson Crusoe.

'But you're too heavy for me to drag you out today. Also, I'm not in the mood for rowing you, you big old beast,' she said.

She loosened the ties for the little boat, threw in one of the otter boards and started pushing it.

Frikk watched from the outside as she pushed her boat down the little slope next to the pier. The old outboard engine was heavy, but not so heavy that she couldn't carry it.

The water lapped over her trainers when she made the final push to get the boat on the water. She wasn't sure just how cold the water was, but she didn't mind. She climbed up to the pier again and secured the rope after pulling the boat alongside it. Frikk barked twice. She looked at him. The dog was standing on the edge of the pier, knowing full well what was about to happen.

She pulled off her clothes, down to her underwear. There was no one around now anyway. Then she ran onto the diving board and jumped, screaming as the cold water hit her. She was grinning when she swam up to the surface and discovered Frikk was still standing on the pier, wagging his tail.

'Get in here, you chicken.'

The dog jumped and splashed around her while she swam towards the pier again.

This was the way to rid herself of Karl and all that had happened.

A piercing scream followed by a big splash woke Jack up. He looked around, wondering what the hell was going on and where he was. A dog was barking and then there was another splash.

Shocked, he stood up from the deckchair he had slept in when he couldn't get himself to sleep inside the house. He was stiff and cold, and felt like the biggest idiot on the planet. No one could ever know that he had been too spooked to sleep inside.

He pulled the blanket over his shoulders and peered over the fence. It took him a second to realise the noise came from one of the boathouses on the beach.

Jack shaded his eyes. He recognised the dog and knew it was Ninni splashing around in the water. What was she doing? Was she in trouble?

He walked towards the gate in the fence, not very keen to jump into the water after her, but if she really was in trouble then he had no choice.

Before he managed to open the gate she came up from the water, calling the dog to follow her. She was wearing nothing but a bra and a flimsy pair of knickers, obviously not expecting anyone to see her. Jack couldn't look away. Especially when she stretched her arms in the air and he was sure his heart stopped.

He couldn't take his eyes off her. She jumped out into the water again, splashing about with the dog swimming around her like a barking seal. Finally she pulled herself up into a yellow plastic boat and dragged the dog after her.

She pulled on a sweater, then started the engine of the boat.

Jack stood there until the boat disappeared around a headland. He let his breath out slowly.

I'm now reduced to a Peeping Tom, he thought, grinning at the image. But she was worth it. Mad woman, though. The water was probably freezing this far north. He shook his head. Who in their right mind would go swimming this early? He thought about Vikings and trolls, and all the other things about Norway he had no idea about. Perhaps the women were all mad from the cold weather? Or perhaps they all went mad as soon as the sun warmed their brains? Hopefully she would do this every morning. It would be worth getting up early for.

Jack looked at his watch. It was far too early to call an estate agent who could take a look at the property and tell him what it was worth. The lawyer had given him loads of paperwork, and the name of someone who'd shown interest in buying, but he wasn't going to be stupid. He would get a second opinion, to be sure.

Jack yawned and stretched his back. He couldn't sleep another night in the chair without doing some serious damage. Sooner or later he would have to sleep inside. Or perhaps he could get a tent and sleep in the garden.

He chuckled. The first thing he had to do was go shopping. Ninni had said the shop opened at ten. In the meantime, he could have another look around the house, take a look upstairs to see if there was a decent bedroom he could use. In case the garden tent didn't work out.

There were bushes along the fence – some sort of berry bushes, he wasn't sure what kind. And something else caught his eye.

Jack bent down and pushed aside something that looked like weeds. 'Chives,' he muttered.

He pulled a small leaf of something else and rubbed it between his fingers. Basil. Did Agnar cook? It seemed he had a kitchen garden of sorts.

That was interesting. A cook. But not for a living, he thought. Agnar had been a farmer and a fisherman. He was nothing like him. Lots of people liked to cook. It didn't mean anything.

Jack picked up the blanket from the chair and walked inside the house. He ignored Agnar's TV lounge and went into the kitchen. All of a sudden he saw signs of someone with more than just a casual interest in cooking.

The knife rack on the side was top-notch. Inside the cupboards he found spices, all sorts of dried herbs and lots of garlic. Everything had been put in small glass jars and carefully labelled with a felt pen.

Jack took down a jar and looked at it. *Estragon*, the label said. He opened it and the sharp smell of anise filled the air.

'Not too bad,' he said aloud, enjoying the smell of tarragon.

He opened the fridge and took out the leftover fish burger Ninni had sold him. The bun was a bit soggy, so he peeled it off. The sauce on the burger was interesting. Not mayo, he thought. It was tart and sweet, with a definite hint of dill. His stomach reminded him it was breakfast time and he wolfed down the food.

'This is so good,' he said to himself, making a mental note to ask Ninni how they were made.

He put on the kettle and sipped the cold drink while he waited for the water to boil. It was orangey and fresh, and a bit sweet. Better than nothing, he thought.

Without hesitating any more, he went upstairs to see what was up there.

He almost hit his head on the ceiling beams. Apparently Agnar's people were shorter in the olden days, he thought. On the landing there were only two rooms, the doors wide open. Inside the first room he found an old-looking double bed with white covers. Someone had put sheets and furniture covers on almost everything.

Jack pulled the covers off the bed. The mattress didn't look too bad. He pushed at it with one hand. Firm. Perhaps this was a better place to crash than in a rickety old deckchair.

From the window he could see the whole bay. Far out he spotted Ninni's boat. She seemed to be just sitting there. Mad woman, he thought.

He took a quick look into the second room. It had two single beds and a tallboy in a corner. The whole room had last century written all over it. Or the century before the last. There were thick layers of dust everywhere. Dust and dead flies.

Jack walked back to the larger bedroom, opened the windows and lay down on the bed. He closed his eyes. It was after all barely six o'clock and the shop wouldn't open for another four hours.

He fell asleep in seconds, the thin curtains wafting in the wind, bringing in the sweet smell of spring.

Ninni looked down into the water. It was so clear she could see all the way to the bottom where the line from the otter board was visible only because of the colourful fishhooks.

'No fish today, Frikk. Have we scared them away?'

The dog peered down into the water, just like her. He barked a couple of times.

'That's not helping,' Ninni said.

She pulled up the line and started the engine. 'I think we'll try further out.'

The boat dipped and jumped on the water and the seawater hit her face. Ninni laughed. It felt so good.

Frikk stood in the front of the boat. His tail wagged like mad.

Ninni turned the boat into the next cove and slowed down, finally stopping a few lengths from land.

She dropped the line again. Once in a while she pulled at the otter board, hoping to get a fish to bite. She couldn't help it, she started to think about Jack Greene. Alma was right. There was something about him.

What was he doing here? It was so utterly weird that a stranger should just show up out of the blue like that, without explaining anything. As if he had fallen from the sky. Britt had been adamant that he wasn't staying with them. So where was he? Sleeping in someone's barn? In one of the boathouses?

She pulled at the line again and this time something nibbled at the hooks. Frikk barked.

'Okay, okay. I can hear you. Don't scare the fish, please.' Ninni wound up the line and looked into the water at the same time.

'There's two of them. A pair of fine cods for dinner.'

She managed to get the fish into the boat and discovered there were a couple more at the end. Ninni took them off the line and dropped them in the bucket. 'Alma will love these.'

She sat back down in the boat and opened the thermos. The coffee was delicious. 'Later this week we'll put out some crab pots. That would be tasty.'

Ninni sighed. 'Karl loved crabs. The more, the better. He ate the whole thing. But mussels are his favourite.'

She looked at the dog. Frikk lifted his ears as if he understood every word.

The sun was heating up. She leaned back and closed her eyes. It was hard to remember a May that was this warm. It would rain again soon, of course, but that only meant this fine day had to be enjoyed to the fullest.

Another swim, she thought. Then more coffee and perhaps breakfast was a good idea.

She turned the boat towards land and headed back. The best place to swim was in the bay.

Jack stepped out in the yard with a mug in his hand. He sipped the tea and pulled a face. The tea was probably as old as the house. All he had found in the house was a sad box of Lipton Yellow that didn't smell of anything. There was no milk or sugar, of course.

He poured the tea out onto a patch of grass, then left the mug on the step. Time to shop for food.

Jack walked along the path back to the pier. He felt

better after a few hours of proper sleep, a short shower and the knowledge that the house didn't spook him any more. And he was famished.

The shop was open when he arrived. He looked at the sign above the door. *Joker,* it said. Funny name for a store, he thought. He hadn't noticed much the night before.

He went inside and looked around. The shop looked like a mix between a grocery store and a haberdashery. There was a post office desk at the back and an ATM in the corner. There was also a rack filled with magazines and books, another with colourful yarns, and even one with all sorts of DIY tools. The rest was food. He couldn't see anyone in there, but figured they would show up.

Jack grabbed a wire basket by the door and started roaming. Everything was labelled in Norwegian so he had to use his imagination and some wild guesswork. Yoghurt was easy, while butter was more of a challenge. He couldn't find any cheddar, and pulled a face when he saw the price of Jarlsberg.

He was pleased to see that none of the vegetables and fruit were wrapped in plastic. He could squeeze the produce, sniff it even, and the prices weren't half bad. Although the selection wasn't impressive.

'*Trenger du hjelp?*'

Jack discovered an elderly man talking to him. 'I'm sorry. I don't speak Norwegian.'

The man's face lit up in a huge grin and he pointed at him. 'You're the Englishman,' he said. The thought seemed to thrill him.

'I guess I am,' Jack said, taking an instant liking to him.

'I'm Jens Mikkelsen. Pleased to meet you.'

Jens held out his hand and Jack shook it. 'Jack Greene.'

'Nobody knows where you disappeared to after talking to Ninni last night. My wife was quite upset about it. She does not approve of things happening before she knows everything about it. Is it true? You didn't have a place to stay last night?'

'No, not really. I have a place to stay. Is your wife Alma Mikkelsen, by any chance?' Jack remembered the lawyer mentioning Alma. She ran the island, he had said with a sneer. She was the one to ask if he wanted to know anything.

Jens chuckled. 'That she is. She is also the shop manager and the mayor, and usually the one most on top of things. There's no use trying to stop her. She'll just waltz right over you.'

'I have no sense of rhythm, I'm afraid.'

Jens looked in his basket. 'But you do have taste for food. Are you a foodie, by any chance?'

'Something like that. Do you have any coriander or avocados?'

'I'm not sure what coriander is, so probably not.

Avocado I do know, but we don't have any at the moment, I'm afraid. You can order whatever you want and we'll get it from the mainland for you, free of transport charge.'

Jack took out a green pepper from his basket. 'So this is about it?'

'For the more exotic stuff, yes. Most people on the island have their own kitchen gardens, I'm afraid. Oh, and just so you know, the root vegetables, all of them, are grown right here on the island,' Jens added with a happy smile.

'Isn't it too early to harvest anything from a garden? What do people do in the meantime? Watch the seedlings grow?' Jack started to empty the contents of the basket onto the counter.

Jens chuckled. 'I wouldn't put it past some of them. But to answer your question, we do have a good selection of vegetables in the frozen section over there.'

Jack couldn't help himself. He burst out laughing. 'I'll check it out,' he said. 'What about cheese?'

'Well, follow me; we'll see what we've got.' Jens trotted over to a small fridge. 'I'm afraid we don't have any Stilton or cheddar; Norwegians don't like it much, I think. But we do have Norzola, which is as close as you get to blue cheese. Not sure what you would make of Old Cheese,' he said with a wicked grin.

'I guess that depends how old it is,' Jack said, intrigued now.

Jens chuckled and pulled a small black package from one of the shelves and held it up.

'This, my friend, is a fresh mould cheese, made from cultured milk. You will not get it anywhere else in the world. You see, this is proper Viking cheese, and only the bravest dare taste it,' he said, his eyes challenging him.

'Viking cheese?' Jack took the cheese from him. 'I'll give it a try.'

'Oh, yes. The Vikings used it as an aphrodisiac. However, I doubt that would work today. The smell of the cheese is a bit pungent.'

'How do you use it?'

Jens smiled. 'I put some on bread with lots of butter and perhaps a dollop of lingonberries. Alma refuses to eat it if there's no bacon. Other people eat it with mayo or just put lots of butter on it, or eat it as it is.'

'Do you have any eggs?' Jack dropped the cheese in the basket.

'Not yet, I'm afraid. Perhaps later today. We get them fresh from one of the farms, and the hens can be temperamental.'

Jack hid a smile. 'But you have oils, right?'

'Of course, over here.' Jens showed him a small rack with a few bottles of Greek olive oil and some rapeseed oil. 'When I tell Alma you have been here, she's going to want to know where you are staying. Everyone is wondering about that!'

'Are they?'

'Oh, yes. Some people think you may be a burglar and will murder us in our beds. Not me,' he added.

Jack smiled. 'You can ease everyone's curiosity. I'm staying at the Bergets farm.'

For a second Jens stared at him. 'Oh,' he finally said. 'Really?'

'Yes. So you can tell people that I'm harmless and don't sleep in a ditch.' Jack was enjoying himself.

Jens shook his head. 'I'm sorry. I'm just so very surprised. We thought the lawyers who run the place now, such as it is, couldn't rent it out. They are doing a poor job looking after the farm, by the way. Mostly we have taken care of the necessary things.'

'Like what?' Jack put the groceries on the counter.

Jens shrugged. 'We've kept up with the grass.'

He looked at him as if he expected Jack to know what he was talking about.

'Sorry?'

'The winter grass. It needs cutting at least twice every season and now, because of all this fine weather, it has been growing a lot faster than normal, so we have cut it a bit earlier than usual. You won't have to cut it again now until July, I should think. And if you're really lucky, and the weather stays nice, you can cut it again in September.'

'Okay,' Jack said, wondering what the man was talking about.

He watched as Jens put the groceries through the ceremony of the till, and followed the instructions on the pad with a little help from the shopkeeper.

'*Pin kode* is the same as a pin code, you know,' Jens explained.

It looked like a spelling mistake to Jack. He stuffed everything in an old backpack he had found in the house and walked towards the door. In the doorway he turned.

'Why do I have to cut the grass?' he said.

'Because of the animals, of course,' Jens said, beaming at him.

'It's something we all do. You'll save a fortune on it in the winter.'

'Do you have animals to feed?' Jack asked.

'Not us. Alma and I have a cat, but he doesn't eat grass, of course. But we all help. You will find that in rough times we tend to stick together and when someone needs help we do a *dugnad*.'

Must be some sort of Norwegian custom, Jack thought when he headed back. Jens seemed to think he knew what it meant. No matter. He was leaving soon.

Chapter 5

Ninni decided to stay around the house. There was work to be done and she had a deep respect for deadlines. It had nothing to do with the Englishman at all.

There was no need to go anywhere. The freezer was filled to the brim and she had everything else she needed from Alma. All she needed first was a morning swim.

She felt better every morning. Because of her parents, she couldn't throw the phone in the bin, but she could leave it in the house and ignore it. She knew she should delete the pictures. Not only every one she had of Karl and her, taken when she'd thought life couldn't be better, but also that last one: the one that changed everything. But she wasn't ready to look at it again and she couldn't get herself to delete it.

Never mind that she had told Karl to go to hell. It hurt too much. She hadn't given him time to explain himself and that gnawed at her. Should she give him the benefit of the doubt? Except there was no doubt in this case. That picture said all there was to say.

'I would never give him a second chance,' she said to Frikk as they walked down to the beach. The dog looked unimpressed. 'I just want to know how he could be such a bastard.'

The dog suddenly stopped and started barking his head off. He was a few steps ahead of her. Ninni hastened up to him.

'What? Why are you barking, you silly dog?'

Frikk barked again. Only it was more of a growl than a bark, and she realised he was warning her.

'What's going on?' Ninni stepped towards the tall grass and peered carefully down. 'Is it a squirrel? Or a mouse?'

A steel-grey snake squirmed past them and disappeared underneath a small rock.

Ninni looked at the dog. 'That's a slow-worm, not a cobra, and it's not dangerous at all. Leave the poor creature alone.'

Frikk kept his ears perked, staring in the direction of the worm in case she needed defending.

'Come on, we have things to do today.' Ninni ran across the hillside until she stood on the edge. She held out her arms and yelled into the wind. Frikk grinned with his tongue hanging out.

The sun was baking, so hot it was almost unnatural. Ninni didn't hesitate when she came down to the beach, but jumped straight into the cool water. It was so clear she could see the bottom. Small crabs darted across the pebbles, hiding in the flowing seaweed. A shoal of young fish swam away when she tried to touch one of them.

She spluttered when Frikk jumped in after her, splashing and panting like a maniac. He was grinning and getting water in his mouth, then sneezing.

'You are a mess,' Ninni said, grabbing hold of his collar. 'Go on land and wait for me.'

The dog paddled towards land and climbed up on the slippery stones, then settled nicely on the pier, watching her swim.

When she climbed out of the water she thought she saw movement from Agnar's house, but when she looked again there was nothing there. Just the sun on the windowpane, she thought, shrugging. As far as she knew, there were no ghosts in Agnar's house.

She lay down next to Frikk and rested her chin on her hands. The wood was warm and comfortable, reminding her of all the summers when it seemed that was all she was doing.

A plastic bottle floated past, catching her attention. 'Oh, the bastards,' she said.

Ninni stretched out her arm and caught the bottle. Just an ordinary fizzy water bottle, thrown overboard by some useless bastard who couldn't be bothered to bring it to shore and throw it in the bin like a normal person.

She got up and put the bottle in her backpack. 'Come on, Frikk. Time to inspect the beach.'

The dog was up at once and followed her down to the beach. Among the patches of sand and pebbles, she found another bottle at once. Carefully she walked towards the other side, picking up rubbish on her way.

Jack saw her from the window, wondering what the hell she was doing. He longed for a swim, but didn't have any shorts to swim in and he wasn't very keen on swimming in his underwear. Not with her there almost all the time. He hadn't brought a lot of clothes, only enough to last for a few days. Agnar had a washing machine, but there was no detergent anywhere that he could find. He added that to his list.

He brought a cup of tea out in the garden, together with the papers from the lawyers. They had translated the will and he had read all of it at the office, not wanting to sign anything that would make it impossible to sell the farm or get him in debtors' prison in Norway. If they had anything like that.

He found a listing of estate agents online and called the first. He explained the situation and ended up explaining it to another two agents, until someone finally said he would come and take a look. They specialised in farms, and the agent gave him a list of things he needed to know.

That was when Jack discovered that the envelope

given to him by the lawyers contained papers that looked like lists but that he couldn't read. Why the hell hadn't they translated them?

The estate agent made him read aloud the first things on the list, being polite enough not to laugh at his pronunciation, then said it was an inventory.

'Bloody hell, it's six pages long,' Jack said.

'That only means they have been thorough.'

He made an appointment for the following day and was pleased with himself. Afterwards, he opened Google Translate and started to translate the list, word by word.

'I have a boat,' he said out loud. That would probably be in the boathouse. Cool.

'Hello?'

Jack looked up to find a man about his own age, standing on top of the little stairs that led down into the garden. The man was dressed in a faded pair of cargo shorts and a T-shirt with a huge print of a cannabis leaf. He lifted a hand. In the other hand he held a brown paper bag. 'Are you the Englishman?'

'I guess I am. Hello.'

The man pointed at the garden. 'May I talk to you?'

'Sure.' Jack stood up and shook his hand. 'Nice to meet you. I'm Jack.'

'Olav. My partner and I have a smallholding on the other side of the island.'

Jack pointed at the chair. 'Sit down. How did you know I was here?'

'Jens told me when I popped into the shop,' Olav said.

Jack smiled. 'Are you the one they send out to see if I'm dangerous?'

'Not really. I just need to know one thing,' Olav said.

'And what is that?'

Olav scratched his ear. 'Are you a tourist? I'm asking because it sounds really ... unlikely. The property has been empty since Agnar died, and I don't think they can rent out a property where there's no owner. All they told us was that they were looking for an heir and, as far as anyone on the island knows, Agnar didn't have any family left.'

'I see.' Jack didn't hide his amusement. 'And you want to know what I'm doing here. Is that so?'

Olav nodded. 'Yes, if you don't mind telling me. Of course, you're under no obligation to do so.'

'Do you want some tea?' Jack lifted his cup. 'I'm happy to get you some.'

Olav shook his head. 'No, thank you. I don't really drink black tea.'

'That's fine. I don't have any biscuits to offer you, I'm afraid.'

The mention of biscuits triggered a reaction with Olav. He held out the paper bag he had been holding. 'Sorry, these are from my partner, Sigrid. They are healthy, I'm afraid,' he added.

Jack opened the bag. The contents looked like biscuits. He took one out and looked at it. It was round, had bits in it and smelled delicious. 'What kind are they?'

'Oatmeal cookies with hazelnut, honey and raisins. We make our own honey. Small scale, but still.'

Olav grinned when Jack carefully took a bite, chewed it and nodded. 'Not bad, actually. Do you want one?' Jack held out the bag.

'No, I had to promise Sigrid to leave all of them for you. It would be rude. She is very partial to hospitality.'

Jack wasn't sure how to respond to that, so he put the rest of the biscuit in his mouth.

Olav looked at him, obviously waiting for something.

Jack smiled. He had nothing to hide. 'I'm the new owner of the farm,' he said.

'Oh,' Olav said. 'That's certainly unexpected.'

'Do you want to see the paperwork?' Jack nodded towards the pile of paper on the table.

'No, of course not. I have no reason not to believe you. I'm just surprised.'

Not as much as me, Jack thought. He could see Olav trying to figure out what to ask next.

'Did you buy the farm?' Olav said after a small pause. Jack smiled. 'No. Agnar left it to me in his will.'

'Well, then that changes matters, I think.' Olav cleared his throat. 'I've been cutting your grass,' he said, waving a hand at the fence towards the field.

'Okay,' Jack said. What was it with these people and grass? Jens had gone on about the same thing. 'That's nice of you, I guess. Did you make those things on the field with the hay?'

'They are racks to dry grass on, yes. It's called *hesjer*,' Olav said. 'I cleared it with the lawyers first, of course; I have been doing it for the last five years. Agnar and us, we shared the grass. This farm is organic, just like mine, so we cooperated.'

'Right. And you want to know if the arrangement can continue?'

Olav nodded. 'Yes, I do. We depend on the grass as winter fodder for our cows and sheep, and for the donkey, of course.'

Jack wasn't sure if he was joking or not. Olav looked serious. It surprised him that Olav didn't ask about why Agnar had left him the farm. He wouldn't volunteer any information. If people wanted to know, they could bloody well ask directly.

'I see. Whatever you and Agnar did, you are welcome to keep doing it until I decide what to do with ... everything.'

'Oh, so you are selling the place?' Olav looked surprised again.

'I'm not sure what I will do with the farm, to be honest.'

'Not a farmer, then.' Olav's face suddenly lit up in a wide grin.

Jack grinned back at him. 'Not even the slightest. I have absolutely no knowledge of farming, Olav. This is the first time I'm on anything resembling a farm. And this place is nothing like I expected.'

Olav looked puzzled. 'Oh. What do you do, then? For a living, I mean?'

'Actually I'm a chef, so I know all about produce and how to cook it,' Jack said with a grin as Olav's eyes widened. 'But that doesn't mean I want to run a farm. I wouldn't know where to begin.'

Olav looked around. 'I hope you don't sell it to developers. They'll ruin the beach and the fields, and all the hard work Agnar put into running this farm will be lost. It would be such a shame. There are so few small-holdings left in this country, and even fewer who farm organically. There's a lot of commitment, hard work and love of the land in this farm.'

'Like I said, I don't know what I'll do. I've only been here for two days,' Jack said.

'Of course, of course. I'm sorry to be nosy, but you know, we are all curious about you. And even more now that we know you're the new owner.'

I bet, Jack thought. 'I understand that.'

Olav looked like he wanted to say something else, but hesitated.

'What?' Jack smiled.

'Well, if you decide to sell, perhaps you could consider another option. You could sell the house as a holiday house, then the fields to the rest of us. I'm sure some of the others would be interested.'

'There's a thought. I'll certainly consider that,' Jack said.

It didn't matter to him who bought it. He wanted the highest price he could get. He had plans for that money, depending on how much he could get for the place.

'Thank you, that's awfully nice.' Olav stood up, apparently finished with the visit. 'Oh, and please come and visit our farm, if you like.'

Jack nodded. 'I would love to. Thank you.'

Olav pointed south. 'We're at the other end of the island.'

He disappeared and Jack leaned back. He put another biscuit in his mouth. It was delicious, he thought, wondering if he could get the recipe. And then the phone buzzed.

Jack looked at it and frowned. Fedra. Yeah, he was not talking to her. He wasn't talking to any of them. Without hesitation, he muted the phone. She immediately texted him.

Where are you? Don't be a child. Pick up the phone.
I want it back! You bastard thief!

Jack grinned and looked up at the tree. It had small knots of fruit all over the branches. What was that?

Pears or apples? He had no idea. Some farmer I'd be, he thought.

Later that afternoon, Ninni climbed up the stairs to Jens and Alma's house. The main entrance was at the back, with the shop on the ground floor.

The door was open. Most people never locked their doors.

'Hello?'

No response, but she heard voices. She kicked off her shoes in the hall and walked in.

Jens sat by the living room door and smiled when she popped her head in. 'We are having a serious discussion about what to do about the Englishman who is roaming the island,' he whispered.

'Why?' Ninni had received a text, telling her to be at the meeting, but it didn't say for what reason. 'Did he do something?'

'Turns out he inherited the place,' Jens whispered.

'What?' Ninni wasn't sure if he was joking.

Jens winked at her, then lifted a finger to point at his wife.

Alma sat in the recliner on the other side of the room, with a cup of coffee in her hand. 'He's not roaming the island. He's an imposter, for God's sake. It's clear as day.'

Ninni looked around the room. Those present formed the island's council. Although the total population was barely over a hundred people, the island governed itself.

She smiled at the school teacher, Britt, who beamed back at her. Olav and Sigrid sat close together on the sofa, and on the other side was the third farmer on the island, Tobben. He nodded at her too, looking grim.

Jens made room for her next to him. 'We have waffles,' he said, pointing at the table.

A lot more than waffles; there were also biscuits and one of Alma's pound cakes. Lemon, Ninni guessed.

'Jens, please. We're not having a coffee party,' Alma said.

Ninni sat down next to Jens and looked at Alma. 'Why do you think Jack is an imposter?'

'Isn't it obvious? How else can he claim to be the owner of Agnar's farm?' Alma said.

Everyone stared blankly at her. She shook her head, exasperated at their thickness. 'He somehow got wind of Agnar's death and thinks he can make a fortune selling the land before anyone discovers he's a criminal. He's stealing a dead man's property.'

'That sounds highly improbable. For one, it would take an enormous amount of planning,' Britt said.

'Not if he's in cahoots with Haldorsen,' Alma said with a grim smile. 'Haldorsen probably has done all the planning and then hired this man to play a role. Perhaps he's an actor of sorts. It's possible.'

They all exchanged looks. Ninni secured a piece of the lemon cake. She cleared her throat. 'Do you really think Erik Haldorsen would produce a false heir, just to get his way? Wouldn't it be easier for him and his partners to wait until the farm went to state hands and then buy the land?'

Alma shook her finger. 'I don't think so. I think they want Agnar's land as soon as possible. This man can sell it whenever he wants. There's no waiting time, no bureaucracy and no competition.'

Jens leaned forward. 'I talked to him when he came in to do his shopping the other day. He seems nice. I don't think he's a fraud.'

Alma made a sound and everyone looked at her. 'And you didn't ask him anything useful, did you, Jens?'

'No, because I'm not the bloody Gestapo, am I?' Jens replied with a wide grin.

Olav cleared his throat. 'Actually, I've just been to see him.'

Everybody stared at him. Alma nodded; obviously she already knew. Olav looked uneasy.

'How did you know he would be there?' Ninni suddenly realised Jack had stayed at Agnar's farm for two nights. That was too close for comfort.

'Jens told me. Jack was in the shop, they talked, and he told him where he was staying. And I thought Jack should know about the grass. Being the new owner and all.'

Sigrid put a hand on his arm. 'We thought it was best to inform him since we can't be sure of what he knows or not.'

'Well, what did he say?' Tobben said.

'He said the arrangement we had with Agnar still stands, and that he has no idea what to do with the farm. And that he's only been here for a few days, so it's too soon to say anything,' Olav said.

'That sounds reasonable,' Jens said.

Alma sent him a dirty look. 'But it's not really proof of anything. How do we even know who he is? How is he related to Agnar? How can he take over the farm without any of us knowing who he is? And how did the lawyers find him?'

'Why don't you ask him?' Ninni said.

'Yes, that's what I think too,' Olav said. 'Someone should just ask him. He seems like a nice bloke.'

'Good. Then you can talk to him tomorrow,' Alma said, looking at Ninni.

Ninni had no intention of being Alma's errand girl. She'd be mortified. 'Not on your life, Alma. If you want to know something about Jack, please ask him yourself. I'm sure he'll answer you.'

Alma sighed. 'I'm too angry,' she admitted.

'If I go, I'm not going to ask him all the questions you want to ask him, you know that.' Ninni smiled at her. 'And you're the mayor. It would make a lot more sense if you go.'

'Right. Then I will. Since you all seem to think that's the best solution, I'll go and see him after work.'

She seemed satisfied with the decision, as everybody

knew she would be. Ninni scratched her nose. 'Have you called the lawyers?'

'No, not yet. I've just learned of his preposterous claim. I haven't had the time, to be honest.'

Tobben looked surprised. 'Perhaps we should talk to the police on the mainland. They could check him out for us. You know, if it's a scam.'

Britt waved her phone in the air. 'Wait, I found him online. He really is a chef. He used to work at this fancy French restaurant in London, but has just quit.'

She scrolled the screen. 'Wow, they almost have a Michelin star. That's amazing. That means he's an excellent chef.'

'Why would he leave a job like that?' Ninni wasn't the only one wondering.

'Not sure. The owner of the restaurant only says that they had "creative differences", whatever that means.' Britt held up her phone again and Ninni leaned forward to look at the screen. There was Jack standing next to a stunning woman. They had their arms around each other, laughing at the camera.

'She's the owner?'

'Says here, her father owns the restaurant but she has taken over as head chef and manager. She must be a good cook too. Although she looks like she hasn't eaten in years,' Britt said.

Ninni took an instant dislike to the woman, but stopped herself. It wasn't her business who Jack had his arm around, was it? If skinny stick women were his type, then that was his problem, wasn't it?

Tobben looked too. 'She looks like she's preserved in plastic,' he said, making everyone laugh again.

Alma looked at them. 'Listen, our island is under threat, we have to protect it from greedy developers like Haldorsen before it's too late. And if this man is not his puppet, he might soon be. It's obvious that a man like that will want to sell the farm to the highest bidder, and we know that's not going to be any of us. So what do we do?'

Ninni nibbled on the cake, finding comfort in the tangy taste of the lemon. It was soft and sweet and with just the extra lemony twist from the glaze. Damned if she was going home without an extra piece.

Britt put up her hand. 'But if this guy sells the farm, would that really be so bad?'

The silence that fell was so thick it could be cut with a knife. Ninni swallowed the last piece of the cake and held her breath.

'They will tear down Agnar's farm buildings, build a huge marina for sailing boats and yachts, and whatnot. Turn the island into a playground for people who will look down upon us and the island, and treat us like dimwits. It will be a disaster for us,' Alma said, clearly not expecting to be contradicted.

Britt wasn't that easily deterred. 'Yes, but I mean, it might bring more tourists and holiday people here, and we can sell our goods. Perhaps even open a place to sell them from. Would that really be so bad? We could bring mainlanders out here, and perhaps more of us could make a decent living out here.'

Ninni liked that idea. 'A bistro or something like that would be nice. Britt's beer is amazing, we all know that. You could extend your shop, Alma. You could sell more of the local produce and baked goods.'

Alma was fuming. 'We all know that Haldorsen will destroy everything. Think of all the rubbish a marina brings with it. We will lose arable land and God knows what else. What if the tourists don't come? And, if they do, Haldorsen and his people will keep the profits from any endeavours they come up with. He will make sure of that. If there is to be a restaurant or an artisan shop, you can bet neither of us will be involved. No, we have too much to lose.'

Britt looked like she wanted to say something else, but restrained herself.

Alma spoke again. 'We need to know more about this man. I will go and talk to him myself and if anyone else could also check him out, that would be much appreciated. The more we know about him, the better it is. All agreed?'

The others nodded, and Alma looked relieved.

'Good, and since that's settled we have to decide what to do after we have the information. It's imperative that we stick together now. This could change our island for ever.'

Ninni leaned towards Jens. 'It sounds terribly dramatic,' she whispered.

Jens nodded, a smile lighting up his face. 'Oh, it is.'

Tobben seemed to think the same thing. 'Do we have to get out the torches and pitchforks, Alma?'

Everybody laughed and Alma couldn't help smiling herself. She waved her hand. 'Fine, I get the point. We're not going to throw him off the island, unless he really is an imposter. Then we can discuss it again. Agreed?'

Ninni snagged another piece of the cake. 'Alma, this is so good. I think you have outdone yourself with this one.'

'That's not mine, it's Britt's,' Alma said.

Britt waved a hand. 'It's just an experiment.'

'Then it's the best experiment since the light bulb,' Tobben said, tucking in.

Ninni noticed Tobben looking at Britt, and Britt giving him a radiant smile. Perhaps other things had happened while she was on the mainland.

Britt came over and sat next to her after the discussion turned to summer plans. 'Did you meet this man?'

'Yes, he hit me with his car in Bergen. He actually came the wrong way around the roundabout.'

'Really? I did that once. In Sheffield. I was so scared, I just stopped in the middle of the road and closed my eyes.'

'You're joking, right?'

Britt shook her head. 'I wish. Every other car stopped and honked, then people came out of their cars and yelled at me. Finally someone realised I wasn't British. Changed the whole atmosphere. They couldn't have been nicer.'

'So a happy ending, then. Not so much for this idiot.'

Britt smiled. 'At least I didn't hit anyone.'

'At least we don't have cars here. That makes us all safer.'

'Yes, but what's he like? Have you talked to him since he arrived here?'

'Just once, on 17th of May when he bought some food from me,' Ninni said.

'It said online that if he had stayed at the restaurant he would have been one of the youngest chefs to get a Michelin star. It makes me wonder why he would leave a restaurant when he must have worked so hard to achieve that.'

Ninni noticed several of the others listening in on the conversation. 'I don't know. He didn't tell me he was a chef. Perhaps that's something you can ask him.'

Britt nodded. 'I certainly will. I don't like Haldorsen any more than the next person, but it would be nice to have a few more business opportunities on the island.'

Alma clapped her hands and they all fell silent. 'Okay, people. We have a plan. We'll meet here again over the weekend.'

Ninni secured herself an extra slice of cake, happy she didn't have to talk to Jack again. She was pretty sure she could avoid him altogether if she put her mind to it.

Chapter 6

The estate agent arrived a few days later, dressed in a T-shirt, jeans and sandals. He also had a backpack.

He greeted Jack as if they had been at school together. 'I'm Mats. Can I call you Jack? It's been a long time since anyone used the equivalent of mister in this country, I'm afraid. We're not that formal.'

Jack nodded. 'Right, I see. I'll get to it then. Can you tell me what this property will be worth on the market? Is there even a market for farms like this? Not speaking Norwegian, I couldn't find anything useful online.'

Mats pulled out a folder and handed it to him. 'I can tell you right away that these properties might take a while to sell, I'm afraid, so if you're looking for a quick sale you might be disappointed.'

Jack sighed. 'That's not what I was hoping for. I'd like to return to London as soon as I possibly can.'

Mats smiled. 'Of course. I fully understand that, and

I can promise you that we will do our best. Do you have the paperwork for the property?'

'In the kitchen. Follow me.'

He noticed that Mats paid attention to everything he saw when they went inside.

'If you want to take a tour of the house, please do. Tea or coffee?'

'Coffee, thank you. I'll be right back.'

Leaving his backpack on a chair, Mats disappeared upstairs and Jack filled the kettle. I need a toaster, he thought. Better put that on the list too, as soon as he found something to write a list on.

The tour of the house didn't take long. Mats was soon back in the kitchen. 'The paperwork?'

Jack pointed at the table. 'It's all yours.'

Mats skimmed through everything while he hummed. 'Right,' he said. 'This looks fine. There's a lot of valuables here. You can sell things like the live-stock, the boat and the boathouse, which is good, people are always interested in those. Unfortunately, it looks like the fields can only be sold together with the house and the barn. There's also the produce that can be sold as it matures. If you need money more quickly, I mean.'

He looked up to see Jack's horrified face. 'What? Did I say something wrong?'

'You said livestock. What does that mean?' Jack was hoping for a few chickens or perhaps he meant the fish

84

in the sea. He also remembered that he had never gone inside the barn, and got a horrible image in his mind of a pile of dead farm animals.

'It's a nice flock of sheep. They're grazing on the islet,' Mats said.

'I don't think I understood one word in that whole sentence,' Jack said.

Mats looked shocked. 'You didn't know?'

'Do I look like I know?' Jack sank down on one of the chairs. 'Nobody said anything about sheep. It wasn't in any of the paperwork they sent me, or the paperwork I had to sign at the lawyer's office. And I would have remembered anyone mentioning sheep.'

Mats pointed at the papers in front of him. 'It says so right here on the inventory list. About twenty animals, probably more now that lambing season is over. Nobody told you?'

'The lawyer never said a word. He handed me all the papers Agnar had prepared, and apparently he didn't check to see if everything had been translated. I'm in a bit of shock here. Did you also say islet? That's not Norwegian for barn, is it?'

'No, of course not; it's a small island not far from here.'

'So, there are no animals in the barn?' Jack wasn't about to be responsible for dead animals.

Mats grinned. 'There could be mice, but they are not on the list. And you don't have to worry, I think. The

85

sheep stay outdoors all year. I'm assuming they get checked on once in a while, although it doesn't say here how often or by whom. I sure hope they have been attended to by someone. The lawyers have definitely not done their job on this one. You should tell them that.'

Jack remembered Jens' talk about grass, and Olav mentioning the same. Why on earth hadn't they said anything? They must have assumed he knew.

'This is ridiculous. I have to see the animals for myself. How can I get out there?'

'By boat, of course.'

Mats said it as if it was the most natural thing in the world. Jack chose not to tell him he hadn't handled a boat in his life. It was probably something everybody here knew. Ninni certainly did. The only boat he had ever been in was a Thames riverboat.

'Right. Just tell me one thing. Are the sheep safe where they are?'

'Oh, absolutely. Like I said, they live there all year round. Mostly they graze on fresh grass and heather, and whatever else sheep eat. But they should be checked on regularly. I'm assuming the former owner did so.'

That didn't really comfort him. 'Yeah, well, Agnar's been dead since January. It took the lawyers some time to find me.'

Mats looked uncomfortable. 'Then perhaps you should call the lawyers and ask them about the sheep.

They knew about them, of course, otherwise they wouldn't have been on the list.'

'I've never even had a cat,' Jack said, overwhelmed by the thought.

'I suspect a flock of sheep are a lot easier to deal with than a flock of cats,' Mats said, smiling now.

Jack smiled slightly. 'I wouldn't really know.'

Mats handed him a paper. 'If you choose to sell through us, please fill out this form and email it to me. Or just pop by the office in town. We're in Haraldsgaten, close by Hotel Saga. Easy to find. Our expenses are clearly marked on the form. You won't get any nasty surprises from us, I promise.'

Jack took the form. To his relief it was in English. 'Thank you. Is there anything I should do to make it more interesting for potential buyers?'

'Tidy up, get rid of personal effects, old furniture that's not very interesting, all those old magazines and stuff by the walls, and make the place look roomy and light.'

Jack looked around. 'Do I have to paint the place?'

'Only if we're desperate. People who buy places like this are either farmers themselves, and would be more interested in the farmland, or they will be property developers and if that's the case they will most likely want to build something else. The value is in the land, Jack,' Mats said.

It was hardly a manor house, Jack thought. 'Okay.'

'Also, I'm sure there will be lots of paperwork concerning the business of the farm somewhere. Bank papers, tax forms, those sort of things. If you could gather it up and send it to me, that will give us a much clearer picture of the farm's value. And you should make a proper inventory list, get that one translated, perhaps, and then let us know as soon as possible.' Mats put everything else in the backpack.

'Do I have to do all that before you can give me an indication of the value?' It sounded like an impossible task.

'At least before we show the house to anyone. I'll need your signature on the authorisation form before we talk about all the other things, like registers and so on.'

Mats stood up and handed him the folder. 'It was really nice meeting you, and I hope we'll speak again soon. Any questions, feel free to call me any time. My card is in there.'

Jack left the folder on the table and followed him outside.

Mats looked around the yard and smiled. 'This is a really nice place, Jack. Are you sure you want to sell?'

'More sure now that I have sheep,' he replied.

He watched the agent make his way through the gate and shook his head. Sheep. He needed to see this for himself.

On one of the hooks by the door there was a key

labelled *"båthus"*. Close enough. Let's see what we have, he thought.

Ninni ran down the field with Frikk at her heels. The *hesjer* holding the drying grass were the perfect hiding spot for a dog. Frikk would hide underneath one of them, then jump out and bark at her, being goofy.

When she came down to the beach she stopped. The doors to Agnar's boathouse was wide open. She held back Frikk, who was trying to catch the waves coming in. Sounds from someone swearing came from inside.

Hiding a smile, she walked closer and looked in. 'What are you doing?'

It was a legitimate question. Jack was in there, muttering to himself while struggling with the chain. 'I'm trying to get this stupid boat out in the water,' he said through clenched teeth.

Ninni climbed in the boathouse. 'Do you have the key?'

Jack looked up at her. His hair was tousled and he had a black mark on his cheek. 'I have a key and I have used it to unlock the bastard lock, but it's still not budging.'

Ninni leaned against the open door. 'Why are you taking out the boat?'

He pulled at one of the chains. 'I learned today that I am the owner of a flock of sheep and that they live on an islet. I would like to go out there and check how they are doing.'

Ninni folded her arms over her chest. 'You didn't know before today about Agnar's sheep? How is that possible?'

He straightened his back and looked at her with a mad look in his eyes. 'You know, I have asked myself the same question. It turns out that the law firm that translated the will didn't bother with the inventory list and never told me about them. So, no, I had no idea.'

He was flustered and angry. Ninni was enjoying herself; she couldn't help it. 'Do you know where they are?'

Jack waved his arm towards the water. 'Out there. I will go there, if I can get this blasted boat out of here.'

'Agnar used this boat when he put out his fishing nets. It's hard to handle, even if you know what you're doing. Do you even know how to drive a boat?'

Jack looked annoyed. 'How hard can it be?'

'I'll take you.' Ninni could hardly believe she'd said the words, but she couldn't in good conscience let him go out there alone. Most likely he would get lost and drown.

'No, thank you,' he said, followed by a yelp when he managed to get his finger stuck in one of the chain links. 'Bloody hell.'

Ninni walked over to him. 'Let me see.'

Jack stuck his finger in his mouth. 'No,' he said between his teeth.

'Don't be a baby. Let me see.' Ninni held out her hand.

He showed her. The cut was small and not bleeding very much. 'You'll live. Come on, let's go see how your sheep are doing.' She turned around.

He followed her without a word. The boat was ready, but he wasn't. Ninni popped into their boathouse and picked up the lifejackets. She handed him the largest. It was pretty old and bulky. But it was the only one in his size. 'Here, put this on.'

Jack eyed it suspiciously. 'I'm not putting on that,' he declared. 'I know how to swim.'

Ninni frowned. 'Then you're not going in the boat. First rule at sea: always wear a life jacket.'

She dropped the jacket at his feet, then put on her own and zipped it up, before getting Frikk into his. The dog stood perfectly still while she fastened the Velcro around his belly and neck. Jack hadn't touched the jacket. Ninni sighed.

'We always use life jackets in the boat when we are going out to sea. The currents here are dangerous and the water cold, and it doesn't really matter if you're a strong swimmer or not. If you want to see your sheep, put it on.'

He did what she said then. 'I look like a twat,' he said.

Ninni smiled sweetly. 'Yes, you do, but if I push you out of the boat for being annoying, at least you'll float.'

Jack looked at Frikk with a wary expression on his face. The dog looked back at him, ears up, tail down.

'Are you sure he's friendly?'

'Are you scared of dogs?' Ninni smiled at him.

Jack kept a watchful eye on Frikk. 'No, not really. I'm not used to them, that's all. We never had any pets. My brother is allergic.'

Ninni turned to Frikk. 'Say hello to Jack, Frikk.'

The dog lifted a paw and Jack, after a moment's hesitation, shook it. 'That's pretty good,' he said and smiled.

Ninni laughed. 'He has excellent manners. Better than most people, I think.'

She climbed into the boat, keeping it steady by standing with her legs apart. 'Come on, Frikk, jump in.'

The dog looked at Jack, seemed to grin at him, and then jumped. Ninni grabbed him and lifted him to the front. She looked up at Jack. 'Come on.'

Jack hesitated. 'Are you sure that thing is safe?'

'My word, you are a scaredy-cat. Don't worry, if you fall while getting into the boat you can't drown. That's what the life jacket is for.'

She held out a hand, but Jack ignored it. Copying her, he carefully stepped into the boat, then sat down.

He stretched out his hands and grabbed hold of the gunwale on both sides.

Ninni didn't say anything. It wasn't nice to make fun of someone sitting in a boat for the first time, no matter how hilarious he looked. He seemed so sure of himself on land and now he sat there, staring at the water as if it was going to attack him.

She sat down in the aft and pulled the cord to the engine a couple of times. It spluttered and then started.

The wind was coming from the south and the water was a bit choppy. The bow jumped on the waves and Frikk had a grand time barking at them.

Jack turned pale.

Ninni leaned forward. 'Are you seasick?'

'No.' He shook his head, then turned a shade greener.

'I'll slow down. It's not far, just about ten to fifteen minutes south of here,' she said.

He looked slightly better at the thought. Ninni slowed down. Best let him get used to the rhythm, she thought. He needed a distraction.

Ninni pointed at her left. 'Do you like birds?'

Jack looked confused. 'What?'

'If you follow the shoreline to the other side, you'll come to a small cliff wall with nesting birds. You're not allowed to get too close because the birds might freak out, but it's nice to see.'

'Unless I can eat them, I'm not into birds,' Jack said.

'Really? I thought that was a British thing. Lying in

fields, gawking at birds through binoculars and writing it down in a little book.'

Jack looked at her. 'Sorry?'

Ninni was surprised. Apparently they had got the only Englishman with no sense of humour. How sad, she thought.

Frikk barked again and Ninni stretched her neck. 'Here we are.'

The islet was mostly a huge cliff with patches of grass and shrubs.

Jack turned around. 'I thought it was a small island,' he said.

'It's just an islet, but more than big enough for your sheep, as you can see.'

Jack shook his head. 'I can't believe I have sheep,' he said.

Ninni turned off the engine and let the boat float freely.

'We can't go on land, I'm afraid. Frikk is not allowed at all, and also the sheep don't know us and they might panic. If they panic and start to run, they might actually fall over the edge of the islet,' she explained. 'Can you see them?'

She watched him, to see his reaction to them. Jack spotted the animals quickly and stared at them for a long time without saying a word.

The ram stood at the edge of the water, keeping a watchful eye on them. He was big, with curly horns and small beady eyes. Behind him a larger flock of ewes were also watching them. Ninni smiled at the lambs, jumping around, chasing each other.

'Are you sure we're in the right place?' Jack didn't take his eyes off the animals. 'Those are goats. I do know the difference, you know.'

'No, they really are sheep. It's a breed called Old Norwegian Sheep. Probably Olav has looked after them since Agnar died.'

'How do they survive out here on their own?' Jack waved his hand at the islet. 'It's hardly more than a rock.'

'They eat whatever grows out here, get plenty of hay supplied in the winter, and they probably fish when the urge takes them.'

Jack looked at her with raised eyebrows. 'I know sheep don't eat fish.'

'I was just testing to see if you have a funny bone.'

'Very amusing. Agnar kept them for the meat?'

He stared at the sheep again, this time taking photos with his phone.

Ninni kept the boat steady for him. 'You can taste for yourself. Agnar smoked the meat in his smokehouse. He produced cured meat for sale, together with Tobben and Britt.'

'There's a smokehouse?' Jack looked interested.

'It's down by the water, on the far side of the house. Agnar would salt the ribs, smoke them and then let them hang to mature. Mutton ribs is a big deal here for Christmas. It's really delicious. And then, of course, there's the *fenalår*.'

'What's a *fenalår*?' Jack managed to pronounce it almost perfectly.

'Leg of mutton. It's a bit like Serrano ham, but darker, and so tasty my father almost cries when he eats it. You'll most probably find some hanging in *stabburet*.'

Jack raised his eyebrows. 'In the what now?'

'*Stabburet*. You know, the building that's not built on the ground?'

His face lit up. 'I was wondering about that. I haven't been in there yet. Why is it built on cairns?'

'It was built that way to keep out mice and rats. Most farms had those in the old days, to keep their grains and food safe during winter. Agnar modernised it at some point and some of the others invested in the business. That's what they do on the island. They work together.'

Jack smiled suddenly. He looked different when he smiled, Ninni thought. It was … unsettling. She turned the boat away from the sheep.

She kept an eye on him. He had a faraway look on his face, and looked back at the islet. The ram still stood his ground on the narrow beach.

Jack couldn't get over the sheep. They looked so strange. Like woolly goats with long fleeces and spindly legs.

Ninni was having him on. He was pretty sure she was laughing her head off now.

The idea that Agnar kept them for the meat intrigued him. He was curious to taste it.

'Can you drop me off at the smokehouse?' he asked.

'Of course. No extra for the trip,' Ninni said.

She was joking. It dawned on him she had been joking earlier. Did that mean she didn't hate him any more? He hoped so.

The boat jumped and dipped and skipped on the waves. The dog barked like a maniac.

Jack held onto the gunwales and didn't mind the trip so much any more. The air was so crisp, so clear it made him smile just to sit there. Even if he was getting sprayed with water every time the boat jumped. He took a deep breath and felt the tension melting from his shoulders.

The shoreline suddenly burst into sight. He tried to hide a sigh of relief, but Ninni caught it and smiled from ear to ear.

'You'll get used to it,' she yelled over the engine.

'Don't bet on it,' Jack replied.

Hopefully, Olav could keep looking after the sheep. He wasn't sure he was up to the task of taking care of the poor animals.

Ninni slowed down the speed and followed the shore past her boathouse, then his, and finally had the boat glide along a small pier. He could see the top of a building half hidden in between the bushes.

'That's it?' It didn't look like much.

'Yes, that's the smokehouse. Agnar always stacked firewood in the back, mostly juniper and birch. It always smelled so good.' She looked at him. 'Do you want me to show you, or are you fine on your own?'

Jack hesitated. He wouldn't mind her company, but it was probably not a good idea. He reminded himself that he would only be there for a short period of time.

'It's on land. I'm sure I'll be fine.'

He watched her as she manoeuvred the boat closer to the small pier. She grabbed hold of one of the pier posts to keep the boat steady. 'Can you get up?'

Jack discovered a makeshift stepladder on the side. It didn't look trustworthy.

It was clearly a challenge. Jack stood, carefully so as not to lose balance, and grabbed hold of the pier. The wood was dry and crumbly underneath his fingers. The boat wobbled underneath his feet. He managed to get one foot on the ladder, hoisting himself up on the pier. He couldn't help feeling pleased and smiled at her.

'Can I have my life jacket back, please?' Ninni stood up in the boat too, holding out her hand. Her balance was perfect.

Jack pulled it off and handed it to her. 'Thank you for taking me out there. I needed to see for myself that the animals were okay. And real,' he said.

Ninni laughed. 'Any time. You know where to find me. I mean, if you want to see the sheep again.'

She pushed off and the boat floated away. Then she started the engine. She waved at him and then turned the boat around. The sound from the engine overpowered the dog's barking.

Jack stood up, relieved to be on solid ground again, even if it was a half rotten old pier. He walked over to the smokehouse, surprised to find it unlocked and curious as to what he would find. Hopefully not a slaughterhouse of some sort.

It was dark and cold inside, and he left the door open behind him. The smell of burnt wood was sharp, but not unpleasant. Across from the door he spotted an oven of sorts, built into the wall. There were pipes going from the oven through the wall. From the ceiling an assortment of hooks made him feel a bit uneasy.

Jack fumbled at the wall next to the door and found the light switch. He turned it on and a single bulb lit up the room. Agnar wasn't much for lighting, he thought.

He walked over to the oven and inspected it. It was built with slabs of grey stone, carefully put on top of each other, making it look like a dome with two doors in it. He was curious and opened it. Inside, it was black with soot. He touched it and his fingertips turned black.

'Brilliant,' he said.

He wondered how it worked. Olav or any of the others would know. Maybe Ninni. She seemed to know everything about everything on the island, yet she didn't really live there. He wondered about her story. She seemed happy enough, but there was something guarded in her eyes.

On the way to *stabburet*, he stopped at the house to pick up the keys. He almost stepped on a box of eggs, placed on top of the steps.

Jack looked around. There wasn't anyone there, nor was there any sign of where they'd come from. He picked up the box and brought it into the kitchen. The eggs seemed fresh. A welcoming gift? He hoped so. He left the box on the counter and went outside again.

Stabburet towered over him. He climbed up the narrow steps and unlocked the door. The smell of meat was strong when he stepped inside and he almost hit his head on something hanging from the ceiling. Stifling a scream, he searched frantically for the light switch and for once there was more than one single lightbulb.

He looked up. Bundles hung from the ceiling, wrapped in some kind of gauze. Jack reached up and touched one of them, surprised at the weight.

Cured mutton, he thought and grinned. *I have a room full of cured mutton.* He discovered that each bundle was labelled with a date, presumably when they were hung up there. Each one was also marked with names. The owners, he guessed. He reached up again and unhooked one of the bundles bearing Agnar's name. It was surprisingly heavy. The date was last September.

He put it to his nose. 'Oh, my God, this is wonderful,' he muttered.

Back in the kitchen, he took one of Agnar's knives and cut the gauze open. He cut a small sliver of the dark meat and put it in his mouth.

'Oh, my word,' he said while he chewed. Sweet and salty, and chewy enough to be interesting. It needed some cheese, he decided. Unfortunately, the cheese desk at Jens and Alma's shop wasn't much to brag about. There was the Jarlsberg, of course, which the Norwegians seemed to treat like any regular cheese, not the slightest piece of a decent cheddar, not to mention the absolute absence of Stilton or any French cheese to speak of.

He remembered the Viking cheese Jens had given him, and pulled the box out of the refrigerator. It was worth a try. He opened the package and smelled it. That one could give any French smelly cheese a run for its money, he thought. Then he cut a piece of cheese and another piece of the meat.

'Good,' he muttered.

But it needed more. Something sweet, something sharp to complement the saltiness. Figs, maybe, if it was possible to get any, and fresh mayo and herbs from the garden, he decided.

There were possibilities here, he thought. Chewing on another piece of cheese and meat, he went into the garden and started rummaging around in the weeds to see what would taste good in a mayo.

Chapter 7

Ninni held the box carefully and headed up the small pathway to the hill. She walked slowly. Her stomach was not in a good mood and she hoped the fresh air would take care of it.

Frikk took his time, sniffing at every bush and stone on his way. She knew he would follow. On top of the hill, she looked down at Agnar's farm, or perhaps it was time to start calling it Jack's farm? How was he doing after his ordeal at sea? Hopefully she hadn't been too rough on him.

'I couldn't help it,' she said aloud. 'He's so damned smug.'

Frikk caught up with her and cocked his head as if he was listening. A movement in the garden made her stretch her neck. What was Jack doing?

Jack was on his knees in the flower beds, digging at the plants. Sometimes he put something to his nose, then tossed it aside. Other times he sniffed something again, then put it on the ground next to him.

Not only smug but a bit insane, Ninni thought. At least he wasn't harmed after the boat trip. She turned her back and walked along, avoiding the pits and holes in the ground. It was a grey day, clouds floated over the island and there was a promise of rain in the air later.

Soon she forgot all about Jack. She stopped outside the little school: a small white house behind the only slightly larger chapel that occasionally was used for the formal part of weddings and christenings.

Britt's house stood next to the school. The front wall was covered in small pink rosebuds with some tulips nodding their heads beneath the window. All the windows on the first floor were wide open, bedclothes hanging over the windowsill in preparation for B&B guests.

Ninni was about to press the doorbell when Britt came around the corner.

'Hi,' Britt said, her face brightening at once.

'I have come on an important errand,' Ninni said.

'Okay. What's so important?' Britt grinned, then frowned. 'Frikk, get out of there! Please keep that silly dog of yours out of my flowers.'

Frikk stepped back from the hole he was digging between the sad-looking tulips. He had a perfectly innocent look on his face.

Ninni lifted her finger at him. 'No,' she said. 'Say sorry to Britt.'

The dog sat down and lifted a paw to Britt. He grinned with his tongue hanging out.

'Cheeky bastard,' Britt said and ruffled his ears. 'Come on, I'm around the back.'

Frikk and Ninni followed her. A ladder leaned against the wall.

'What are you doing?'

Britt wielded a paint scraper with a determined look in her eyes. 'The windowsills need repainting and I don't want to spend my summer holiday doing this. Better do it now, before school ends. I have plans for the summer. Hopefully, I can keep my rooms let most of the summer and make extra money that way.'

'Don't let me keep you. I just came to see if you have any eggs.'

'That's the important errand?' Britt smiled.

'Yes, I'm all out. Do you have any?' Ninni held out the cardboard box and Britt laughed.

'I have about twenty today, if you want that many. The children are feeding the chickens too much and in return they are laying eggs as if it's an Olympic challenge.'

Ninni wrinkled her nose. 'I think ten will be more than enough.'

'Are some of them for your Englishman?' Britt walked towards the end of the garden where the henhouse stood under the shade of a tall spruce. On the other side of the garden was the brewery building.

'Why do you ask me that?' Ninni was surprised.

Britt shrugged. 'You're his closest neighbour.'

'Sure, but I don't run errands for him. Jack can get his own eggs,' Ninni said.

'Actually, he already has. I went by the farm yesterday to see if he was there, doing my civic duty before Alma lost her cool, and I brought a carton of eggs as a neighbourly gesture. Except he wasn't there.'

Ninni smiled. 'I took him to see the islet. Would you believe nobody told him about Agnar's sheep?'

'That's ridiculous. How is that even possible?' Britt shook her head.

'Someone didn't translate all the legal papers.'

'You should have done it.' Britt dried her hands on her shorts.

Ninni shrugged. 'I wasn't asked.'

Britt put the paint scraper on the ladder. 'I have coffee, if you want.'

'Do you have any more of that lemon cake?' Ninni didn't wait for a reply. She sat down on one of the garden chairs. There was a thermos on the table and a mug.

'No, they gobbled it all up, I'm afraid. You can take the mug; I have the thermos.' Britt sat down on the other chair, leaning back with a happy sigh. 'I am so looking forward to June. Barely a month left now and the little monsters are off on their holidays. Then I can focus on my fun.'

'Making beer?' Ninni smiled.

Britt laughed. 'You know, I'm looking at possibly starting producing aquavit at the moment. It's very popular and really profitable. I think I've had enough of being a teacher.'

'You love those kids.' Ninni knew she was right. Britt doted on all ten of them.

Britt smiled. 'Of course I do. I'll have a new one in the autumn; Sigrid and Olav's youngest is six. Which is good, because next year two of the big kids have to start going to school in town.'

Ninni stretched her legs. 'Why did you bring Jack eggs?'

'He's a chef. I'm sure he would prefer eggs to flowers, and besides, I can't take flowers to a man I haven't said hello to yet. It might be misunderstood.'

'And eggs will not be?' Ninni laughed at her, and Britt looked mortified before laughing so loudly that Frikk sat up and looked at them.

'Oh, I didn't think of that! Do you think he might take offence?' Britt couldn't hide her delight.

'Not really. It's the perfect welcome gift for a chef and, besides, I don't think Jack gets offended so easily.'

'What's he like? Olav said he looked okay, but what does that even mean?'

'He's tall, with blond hair and blue eyes, if you can believe it. He looks more Norwegian than I do.' Ninni pulled at her dark curls. 'He's tense, if you know what I mean.'

Britt was amused. 'No. Explain. In detail, please.'

'Like he's angry about something. Also he's jumpy and he has obviously never been on an island in his life. He has no idea how to get into a boat, for God's sake. Who doesn't know that?'

Britt brushed it aside. 'Anyone from a huge city, I guess. There are loads of people in Norway who don't know their way around a boat. What I want to know is, is he good-looking? Is he sexy?'

Ninni thought about Jack. Her stomach tingled. 'I suppose so,' she admitted.

'I'll absolutely have to go see him for myself now. Sexy men are few and far between, especially here.'

'What about Tobben? I saw how he looked at you at the meeting, and I saw that smile you gave him,' Ninni teased.

Britt pulled a face. 'Tobben is a nice man, but not very exciting. All he talks about is the price of meat, and whether or not I think he should plant broccoli this year.'

'Perhaps he has hidden depths,' Ninni said.

'If he does, I haven't found them and I wouldn't be bothered to look either.' Britt looked at her. 'What about you? Is Karl coming later?'

Ninni had expected the question, but it still stung. 'No, he's not. It's over between us.'

Britt's jaw dropped. 'I'm so sorry. I really thought you'd make it. You seemed to have it so together, you know. You both seemed so happy whenever you came here. What happened?'

Ninni couldn't bring herself to say it aloud. The truth was too raw, and even more embarrassing.

'It just didn't work for me any more. You know, with his flying schedule and being away all the time. It was too demanding, and he doesn't want to give up being a pilot. I wouldn't want him to either,' she said.

Britt nodded. 'I get that. You know I had the same thing with my ex. Geir was travelling all the time and when he was here he was always complaining about how much he hated working on the oil platforms, and I was alone with all the responsibilities. I got fed up with the whole thing.' She leaned forward and put her hand on Ninni's. 'So that's why you seem so under the weather. I'm so sorry, sweetie. It must hurt terribly. If there's anything I can do, anything, you let me know.'

Ninni nodded, afraid to speak in case she started crying. It was the sympathy thing, she thought. It was deadly. She took a deep breath and smiled.

'I'm fine, truly, I am. The island is the perfect place to stay right now. In a few days, a few weeks, I'll be even better.'

Britt frowned. 'That sounds awful. But I understand. You're not ready to talk about it. But don't wait too long or you'll end up old, miserable and dead, surrounded by fifteen dogs and a house filled with empty cake cartons.'

Ninni grinned. 'Oh, thank you. That's a future to look forward to.'

'Tell you what, I'm going to town tomorrow. I'll stock up on wine, and you and I'll get sloshed. We haven't done that in ages, have we?'

'Excellent idea. I could do with a massive hangover.'

'If that's what you want, we should stay here and drink my beer.'

Britt looked at her, and Ninni couldn't help laughing.

The mayonnaise didn't turn out as expected. Jack frowned. Something wasn't right with the flavour. Was it the eggs, perhaps? Or the oil wasn't good. He sniffed it and put it down. No, not that. The sauce on the fish burger Ninni had made for him on the first day was different. He wasn't quite sure why and that annoyed him.

His thoughts drifted to Ninni. For some reason he kept thinking about her. She had edges, he thought. He liked that. And he liked her curls. She had a funny way about her. Charming, even. And she looked amazing in her underwear.

To distract himself, he rummaged through the cupboards and discovered a row of old exercise books in the back. He pulled one out and was about to open it when the phone rang. Jack picked it up and looked at the screen. Fedra again. She wasn't taking no for an answer, of course she wasn't, but he didn't want her to start bothering Danny and Holly, or his dad.

This time he answered. 'What do you want?'

Fedra was silent for a second, unusual for her, but Jack didn't take the bait.

'Why haven't you responded to my calls?' she finally said in her usual demanding voice, the one he used to think was sexy. Now it was annoying.

'Because I don't have anything to say to you,' Jack said.

'That's so insensitive and so typical of you. You are so selfish, Jack. The moment something doesn't go your way, you quit. I do hope that your little travel adventure has made you think about your behaviour.'

Jack wondered, and not for the first time, if she was able to hear herself. 'Get to the point, Fedra. I'm busy.'

While he spoke, he pulled out one of the exercise books and put it on the counter. The pages were yellow at the edges. When he opened it, the pages were filled with spiky writing, clearly recognisable as recipes of some sort, and done mostly with pencil. Some of the pages had simple drawings. There were a few landscape sketches, quite a few of meat cuts and also of sheep, and a few of a young boy.

'I want it back, you bastard,' Fedra hissed in his ear.

Jack had almost forgotten she was on the phone. 'Want what back?' He knew perfectly well what she was talking about.

'The book, of course. The recipe book. I know you took it. It belongs to the restaurant.'

'Every recipe in that book I developed. I created them. It's my book.'

'Yes, but it was done while working for us, in this restaurant, so it belongs to us. And I want those recipes back.'

Jack remembered the humiliation they had put him through, and snorted. 'How is Pierre doing? Is he getting you one of those pesky Michelin stars you're so hungry for?'

'Pierre is doing fine, thank you. He's doing his best, but he's not you, Jack. Nor am I.'

And there it was, Jack thought. There was a certain amount of satisfaction in hearing her admission.

'Are you sure? He took over pretty quickly – both you and the restaurant, as I recall.'

Fedra narrowed her eyes. Oh, you're such a bastard. I didn't cheat on you, and you know that. So don't play hurt, if you don't mind.'

She was right about that. They'd had a short affair, it had burned hot for a few weeks and then it was over. They'd parted as friends. Or so he'd thought.

'There are many ways to cheat on someone, Fedra. Roland made sure he and I never had a contract, and that means the book is all mine. You can go to hell and take bloody Pierre and your father with you.'

'Jack, be reasonable. I don't deserve this. You

threatened Daddy and he doesn't deserve that,' Fedra pleaded now, and he knew how she hated to ask for anything.

Jack closed his eyes for a second. Fedra's father had been his mentor, the man he'd trusted almost as much as his own father, and to be so snubbed by him had been such a blow.

'Roland did deserve it, all of it. He made a promise to me, repeatedly if you recall, and then he changed his mind. He then used the lack of contract to fire me on the spot. And now he sends you to make nice because it has backfired on him.'

Jack paused to calm down. Fedra tried to say something, but he cut her off.

'Listen carefully, Fedra. I don't owe either of you anything. Now, if you ever dare to call my dad again or anyone else, I'll report you to the police for harassment.'

He ended the call and put the phone in his pocket. 'Chew on that for a while.'

He leafed through a few more pages of the exercise book. It was all completely incomprehensible, apart from the occasional word. Egg, he understood that, and "*melk*" had to be milk, and "*sukker*" probably meant sugar. So not too far off. Jack grinned. I'm practically fluent, he thought.

Whoever wrote these books had been talented. Somehow he didn't think it was Agnar. It looked like a diary, although there seemed to be no continuity in how often entries were made. He looked for a name, some clue as to who had written it, but there was nothing. Most likely most of the recipes were about mutton and pork, and loads of cakes, judging by how often sugar was mentioned.

'Why are you here?' a commanding voice said right behind him.

Jack almost dropped the book he was holding. He turned around and looked at the woman standing in the doorway while his heart raced. She had a deep frown on her face.

'Where the hell did you come from? You scared me half to death.'

She pointed behind her. 'The door is open and you didn't answer when I called.'

'Right. And who are you?'

'Alma Mikkelsen, Jens' wife. I'm the mayor.'

'Of course you are. I ... can I help you?' Jack knew who she was now. The bossy one, the lawyer had said.

Alma eyed him with suspicion. 'I would like to know why you are here on the island and why you are in this house for starters. Who are you?'

'Jack Greene,' Jack said.

'I know your name. What I don't know is why you told Olav you own this farm. Are you a fraud? If you have somehow managed to fool Agnar's lawyers or bribed them, for all I know, you should be aware that we will fight you. Haldorsen will not find it so easy to deal with us as he thinks.'

Jack listened carefully. Alma quivered with anger. He didn't reply at first, just took the file with Agnar's will from the kitchen table and handed it to her.

'This is why,' he said.

She took it with an expression of deep mistrust.

'Please read it. It will answer your questions.'

He watched her as she read through the papers. She first became pale, then flushed. Then she looked at him. 'You can't be,' she said.

'And yet I am.' Jack smiled at her. 'Sit down, please.'

Alma's hands were shaking. 'I refuse to believe this. I have known Agnar since he was a little boy. He would have told me if he had a son.'

'Wait here,' Jack said.

He went into the TV lounge and found the pictures he wanted to show her.

She was still reading through the will, as if she needed to understand every word. But at least she was sitting down.

'I also have it in Norwegian if that helps,' he said as he sat down opposite her.

'Yes, I would like to compare the text. If this is a fraud, it's done well.' She looked up at him.

Jack put the photographs in front of her, one by one. 'This is my mother and me, this is me on my first day at school, and this is Agnar and my mother together. I don't know how much Agnar knew about me, or even if he wanted to know anything, but she sent him these pictures. My mother died when I was twelve, and I guess nobody sent Agnar any pictures after that.'

Alma touched the photographs. Her face was a mixture of emotions. 'I never saw these,' she whispered.

'They were on the table in the lounge across the hall. I'm guessing Agnar used that as a bedroom.'

'Yes, he did. He never let anyone in there.' Alma took a deep breath. 'The lawyers had a professional company close up the house after Agnar passed. He had a heart attack while shovelling snow from the road. Jens found him. We took Agnar to the hospital and we all stayed with him. He never regained consciousness.'

'That must have been hard for you,' Jack said.

'Yes, it was. He was a dear friend. How old are you?' Alma looked at him.

'I'm thirty-five. I was born in 1985.'

She pushed the papers over the table towards him. 'I see. Well, I got what I came for. Thank you for being so frank.'

Jack smiled. All the bluster had left her. 'Would you like some tea?' he asked.

'Tea? If I have to.' Alma folded her hands on the table. 'Agnar wasn't here much in the eighties. His mother was still alive then and took care of the farm, and he went to sea for a few years.'

'What did he do? When he returned home, I mean.'

'Like most farmers in this country, he dabbled in bits of everything. The traditional fisheries weren't that lucrative back then. The shipping was in decline. He worked in the North Sea for a while, on the oil fields, and also sailed with some of the oil tankers. Jens would probably know more about that, or Petter, Ninni's father. What do you know about him?'

'All I know is that my mother met him in 1984 in London. They had a short affair, and some weeks later my mother realised she was pregnant. By then Agnar had returned home and my mother didn't want to follow him. She wanted to stay in London.'

'You can't blame her. Boys here, on this coast, have always gone to sea, but they always come home again. Especially boys like Agnar who had a farm. He was an only child and I remember his mother being so worried for him. Magni would have loved a grandson.' Alma smiled a little.

Jack rose and put on the kettle. He needed something to distract himself. 'Did you know Agnar well?'

'As well as anyone. I certainly knew him the longest. Petter, Ninni's father, was a good friend to Agnar, so he will have other memories if you're interested.'

Jack poured hot water in two mugs and dropped a teabag in each. 'Sorry, I don't have any coffee.'

She didn't seem to care, putting two spoons of sugar in the mug and stirring with a faraway look in her eyes.

'I can't believe Agnar never told me about you,' she said again.

'If it's any consolation, nobody told me about Agnar either. I never thought to ask Mum about him, and by the time I started wondering about Agnar, she was gone,' Jack said.

Alma took a sip of the tea, frowned and put the mug down, pushing it a bit away. 'Agnar kept to himself. He worked with Olav on the fields, and in the last few years Tobben, Olav and Britt worked with him on the meat production. Men barely talk about much apart from the weather and football, so he probably didn't talk to them about you either. Men are strange creatures, sometimes, Mr Greene.'

It was the first time she had referred to him by name. Jack smiled. 'Please call me Jack. Everyone else does.'

Alma nodded. 'Tell me something, Jack. You said your mother passed away when you were twelve. What happened to you afterwards?'

'My mother married my dad when I was five. Paul treated me as if I was his son, and before Mum died she made him my legal guardian. Pauls family wasn't too thrilled, but he couldn't care less. I stayed with him and my two siblings.' Jack smiled.

'I can't help wondering if anyone told Agnar about your mother passing. It seems strange to me that he would not make some kind of claim on you,' Alma said.

Jack thought about it. 'I wouldn't know. Paul is my dad in every way. From the first time I met him. He never treated me differently from my siblings. And I wouldn't have left him on his own anyway. He needed me. Holly was four years old and Danny was just a baby. Perhaps Mum didn't want us to lose each other.'

'Or to send you to a stranger in another country. I can understand that. I just wonder if Agnar was asked what he thought.'

Jack shook his head. 'I don't really know.'

He realised he hadn't asked his dad about this. Perhaps he should have.

Alma put a finger on the small exercise book and smiled. 'I haven't seen one of these in years. Your grandmother was a great cook, you know. So was Agnar. So perhaps you have inherited more from them than you think.'

Jack stood up and followed her outside. She looked up at him.

'You look like Agnar. I didn't realise why you seemed so familiar until now.' Tears welled up in her eyes and she turned abruptly. 'I should leave.'

Jack leaned against the doorpost, watching her go. That was a first, he thought. He was used to not looking like anyone.

Ninni climbed up the path from the beach with a bucket full of nice fat mackerel. She wondered what to do with them or, even better, who to give them to.

She stopped when Frikk started barking, then wagged his tail.

Alma came up the road from Agnar's farm. She was pale and looked like she had been crying.

Ninni hurried over to her. 'Alma ... what's wrong?'

The older woman shook her head. Her lower lip trembled.

Ninni dropped the bucket and put her arm around her. 'Come on, sit with me. You look like you've had the shock of your life.'

They sat down on the grass and Alma shook her head again. 'I've just come from Agnar's farm. I talked to the boy,' she said.

Ninni didn't like the sound of that. 'What did Jack do? Did he insult you in any way?'

Alma shook her head again. 'No, of course not. He's a nice man. It's not his fault.'

'Tell me, please.'

'He's Agnar's son, and it breaks my heart that Agnar didn't trust us, trust me, enough to tell us. I would have begged him to bring the boy here, at least for holidays. He's one of us and we should have been allowed to get to know him.'

'Agnar's son?' Ninni said. That was unexpected. 'Are you sure?'

Alma nodded. 'Absolutely. He let me read Agnar's will. It's all there. Name, date of birth, his mother's name. Agnar knew all about him. He even had pictures of himself and the boy's mother, for God's sake.'

'I thought there was something strange about him,' Ninni said slowly.

'Yes, well, you didn't know Agnar when he was young, but Jack looks so very much like him. I should have recognised him at once.'

'Perhaps you should ask for a DNA test,' Ninni suggested.

Alma shrugged. 'No, he's been vetted by the lawyers, and by Agnar. His name is on Jack's birth certificate. It's all true.'

She fell silent for a moment. Ninni picked up the bucket again and waved Frikk away when he tried to sniff the fish.

'We have to give him a proper welcome, you know. Agnar would have expected us to treat him well.'

Ninni wasn't sure that was a good idea, considering Agnar's secrecy. 'But Olav said Jack wants to sell the farm. Why would you welcome him when he's going to leave, and destroy the island at the same time?'

Alma patted her knee. 'We must be clever. He has never been here before; he feels no ties to the island or to the farm. He is also confused about the whole situation. Our aim will be to keep him from leaving until he realises that he belongs here.'

Ninni looked at her. 'That's your plan? It's not much

of a plan, Alma. He's British, he's from London and he's a Michelin star chef. There is no chance in hell that he will stay here.'

Alma smiled. 'We will win him over by making him feel like he's one of us. Which he is; don't forget that. We will all help, including you. You wait and see.'

'You are sneaky. It's a long shot, though. You know that, right?'

'Stranger things have happened. We didn't think Agnar had an heir, but he did.'

'Okay. What do you have in mind?'

'I'll think of something. In the meantime, we will treat him like family.'

'Well, perhaps not that close,' Ninni said, not sure why she didn't like the idea at all.

Alma took a deep breath. 'Jack told me that his father's family never treated him like one of them. So he needs us. Even if he doesn't know it yet.'

Ninni almost rolled her eyes. 'If you say so.'

'You should call Petter. Let him know. You know how close he was to Agnar. I'm sure he would like to meet Jack.' Alma got up from the grass. She brushed her trousers and smiled at Ninni. 'Don't look so serious. We'll get him on our side. If there's anything of Agnar in him, we'll find it.'

After getting to know Jack a little better, Ninni doubted anything would make him stay on the island. It must have shown on her face.

Alma patted her cheek. 'It will all work out in the end. I promise.'

Ninni picked up the bucket. 'I caught these today. Perhaps you would like them? They're too many for me.'

Alma peered into the bucket. 'I'll take them. Jens loves mackerel cakes. I'll save some for you, if you like.'

'Thank you. I'll pick them up tomorrow. I'm more in the mood for pizza today.'

'You are a funny one. I have to go. Jens is eagerly awaiting the result of my talk. He's in for quite a shock.'

Alma gave her a quick hug. 'Be nice to the boy. At least for the time being.'

Ninni watched her make her way towards the harbour. She turned and headed home. Be nice to the boy? she thought. 'I'll bet someone said that to Mata Hari once too,' she muttered.

Chapter 8

Early in the morning a couple of days later, Ninni rigged up a table in the garden. The old cherry tree showed promise; there were lots of tiny pink buds on the branches.

She scratched Frikk under his chin. 'I think we'll stay until autumn this time. No need to go home, now that Karl is out of the picture, is there?'

It felt good saying it aloud – so good. From now on she would remember that feeling.

Frikk slipped under the table and fell asleep. Dogs were lucky, she thought as she put the computer in the shadow and the stack of reference books on one of the chairs next to her. She had coffee in the thermos and sandwiches on a plate, and a beautiful view to distract her.

Time to get some work done. She placed her mobile next to the computer. Her father hadn't responded to the text she'd sent him earlier, but he would at some point. She wondered how he would react to the news about Jack.

She opened the computer and was soon immersed in a contract between two oil companies. The thermos was almost empty when Frikk started barking and almost toppled the table as he shot out from under it.

Ninni turned around and discovered Jack standing outside the fence.

'You are really good at concentrating,' he said. 'I've been standing here for five minutes.'

'No, you haven't. Frikk reacted the moment you got close,' she said and grabbed the dog by the collar. 'Shush, Frikk. You are scaring the nice man. You know him now. Jack is a friend.'

'I've come to ask you a favour.' He held up a carrier bag as if that explained everything.

Ninni remembered Alma's plea to treat him nicely. 'Of course, come in.'

Jack climbed over the low fence and walked towards her. Frikk sat up, ears perked and tail hitting the ground. Jack stopped. 'We have exchanged paws, buddy, so be nice.'

He patted Frikk on the head and got a lick back.

'Sit down,' Ninni said.

Jack sat down on the only available chair. 'I'm sorry, I just realised that you are working. Do you hold regular office hours out here?'

'No, nothing regular. I work when I want to. Work shouldn't be stressful,' Ninni said.

He seemed amused. 'I have never quite thought about it in that manner.'

'Then maybe you are in the wrong line of work?' Something about him made Ninni want to tease him.

'I love cooking, so I don't think so.'

Ninni shrugged. 'To be a chef in a Michelin-star restaurant has to be stressful. All that pressure to cook perfectly, every time you go into a kitchen? It sounds like a nightmare.'

Jack smiled. 'Do you cook?'

'Enough to keep Frikk and myself alive, but it's not something I do for the love of it. To be honest, I can live perfectly fine on frozen pizza and waffles.'

Jack frowned. 'Now that sounds like a nightmare.'

'That's because you haven't tasted my waffles,' Ninni said.

He looked like he was waiting for an invitation, but one that wasn't coming. Not on your life, mate, she thought.

'What's in the bag?' she said instead.

He put the bag on the table. 'Alma said you're a translator.'

Ninni nodded. 'Yes, but I don't translate fiction, only legal papers, contracts and such: all those things you need notarised. Is that what you need?'

'It's not that complicated, I'm afraid. The lawyers who translated Agnar's will left out the inventory list. I called them, but they tell me it would be a full week

127

before I get it back. I've tried to do it myself with Google Translate, but perhaps there's more I should know about. I don't want to discover I have more goats,' he said.

'Sheep,' Ninni said and held out her hand.

'I'm not convinced about that yet,' Jack said and handed her the bag.

She hid a smile. 'Did you find the smokehouse?'

'I found a lot more than that. I found the meat hanging in the *stabbur*. It melted in my mouth.'

'I told you so.' Ninni opened the bag and pulled out the contents: a thin file and some old notebooks. She started with the file.

'Hmm,' she said.

'What? More goats?' Jack looked suspicious.

Ninni looked at him. 'No, but there's a donkey and a couple of cows, and quite a few turkeys.'

Jack frowned. 'Turkeys?'

'Yes, and a llama.'

He laughed. 'I hope you are a better translator than that.'

'I'm an excellent translator. I've been doing it for seven years.' Ninni read through the list and handed it back to him. 'Don't worry. There's no more livestock or anything like that. But it mentions that the *stabbur* is a joint venture with Tobben, Britt and Olav.'

'I know. They will go through everything with me soon,' he said.

Ninni looked at him. 'If you already know what's in here, why come to me? Do you think the lawyers have cheated you or that Tobben and the others have?'

'No, not at all. They couldn't be nicer. In the last few days I have received visitors and gifts worthy of a king. There's eggs and beer, all sorts of jam and even some dried fish – herring, I think.'

He said it with such delight that Ninni couldn't help but be charmed. 'I heard Jens sold you a package of Old Cheese. He's had great fun with that.'

Jack shrugged. 'I actually like it.'

'Seriously? It's hideous and smelly,' Ninni said and opened the old notebook.

'It has a distinct flavour, yes, but I like Stinking Bishop, so the joke is on me.'

'Stinking Bishop? What's that?'

'The smelliest cheese in the UK. It's fantastic,' Jack said with a wide grin.

Ninni picked up one of the exercise books and opened it to read the first page. She looked up at him. 'Do you know what this is?'

'Those are recipes, right?' He looked at the familiar set-up.

Ninni nodded. 'Yes, but it's a lot more than that. This book isn't just a cookbook; it's more like a journal of the farm.'

Jack leaned forward. 'Really? Who wrote it?'

'Agnar's mother, Magni. Your grandmother, actually—' Ninni smiled at his surprise. 'You didn't know that either, did you? It must be so strange to arrive at a place like this, not knowing anything about the people who lived there before. Especially since they are your family.'

Jack smiled. 'It's interesting, for sure. Tell me more about the book. What else is in it?'

Ninni stopped at one page and pointed. 'Magni writes about the weather. Not surprising, not here on the island, at least. Then there's a recipe on how to prepare *lubbesild*; it's a traditional way of preparing herring, a bit like kippers. She says Agnar brought her some good fat herring.' Ninni turned a few more pages. 'And here are recipes for gooseberry jam and redcurrant jelly. That doesn't sound half bad, actually.'

Jack stretched his legs. 'It sounds ... nice.'

'There's a detailed description on how to butcher and preserve a pig. With drawings. Nasty.'

'I already know how to carve meat.' Jack smiled again.

'There's also a description of how to knit woollen socks. That could come in handy during the winter,' Ninni said.

'Did she make them from the sheep's wool?'

'Maybe. I'm not sure when they started to keep sheep, to be honest.'

Ninni closed the book. 'You should learn Norwegian if you want to read these. It gives you quite an insight into how the farm was run when Agnar was growing up. There's also references to his childhood. She obviously loved him very much.'

He looked like he was considering it. Then he smiled slowly, making heat rise in the pit of her stomach. 'Could you translate them for me? I will, of course, pay you for the work.'

Ninni couldn't help smiling. 'Are you sure you can afford it? My rates are pretty high.'

He grinned back at her. 'Well, I think I can. I'd love to read them. Perhaps there are some recipes I can experiment with.'

'I know Sigrid would kill for these.'

'Olav's partner? Why?'

'She firmly believes that everything was done better before. As if the last fifty years have been wasted on making life easier, especially for women.'

'I didn't get the impression that Olav feels that way. The storehouse is professionally made, with loads of electricity and high tech freezers.'

'He chose to live on an island with no cars, they don't have a TV and the internet connection is hidden in the attic so the children won't be corrupted by it,' Ninni said.

Jack laughed. 'That sounds bloody exhausting.'

'Yes, it does, but they are dedicated to the cause.'

'Now I know I have to go and see them.'

Here's my chance, Ninni thought. 'Why haven't you?'

'I'm not used to imposing on my neighbours. If you do that in London you're considered mad,' he said with light laughter.

Ninni could hear Alma's instructions in her head and almost rolled her eyes. She smiled at him instead.

'You're in luck. Tomorrow night we're all going to plant potatoes at Sigrid and Olav's farm. You could come if you want to. They would love it.'

He looked confused. 'To plant potatoes?'

'Yes. Everyone will be there. There will be a party afterwards.' Ninni felt uncomfortable. Why hadn't any of the others invited him?

'Is this what Jens called *dugnad*?'

'That's the official word, yes. But really it's more of an excuse to have a party on the beach. There will be beer, possibly wine, and I wouldn't be surprised if Tobben brings a bottle of what he claims to be whisky, but is actually some witches brew he concocted in the barn. Don't say I didn't warn you.'

Jack's smile grew slowly and Ninni's heart jumped. She leafed through the exercise book she was still holding to hide her embarrassment.

'When does it start?'

She was so aware that Jack was watching her.

'Usually around three o'clock. It's going to be a long day, I'm afraid. So if you're not up for it, you don't have to come.' Ninni looked at him.

'I would love to come. Since I don't know the customs

here, is there anything I should bring? Wine or food, or something else?'

Ninni shook her head. 'You're new, so you're not expected to bring anything. There will be more than enough food and drinks, so don't worry about that.'

'Is there a dress code to this *dugnad*?'

'We'll be digging in a muddy potato field. I think you're fine in wellingtons and jeans,' she said, regretting her words when his smile broadened. 'And a sweater for later,' she muttered.

Ninni felt uncomfortable and embarrassed and did not like it. She frowned at him. 'I'm sorry, but I have a deadline.'

'And here I was thinking Norwegians were so hospitable,' he said, clearly enjoying himself. He made no sign of leaving.

'You've read the wrong guidebook, I'm afraid.' Ninni pulled the computer closer to her. 'I'll see you tomorrow then,' she said.

Jack stood up. 'I'm looking forward to it.'

He gave Frikk another quick pat on the head, then climbed over the fence and walked away. Ninni tried to look without looking. She slowly let out her breath again. I shouldn't have asked him, she thought. I really shouldn't.

Chapter 9

There wasn't a flag left anywhere, not a banner, no bunting or a *bunad* in sight. Jack remembered the hotel receptionist telling him that they would all go back to normal on the 18th of May. Apparently they had.

Mats waved at him through the window to his office. Jack waved back. The estate agent looked pleased with himself.

'Jack, great to see you again,' he said and held the door open for him. 'I have great news.'

'Here, this is for you.' Jack handed him all the papers he had been able to find in the house. 'I hope that's what you need.'

'Thank you. I'm sure it is. But listen, I already have someone who is interested,' Mats said.

'I thought you said it would take time.' Jack felt a surprising sting of disappointment.

Mats shook his head. 'So did I, but this person rang me up. It's not a farmer, I'm afraid. He's a developer of sorts, although I don't know what his plans are for the property. But I think you should meet him.'

'That sounds brilliant.' Jack smiled at the agent's enthusiasm.

'Wait here, I'll go and get his number for you.'

Jack waited in the main office. It looked like any estate agent's office he had ever been in. Pictures of houses and apartments for sale covered the walls and the windows. He looked at a few and whistled at the prices. Almost worse than London, he thought.

Mats returned, waving a note. 'Now, don't let him know that you are eager to sell. Play hard to get, so we can get a good price for you.'

'Do you want to be there if I make an appointment?'

Mats smiled. 'Well, first we'll see if you like him and what he has to say. Then we'll get him here. That will give me time to go through your papers and all the rest of it.'

Jack nodded. 'That sounds fine to me.'

The note had a name and a phone number. 'Erik Haldorsen?'

Mats nodded. 'He's a big businessman in this town. Don't worry, I'll look after your interests.'

Jack laughed. 'I appreciate that. Let's see what they say, shall we?'

He dialled the number and a chirpy secretary put him through. Absolutely not a farmer, he thought.

It was a brief conversation, ending in an appointment. He smiled at Mats and put the phone in his pocket.

'This should be interesting,' he said.

Mats almost rubbed his hands. 'Let me know how it goes.'

Jack nodded. 'Absolutely.'

On the way back to the ferry Jack discovered a spice shop and walked inside. Oils and spices, and brands he recognised from home. He filled up on necessities like balsamic vinegar and a good olive oil. Agnar's kitchen had nothing like this. This was perfect. He wanted to try a bit of cooking for the beach party. He didn't analyse the sudden need to impress.

On the ferry he called his dad and told him about the news.

'Have you called this developer yet?' Paul asked.

'Yes, I have an appointment with him. We'll see how it goes.'

Paul paused for a second. 'I see.'

'What?' Jack frowned.

'Nothing. I just thought you would be more enthusiastic, that's all.'

Jack smiled. 'It's too early to celebrate, Dad.'

'I see. We're really fascinated by the goats,' Paul said, changing the subject.

Jack stood outside on the ferry deck, enjoying the sun and the wind on his face. 'They're not goats, Dad. They're sheep.'

'Yeah, we're pretty convinced they're taking the piss,

son. I bet they're laughing their heads off whenever you call those goats sheep.'

Jack thought about Ninni's grin. 'I wouldn't be surprised, but I actually Googled them. They are sheep.'

'Bugger, Holly's probably done the same. She tricked me.'

Jack laughed out loud. 'How much do you owe her?'

'A fiver. Well, it's not the first time she's outfoxed me.'

'You should have learned by now. She's smarter than the rest of us put together,' Jack said.

Paul laughed. 'So, how are you doing? Are you settling in?'

'I'm not here on holiday, Dad.'

'There's no harm in enjoying yourself, son. How long can you stay until you need to get a new job? Please don't tell me you're relying on credit cards.' Paul sounded stern.

Jack smiled. 'Of course not. I have my savings, but there's also quite a bit of money in the estate. I could probably live on this island for a decade on that money alone.'

'Really? Without working? You'll be bored out of your mind,' Paul said, but he couldn't hide that he was impressed. 'Sounds like a bloody dream to me.'

'It's more than a bit mad, actually,' Jack said.

He looked up at a pair of seagulls chasing each other across the sky, screaming like banshees. On the deck, a group of kids chased each other too, making almost as much noise as the birds. Nobody seemed to worry about them falling overboard. The parents were leaning against the railing, drinking coffee and watching the scenery.

'Are you bored yet?' Paul asked.

'Not really. Not yet, anyway.' It made Jack smile.

'Well, tell me then. How are you spending your days? Are the islanders nice to you?'

Jack sat down on the deck. 'Yes, Dad, they are. I've been invited to a potato-planting party tomorrow.'

'A potato-planting party? Is this what these people do for fun?'

'I'm not sure. Ninni said there would be some sort of beach party afterwards. Everybody is bringing food and there's home-brewed beer.'

'Scandinavian beer is good. I've tasted the Carlsberg. Pilsner, it's called.'

'I have no idea what type of beer they're making, Dad. It could be dreadful.'

'Bring a bottle when you come home, but only if it's good.'

'I'll have to taste it first.'

'So, who is Ninni? Some elderly neighbour who feels sorry for you?'

'No, I wouldn't call her elderly,' Jack said.

'Oh? Who is she?'

'She's the closest neighbour to the farm. She lives in

Bergen, has a dog and she's the one who took me to see the sheep.'

'And how old is she?'

'She's about my age, and I'm not Danny, so lay off,' Jack said, laughing.

Paul snorted. 'You kids are so secretive all the time. I bet she's gorgeous.'

He wasn't wrong, Jack thought. But he had no intention of discussing her with him. 'How are Danny and Holly?'

'Ah, the good old diversion ploy. Okay. Danny is in love, and I've had to sit him down to explain the birds and the bees again.'

'Dad, no. He hates it when you do that. You've been doing it since he was ten years old.'

'Yes, and does he have any children? No, he does not. I knew girls would fall over themselves with him, and that he would be careless and stupid. He's still both those things, but he's not a father and that's a win to me.'

'God, I remember when you did that to me,' Jack said.

'And I only had to tell you once. You already knew what it meant to have kids. You took care of Danny and Holly a lot more than you should have.' It was an old story, and Jack didn't really want to talk about it.

'I think Danny knows that there are no birds and bees involved by now, you know.'

'Yes, but I love the way he squirms when I force him to listen to me. It's one of the perks of being a father.'

Jack laughed. 'You're evil. What about Holly?'

'She's working far too much. You know how she is. Perhaps I should send her to you for a while.'

'I don't think she'd come. You know what final year medic students are like. The pressure is horrendous.'

'Well, I'm going to try before she works herself sick. At least she used to go down to your restaurant for a meal once in a while. Now she lives off crisps and coffee. It's not healthy. Which is ironic for a doctor.'

Jack talked a few minutes more, then the ferry docked at the island.

His phone pinged as soon as he entered the house. Jack dropped the shopping on the table before he looked at the message. Fedra. Again. This time she threatened legal repercussions. He smiled. As if he hadn't checked that before he'd held the book back. The restaurant could go to hell before he returned the recipes.

Good luck with that, he texted back.

After Roland's betrayal, he had decided to keep the book. It was, after all, his creation.

Jack put the mobile on the table, ignoring the angry beeping from another one of Fedra's messages.

Instead he went down to the beach. He changed to his new swimming trunks inside the boathouse and carefully lowered himself into the water.

'Bloody hell,' he muttered.

It was freezing. He managed to hold back a yelp as he ducked under and took a few strokes. The sensation of cold quickly disappeared. The water was surprisingly clear and he could see the bottom was covered with seaweed and rocks.

He laughed when he spotted a few crabs scatter away from him. Somehow all the tension in his shoulders and back melted into oblivion.

Before he knew it, he had swum to the other side of the beach. He turned around, remembering Ninni's warning about strong currents, and kept close to the shore.

I could get used to this, he thought.

Ninni watched Jack from the path. She was on her way to the beach, and then spotted him going into the water. So now she didn't want to go down there.

Also, she didn't want him to see her. What if he thought she had come down to see him in his trunks? Not that he wasn't worth watching. He looked good.

Her gaze followed him as he swam across, and when he turned to swim back she threw herself behind the nearest *hesjer*. The grass was still green under the upper layer of hay and smelled strongly of Timothy and red clover.

This was beyond stupid, she thought, cursing herself. If she got up now, he would know what she'd done and she would feel like an even bigger idiot.

Frikk came bouncing over to her, delighted with the new game. He crawled under the *hesjer* and she followed, scraping her bottom on the lowest wire.

'Stupid, stupid, stupid,' she muttered.

Frikk ran off, barking in the process, and she closed her eyes. Even Jack would know that wherever Frikk was, she wouldn't be far behind. There was really only one thing to do – stand up and pretend that was what she had intended all the time. Someone has to inspect the hay, she thought.

She stood up, only to discover that Jack was gone.

Oh, thank God, she thought and hurried up the field. Frikk zigzagged through the rows of *hesjer* and ran in front of her up to the house.

Ninni sank down in the garden and breathed a heavy sigh of relief. It took her a minute to realise her phone was buzzing.

'Hi, Dad. No, I'm fine. I was just … running with Frikk,' she said, trying to catch her breath.

'I got your message,' he said. 'Is everything okay?'

Ninni pictured him in the small bookshop on Tyskebryggen, the German Dock in Bergen. Most likely, he would be sitting in a corner, reading a book and ignoring customers as best he could.

'Yes, only I have quite some news for you. Agnar had a son and he's here.'

Petter didn't say anything. Ninni checked the screen to see if she had accidentally turned it off. 'Pappa?'

'I'm here. Are you sure? I mean, that's ... Agnar never mentioned anything like that.'

'Alma thought he was an imposter at first, but she has seen the paperwork and he looks like Agnar. I thought perhaps you'd want to meet him.'

'Of course I do. I'd decided to come to the island after closing hour tomorrow anyway.'

'Do you want me to come and get you? I have taken the boat out.'

'No, I don't want you on the water by yourself; it's not that far, anyway. I'm perfectly happy on the ferry.'

Ninni smiled. He always said that. 'Okay. Everybody will be at Olav and Sigrid's for the day. Planting potatoes.'

'Whatever for? They are perfectly capable of planting their own potatoes. That field of theirs is minuscule.'

'Yes, but that's just an excuse. It's Alma's clever plan to get to know Jack better and give him a taste of island life, I think. Food and drinks aplenty, Pappa.'

'I'll be there, but I refuse to plant anything. Is Britt coming?'

'Of course, and she's bringing beer. Don't worry.'

'Sounds good then. Now you can tell me more about this man. Is he nice? Does he look like Agnar?'

Ninni smiled. 'Yes, he looks like Agnar and he's nice. You will have to make up your own mind when you meet him.'

'I will. Do you have enough books?' Petter was a firm believer that nobody ever had enough books.

It made her laugh. 'The house is filled with books. It might fall down the slope if you bring any more.'

'Then I'll only bring some for me,' Petter said.

Ninni was still laughing when she turned off the phone.

Jack cut the pieces of *fenalår* into small bits. He roasted them slowly in the pan, just to see how they turned out. A crumble, he thought. Now what could he use that for? Still thinking, he opened the box with Jens' Old Cheese and sniffed it.

'Nice,' he said and smiled. This should be interesting.

He cut off a slice and chopped it into small pieces, then threw them in with the *fenalår*, drizzled on some oil and stirred a few times.

'Onions,' he muttered to himself.

Half the fun of his job was the experimentation. To taste things, to smell ingredients and put them together. Just to see what happened.

He shook the pan a few times. On the bench he had a bowl filled with chopped herbs and plants from the garden. He hummed while crushing some garlic from the shop.

The knocking startled him. 'Shit,' he said, and turned around.

A woman in her forties leaned against the doorway and smiled broadly at him. '*Hei*,' she said.

'There's a doorbell, you know,' he said.

'Yes, but I don't think it's ever been used. I'm Britt.'

Ah, yes, the B&B owner, school teacher, beer brewer and also part owner of the meat business.

'Nice to meet you,' Jack said, but he wasn't happy. Perhaps he should get a padlock on the inside of the door. This was worse than Oxford Street.

She held out a bag. 'I bring gifts. Someone told me you are a chef. What are you cooking?'

Jack shook the pan again. 'Not quite sure yet. It's an experiment.'

Britt walked up to the oven and sniffed. 'That smells ... interesting. What have you put in there?'

'Mutton and Old Cheese, some herbs and garlic,' Jack said, watching with fascination how she took a step back.

She looked horrified. 'That's disgusting. Do you have any idea of how exclusive that meat is? What it has cost us in time and labour to perfect it? Why would you ruin good meat like that?'

Jack took a spoon and waved it at her. 'It's good. Please, taste it.'

'Not on your life. English people are weird,' Britt said.

'How do you eat the cheese?' Jack stirred the pan again.

'I would rather eat anything else than that cheese, thank you.'

She held up the bag again. 'Here, try this. Perhaps it will take the taste away.'

Jack smiled when he saw the bottles. 'Is this the famous island beer?'

'Yes, it's a house-warming present.' Britt sat down by the kitchen table. 'Is it true that you're selling the farm?'

'Yes.' Jack opened one of the beer bottles and handed it to her.

She shook her head. 'Too early for me. Please, I'd like to know your opinion.'

Jack sniffed the bottle and enjoyed the faint smell of yeast and something slightly sweet. 'Is it honey?'

'God, no, that would be *mjød*'—she waved her hand—'I mean mead. No, I use yeast and hops, so it's plain pilsner, or lager, made with loving hands right here in my shed on the island.'

Jack tasted it and smiled. 'It's good. I mean, this is really good. Why are you making beer?'

'I started a micro-brewery with my ex, to see if we could make some money and get him off his job on the oil platforms. Mostly I sell to a restaurant in town.'

Jack took another sip. 'Only to one? Can you make a profit from it?'

Britt smiled. 'Not really. I like your style. I would love to make a living from it, but at the moment it's more of a hobby. We've been experimenting for a few years. That is, I have, since my ex decided island life wasn't for him. I pay my bills being a teacher, but there are very few kids now; it's just a matter of time before the school closes down for good.'

Jack shook the pan. 'Why have you come here? Apart from inspecting me.'

'I wanted to talk to you before the potato planting,' Britt said.

'Okay. Why?' Jack tossed the garlic into the pan.

'Most of the islanders don't want you to sell this place. They are worried about the big bad wolf coming and devouring everyone. Changing the way the island has been run since the Stone Age, I guess.'

'And you're not worried?'

'I think there are opportunities in change,' she said.

Jack leaned back. 'Who's the big bad wolf?'

Britt laughed. 'Oh, him. Erik Haldorsen. According to Alma, he wants to destroy the island. Meaning, if you sell to him we are doomed and will be thrown off the island half an hour later.'

She didn't seem worried. Jack watched her. 'Doomed, how?'

'Erik is a property developer, an investor. He's had his eyes on the island for years. He held a town meeting some years back and showed us plans for a wind farm on the west side, a marina right here on your land, and all sorts of other things. We would all be making a fortune from the island, he said.' She shrugged and smiled a little. 'Not sure if that's true, but a little development would be nice.'

Jack thought about it. 'You can't control development. Not once it's started.'

'I know that, but the fact is we are losing people to the mainland every year. There are no jobs out here, of course. Most people work in the oil industry and if you work in town, commuting is a nightmare in the winter. Geir worked offshore and he got fed up with helicopter trips in midwinter. Now he lives the good life in Oslo, doing God knows what. I couldn't blame him. It's bloody dangerous.'

'Are you here because you want me to sell to Haldorsen or to warn me about him?' Jack pulled the skillet away from the hob.

Britt smiled. 'It's not my business who you choose to sell your farm to, Jack. If it was mine, I'd sell it to the highest bidder in the blink of an eye and move to Hawaii.'

'You really like islands,' Jack said.

Britt laughed. 'Yes, I do. I love the ocean.'

Jack finished the beer. 'Listen, I don't know when I'm selling the farm. I've contacted an estate agent and left it up to him. What happens after that is not really my problem, is it?'

'I like your attitude. Perhaps something will change at last.'

Jack looked at the beer bottle. 'Why don't you have a proper restaurant here, on the island?'

'There's not enough people for it and most

Norwegians can't afford to eat out anyway,' Britt said with a shrug.

'It would have to be a restaurant people would be willing to travel here for,' Jack said slowly.

'In that case, the food would have to be bloody sensational,' Britt said.

'No Old Cheese, you mean?' Jack looked at the skillet.

That made her laugh out loud. 'Yes, no Old Cheese.'

Jack leaned over the table. 'But that's where you're wrong. If you have the right ingredients and the right chef, you can make people travel. You don't have to be smack down in the middle of London.'

Britt grinned. 'Are you talking about yourself? Would you consider that here?'

'God, no. My whole life is in London. I don't belong on an island in the middle of nowhere. My family is there, my work.'

'You don't have a job. I checked you out online. There was an article about you. We all read it,' Britt said, undaunted.

'Right. Of course you did.' Even Ninni, he thought.

'It's what you do these days, isn't it?'

'Yes, I suppose it is.' He wondered what Ninni thought about it.

'To be honest, there wasn't that much about you, except that you left your job right before you secured a Michelin star for the restaurant. Did you do that because of the inheritance?'

Jack laughed. 'No, not at all. I didn't know about the farm when that happened. The restaurant owner and I had a difference of opinion. It's not uncommon in my line of work. Chefs can be temperamental, like all creative people.'

'We saw the photo with the stunning blonde. Is she your girlfriend?' Britt wasn't giving up on the questions.

'No, she's not.' Jack had no intention of discussing his love life with a strange woman.

'Sorry, I can be too curious at times,' Britt said and didn't look the least sorry. 'It comes from working with kids, I'm afraid.'

'It's fine. No hearts were broken or anything like that.'

At least nothing he would talk to anyone about. The whole situation was too embarrassing.

Britt got up from the chair. 'I'm sorry. I'll leave you to your experiments. Are you coming to the potato party tomorrow?'

'Yes, I've never planted a potato in my life. I'm expecting a life-altering experience,' he said.

'Don't get your hopes up. Potatoes aren't really that interesting,' she said, laughing.

'That depends on how you cook them,' Jack said.

Britt nodded towards the pan. 'Please take that horror with you. I'd love to see Jens' expression when he sees what you've done to his favourite cheese.'

Jack grinned. 'That's my evil plan.'

'Good. He loves giving that cheese to tourists.'

She left the house laughing.

'I really need a proper lock on the bloody door,' Jack muttered.

He took another spoonful from the pan, wondering what he could use it for. The garlic had improved it, but it wasn't impressive in any way.

Chapter 10

It annoyed Ninni that she kept looking towards the road. The gates were closed to prevent animals and children running off.

She was sitting on the fence watching the donkey trotting around the enclosed paddock with Olav and Sigrid's five-year-old son clinging to the animal's back. He was giggling like mad.

Ninni turned to Sigrid. 'Aren't you scared he's going to fall off?'

'If he does it's not much of a fall, and besides, he's got a helmet,' Sigrid said, clearly not worried.

'I would be terrified,' Ninni confessed.

Sigrid laughed. 'We were with Anja. We sterilised everything and practically wrapped her in bubble wrap from the day we brought her home. Fortunately, Olav's mum interfered before we broke her.'

The child in question was balancing on top of the fence, trying to catch cherries in her mouth at the same time.

'She looks fine now,' Ninni said.

Sigrid threw a glance at her daughter. 'Yes, she does. Anja, be careful. I don't want to take you to the hospital again; we'll miss the party.'

Anja gave them a toothy grin. 'I'm just seeing how many cherries I can catch, Mamma.'

'Do it on the ground, darling. You're freaking Ninni out.'

Anja jumped down at once, and Ninni breathed a little easier.

'Look at those idiots.' Sigrid nodded towards the barn. Half the roof had caved in during the winter, and was now covered with a huge tarp.

Olav and Tobben were manoeuvring an old harrow through the door. 'They insist that's going to make it easier to plant. Seems to me that's an awful lot of work for making something easy,' Sigrid said.

It was fun to watch, though, the men heaving and muttering, and using lots of words little ears probably shouldn't hear.

'They'll give up soon enough,' Sigrid said.

Ninni watched them. 'I hope so. I'm not in the mood to dig furrows all day. Better they do it.'

Sigrid looked at her. 'You know, I'm the only one who hasn't met your Englishman yet.'

'Oh, for God's sake. Why does everyone keep saying that? He's not my Englishman,' Ninni said.

'But you're the one who has the most dealings with him, being his neighbour. Olav said he's not a farmer. What's he like?'

Everyone asked her that question. Ninni sighed. 'He's nice, I suppose. All I know is that he's not familiar with the sea or boats, and a bit wary of dogs.'

'It's more than a bit strange that he shows up out of the blue like that. You could have knocked me over with a feather. Ole, don't pull his ears,' she barked at the boy.

The boy had been hanging over the donkey's ears. 'But he likes it,' he whined.

'I'll come over there and pull your ears soon. See how much you like it,' she said.

Ole let go at once.

Sigrid turned to Ninni again. 'Is he good-looking? Olav had no idea. He's so clueless sometimes.'

They were interrupted by the arrival of Jens and Alma, coming up from the beach and carrying a huge basket between them. Alma shook her head when Ninni took the basket from them. 'I'm getting too old to walk all this way,' she said.

Jens leaned against the fence, breathing heavily. He took off his hat and ran a hand over his head. 'Last time it was this hot, you two weren't even born.'

Ninni smiled at him. 'Didn't you take the boat?'

'Of course we did, but it's a long way up from the beach.' Alma looked around. 'Shouldn't we be in the field by now?'

'We're waiting for Ninni's Englishman,' Sigrid said with a grin.

Jens chuckled. 'I'm looking forward to his opinion on the Old Cheese I gave him.'

'We all are. You haven't stopped talking about it since you forced it on him,' Alma said before handing the basket over to Sigrid. 'It's just a few baked goods.'

Ninni leaned closer when Sigrid peered inside. The golden buns smelled of cardamom and vanilla, and Sigrid smiled. 'Oh, these are going to disappear fast. I'll hide them in the kitchen for now,' she said.

'Wait, wait, wait.' Ninni grabbed a bun. 'Sorry, I'm starving,' she said when Alma gave her a stern look.

'Let's go before she eats all of them,' Sigrid said with a smile.

Alma followed her to make sure everything was taken care of. 'Are you still using that old wood-burner oven? You do know that there are perfectly good electric ovens to get, some of them really good too,' she said.

Sigrid smiled. 'I like the old oven. You will not believe the bread we make in it.'

Alma huffed and muttered something Ninni couldn't hear. It made her smile, listening to the two of them bickering like that.

Jens waved his arm at the two men still struggling with the machinery. 'I'm not going over there,' he declared.

Ninni took a bite of the buttery bun with a satisfied sigh. 'Better you stay here with me and the kids. It's a lot safer.'

Jens patted her knee. 'You're a good girl. How's your Englishman?'

Ninni rolled her eyes. 'He's not my Englishman.'

'Well, have you seen him lately?'

'I saw Jack yesterday. He'd found some old exercise books that Agnar's mother had written and wanted me to take a look at them. I can't remember her. Did you know her?'

Jens smiled. 'Oh, indeed I did. Magni was a scary woman. Tough as nails. Her husband was a fisherman so he was barely at home, and she was in charge of the farm. Ran that farm as if it was a military camp.'

Ninni looked at him. 'You should tell Jack that. He'd be interested, I'm sure.'

Jens nodded. 'Perhaps I will. Is your dad coming today?'

'He left Bergen early and should be here on the next ferry. I told him about Jack and he's eager to meet him.'

'Good, good. It must be quite a shock to him as well. Agnar was a close friend,' Jens said.

Ninni kept an eye on Ole and Anja. They were feeding the donkey carrots and it looked like they had decided to be nicer to him.

Jack put the food in a bag and left the house. The sun was shining and, despite the fact that the wellingtons he had found were a tiny bit too big, he felt good.

He had ended up using the second bottle of Britt's

beer in the marinade for the beef. It would be interesting to see how it turned out.

When he got up to the main road he had no idea which direction was south, but assumed it was opposite to where he stood. He followed the road past Ninni's house and craned his neck to see if she was there. Instead he was surprised to see a man coming out, closing the door behind him.

The man smiled when he spotted Jack. '*Hei*,' he said in Norwegian, then quickly switched to English. 'You must be Agnar's boy.'

Jack wasn't sure he'd ever get used to that expression. 'I suppose I am,' he said.

'You look so much like him, for a minute there I thought you were him,' he said.

The man came down to the road, smiling from ear to ear. He carried a tote bag that looked heavy. He held out his hand. 'I'm Petter Toft, Ninni's father. Ninni only told me about you yesterday. I couldn't believe it and so I had to come and see for myself.'

'Nice to meet you too. I could hardly believe it myself.' Jack took an instant liking to him.

'Agnar was my friend. I have known him since I was a kid. And I've had a hard time understanding why he never said a word to me about you.'

'So do I. He never met me, or even told me he existed,' Jack said.

Petter looked confused. 'I'm sorry,' he said. 'You prob-

158

ably have all sorts of questions. Feel free to ask me, and I'll answer as best I can.'

Jack couldn't help being charmed. 'Thank you. I'll do that. Want me to take that bag for you?'

'God, no, I'm perfectly capable of carrying it myself. It's just books for the children,' Petter said.

'You grew up on the island, didn't you?' Jack let Petter take the lead.

'Yes, right in this house. Agnar and I spent a lot of time together, although he was a few years older than me. There weren't many other children here when I grew up. My father died when I was young and I didn't have any siblings. Agnar became more like my older brother than a neighbour.'

Jack thought of something. 'Why didn't Agnar leave the farm to you? He didn't know me. He never even met me.'

'That I can't tell you but, for one thing, he knew I would never be much of a farmer. Agnar promised his mother before she died that he would keep the farm in the family. Unfortunately, he never married.' Petter smiled, as if he'd suddenly thought of something. 'You know, I remember being surprised he didn't seem worried about what would happen to the farm after he passed away. It must have been because he had you.'

Jack looked around. The landscape they were walking through didn't look anything like London. There were a few windswept spruce trees, juniper bushes and lots of grass and wildflowers.

'What I don't understand is why Agnar never contacted me. He obviously knew where I lived, what I do for a living. He even knew when my mother died.'

Petter shook his head. 'I don't know. Agnar was a hermit, if that's the right word, and got even more of a recluse as he got older.'

'Was he always like that?'

'More or less, especially after he returned and settled on the island once his parents passed away.'

'What was he like?' Jack hadn't asked anyone about Agnar, but now he wanted to know more.

'He drank too much about twice a year, loved this island and he could be funny when he was in the right mood. But he was lonely.'

Jack looked at him. 'Why did he never get married?'

'I asked him once, shortly after Ninni was born and I thought everyone should have a family,' Petter said. 'He said he had been in love once, it didn't work out and he never wanted to go through that sort of thing again. When I pressed him on it, he said he'd had to choose between the island and this girl. And he didn't think she'd be happy here. She was a big city girl. I always assumed it was someone in Bergen. He hated cities. He even avoided Haugesund.' Petter looked at him. 'Now, I'm thinking she must have been your mother.'

'Perhaps. But my mother married Paul when I was five and, as far as I know, they were happy together,' he said.

'Good for her,' Petter said with a smile.

Without Jack noticing, they had arrived at a gate. Petter pointed towards a farm with a scattering of buildings. 'That's Olav and Sigrid's place. It's a bit more isolated than our side of the island, but it's nice, yes? It's smaller than your farm, actually.'

Jack spotted a paddock where a couple of children were riding on a donkey. Frikk barked at them, so he knew Ninni was there.

The buildings were set back: a white house, a red barn that looked like it had fallen apart and a few smaller outbuildings on the side. On the other side there was a sandy beach with a boathouse, a pier and two rowing boats bobbing in the water.

'Most visitors to the island come to this side as the beach on our side isn't sandy. But we'll see our fair share of summer guests in a week or so,' Petter said.

'Doesn't the beach belong to the farm?'

'Technically, yes, but because of the *allemannsretten*, everyone can use it. They do have to stay outside the farm's fences and cultivated fields.'

'How so?' Jack wasn't sure what *allemannsretten* was, although he remembered seeing the word on an Ikea package of meatballs at some point.

'It means anyone can use the beach. You can't sunbathe on someone's pier but, apart from that, it's for everyone. It's to make sure that rich people don't hog all the best outdoor areas,' Petter said with a wide grin. 'Unfortunately, this common right is under pressure in parts of the country, but we do our best to defend it here. We want people to feel welcome.'

'That sounds nice,' Jack said.

Petter opened the first gate and closed it behind them. 'Yes, it is, but it comes with a few rules. Always close gates, don't light fires close to houses or in the fields, take your rubbish with you and always make sure you stay on uncultivated land. So you can't camp in a crop field or where there's livestock, or in someone's garden.'

'And do people abide by these rules?' Jack wasn't sure how they could ensure that.

'Yes, of course.' Petter looked surprised at the idea. 'There are always a few bastards who think they don't have to be considerate of other people, but those are the exceptions.'

Jack couldn't see any rubbish anywhere, so perhaps Petter was right. Although he had also seen Ninni picking plastic bottles off the beach.

'And what do you do if someone doesn't follow the rules? If kids throw a huge party on the beach? Do you make them walk the plank? Throw them out to sea?'

'Nah, usually we talk to them. Make them see sense, and if they're too drunk to go back to the mainland we let them sleep it off in one of the boathouses or on the beach. We're not pirates out here, you know. Not any more,' he said with a wide grin.

Jack caught a glimpse of Ninni by the second gate

and wondered if she had been looking for him. The thought made him smile.

She wasn't alone. Jens leaned against the fence next to her. On the other side of the paddock, he saw Olav standing together with another, heavy-set man. 'Who's that?'

Petter smiled. 'Oh, that's Tobben. The third farmer on the island.'

Ninni hugged her dad. Petter waved a hand towards Jack. 'Look who I found on the way.'

Jack smiled when Ninni nodded at him. 'Nice to see you again,' he said.

'*Takk for sist*,' Ninni said.

'Sorry?'

'It's an expression to use whenever you meet someone again. It means *thank you for the last time we saw each other*. And you use it whether you haven't seen a person in fifty years or in the last few hours. It's a bit formal, like I wouldn't say it to Pappa but I say it to people on the island when I've been gone for a while.'

'Is that what they've just done?' He nodded towards Jens and Petter. The men had greeted each other with a brisk hug and a hearty pat on the back. They were talking excitedly in Norwegian. Jack understood *takk*, but that was about it.

'Yes, but right now Jens is complaining that Pappa only brought books for the kids.'

'Why does he bring books?' Jack took a step closer to her.

Ninni smelled good. Like cardamom and vanilla, he thought.

'Pappa owns a bookshop in Bergen. He always brings the latest books with him for the islanders. During the summer, he sets up a book corner in the shop and tries to persuade me to sit there to sell all the surplus stuff from the bookshop nobody wants to buy.'

'Which you mostly refuse, I guess,' Jack said.

She shrugged. 'I have a job. He also tries to get me to open a permanent bookshop here, and I keep telling him it's a ridiculous plan. People either buy their books in town or online, or get them from the library.'

Jack found her obvious annoyance charming. 'So,' he said, 'How is this potato thing going to happen?'

Ninni nodded towards the barn. 'The field is behind there. They spent most of the morning trying to make an old harrow work, so they wouldn't have to dig furrows.'

Jack watched the men heading towards the barn. 'Where are they going?'

'Looks like they've given up on modern machinery,' Ninni said with a wide smile. 'Just stay here with me and you won't get a shovel in your hands. Those things are murder on the back.'

Jack had no intention of going anywhere without her.

A little girl came running towards them, grabbing Ninni's hand and talking a mile a minute. Ninni smiled and nodded. 'This is Jack. He doesn't speak Norwegian, so this is your chance to show off your English, Anja,' she said to the little girl.

Anja looked at him. 'Hello,' she said.

'Hello,' Jack said. 'How are you?'

'Fine. How are you?' She was giggling so hard she could hardly get a word out.

Jack nodded at the donkey. 'Is that yours?'

'Yes. His name is Olly.'

Not bad, Jack thought. The girl said something to Ninni.

'Her little brother got to name the donkey. She's a bit mad about that.'

Anja tugged at Ninni's arm again. '*Kom nå*,' she said.

'She wants us to come now. There's work to be done.'

She held onto the little girl's hand and chatted with her as they walked across the courtyard and around the barn.

The field was ploughed, or at any rate it looked ploughed to his eyes. At least five or six people were using shovels to turn the dirt. Ninni was right; it looked like hard work.

The field was also mucky and soft underfoot, as he discovered when he walked into it.

A woman holding a heavy metal bucket, filled to the rim with what looked like old potatoes full of sprouts, came towards them. 'Hi, I'm Sigrid. Pleased to meet you,' she said, sounding exactly like the little girl. 'Are you ready to work?'

'I guess so.' Jack couldn't help admiring her bright blue eyes and the long blonde braid over her shoulder.

'Ninni said you haven't done this before. Are you sure you're up for it?'

'I've been looking forward to this since yesterday,' he assured her.

'Good. Follow me.' Sigrid put the bucket down next to a furrow. She picked up a potato and held it in front of him. 'You put them down with the sprouts facing up, then fold dirt over them, making it look like a narrow ridge. About twenty centimetres between them. If there's anything you need, let me know.'

Sigrid left and he looked around. Ninni was in the next furrow, with her bottom in the air and the same kind of bucket next to her. He admired her bottom, and smiled when she turned to look at him.

'Why don't they use plastic buckets?' he asked.

She laughed. 'They don't believe in plastic. Sorry about that. Is it too heavy for you?'

She was teasing him again. 'I can manage.'

He tried to keep up with her, only to realise it was better if he kept a few paces behind. He was enjoying the view too much.

Chapter 11

Finishing the potato field took almost three hours, despite all the people working. Jack was knackered halfway through, but would be damned if he was going to show it. His back, arms and even shins ached. But he kept up with the mad mud people.

Ninni came over to him, rubbing her hands against the dungarees she was wearing on top of her clothes. 'You did well,' she said with a wide smile. 'How are you feeling?'

He looked at the furrows he had finished. They didn't look as straight as the others. 'It's not really precision work, is it?' he said.

'Not really, no. They look fine, though. Are you hungry?'

'I'm starving. Are we done?' Jack couldn't hide his relief and it made her laugh.

'Yes, you can turn in your bucket now. We are going to the beach. Jens started up the firepit an hour ago.'

'Sounds fantastic. Is it for hot dogs?'

'That too. Don't worry, there's plenty of different stuff to eat. You brought something as well, didn't you?'

She had noticed. Jack grinned. 'I couldn't come empty-handed, could I?'

They dropped the buckets by the barn. Ninni looked at him. 'What did you bring? I'm only asking because I don't want you to be disappointed if they don't like it. We're not Michelin-star eaters here, you know.'

He smiled. 'A challenge. I like that.'

Ninni watched him. He had mostly kept pace with everyone else. She hadn't expected anything less. He looked fit enough. He looked damned good, although she wouldn't let him know that.

'There's a bathroom in the house if you want to have a wash,' she said.

Jack looked at his muddy hands and equally muddy wellingtons. 'I'll think I'll take you up on that.'

Ninni watched him as he walked towards the house.

'Oh, dear, he looks a bit stiff in the gait, doesn't he?' Britt slid up to her, following her look.

'Not used to hard manual labour, I should think,' Ninni said.

'But he's a sight for sore eyes, isn't he?' Britt grinned. 'And he likes you.'

'No, he doesn't.' Ninni frowned, which only encouraged Britt.

'He was watching you the whole time you were

digging around with the potatoes. Admiring your bottom. It was so obvious.'

Ninni shook her head. 'You're so wrong. I'm not ready for someone else, and besides, Jack is leaving as soon as he can sell the farm.'

'Well, then, have a summer fling while he's here. Enjoy yourself. You're finally rid of that idiot Karl. It's time to live a little. There's nothing wrong with having a bit of fun. If I was fifteen years younger I wouldn't encourage you,' Britt said.

'Did you bring any beer today?' Ninni pulled her hair out of the scrunchie and shook her head.

'Of course I did. Sigrid put them in the fridge. They'll bring it down later.'

They made their way down the pathway to the beach. Ninni looked at Britt. 'Do you really think Karl is an idiot?'

Britt rolled her eyes. 'God, yes, Karl is so full of himself. Pilots have egos as huge as jumbo jets. And all that flying in and out, leaving you for weeks on end? It never seemed right to me. You're far too good to waste yourself on someone who treats you like that. You deserve so much better.'

She didn't ask what had happened and Ninni didn't tell her. She wasn't ready to tell anyone. Not yet. It was too devastating and too embarrassing to even say aloud.

Frikk came running towards her, tongue lolling and

tail wagging. Ninni patted him on the head. 'You're having a blast, aren't you?'

She was grateful for the interruption. Britt tended to ask questions until she got answers.

On the beach, Jens had the firepit going. He whistled while stirring the coals with a poker, making clouds of embers dance into the air. He looked like some ancient gnome performing a ritual.

Ninni sat down on a patch of grass and sighed with contentment while Britt walked over to the firepit to talk to Jens. Planting potatoes was hell on the back. A mild breeze cooled her face.

'Are you hungry, my girl?' Jens popped up in front of her.

'Yes, I am, actually. What are you cooking?'

Jens scratched his nose. 'There's sausages for the kids, but they'll want to cook those themselves. I have potatoes roasting between the coals, and if someone is willing to go out in the boat to pick some fresh mussels, that would be a kindness indeed.'

Ninni frowned. 'Ugh, no, thank you. I'll take sausages over mussels any day.'

'You're a strange islander.' He patted her knee.

'My mother is a mainlander,' Ninni said. She waved her hand at the pit. 'Haven't you got any proper food in there?'

'A few things, yes. A pork chop or two, and the Englishman brought something that looks interesting,

170

including some delicious-smelling beef. You won't starve.'

'As long as you have enough ketchup, I'm happy.' She laughed at him when he pulled a face at her.

'Ketchup?' Jack towered over them. He looked slightly cleaner.

Ninni's heart gave a jolt. She hadn't heard him coming. 'Yes, I like ketchup.' She became defensive.

He grinned. 'I have nothing against tomato sauce; I just prefer to cook it myself.'

Jens turned his attention on him. 'Do you like mussels, Englishman?'

'Of course I do. Do you need any help prepping anything?'

Ninni almost groaned, knowing what would follow. 'Don't fall for it, Jack. He needs someone to go and pick mussels,' she said.

'From where?' Jack looked intrigued.

Ninni pointed to the water. 'From out there.'

'I've never done that. Can I come?' Jack looked eager.

Jens grinned. 'See? He's willing to help. You don't want me to send him out there on his own, do you?'

No, she didn't. He'd probably drown if he tried. Ninni sighed and got up. 'Come along then.'

Jens rubbed his hands together. 'At least a bucketful, my girl, and make sure you clean them before you bring them in.'

'Yeah, yeah,' Ninni said, stamping towards the pier.

Jack kept up the pace. 'You don't really want to do this?'

Ninni laughed. 'I don't mind. It makes him happy if he thinks he's forcing me. Just look at him.'

Jack looked over his shoulder and Jens waved at him, clearly pleased with himself.

'I see what you mean,' Jack said.

He followed her to the pier and they both climbed into the nearest rowing boat. He put on the life jacket she handed him, without argument this time.

Jack looked around. 'Where are we going?'

'Around that point and into the next bay.' Ninni pushed the boat away from the pier and put out the oars. She smiled when he looked confused. 'Not all boats have engines. This boat belongs to the children and it's a lot easier to handle.'

She soon managed to turn the boat around and started to row. Jack looked fascinated.

'Would you like to try?' Ninni lifted the oars out of the water.

He smiled so suddenly her heart jumped and she almost lost her grip on one of the oars. 'I'd love to.'

'You have to sit next to me,' she said, trying to hide how awkward she felt.

He carefully climbed over and sat down, making the boat rock and himself turn pale. Ninni hid a smile.

'Just hold onto the oar, make sure it stays in the oarlock. If you lose it, we'll have to swim to shore.'

Jack had an expression of fierce concentration on his face. He gripped the handle of the oar with both hands.

'Turn it so the blade goes in the water sideways and follow my rhythm.'

He missed the surface on the first attempt and almost fell over, then, a bit more gently, he got it right. He laughed out loud. 'Oh, this is brilliant.'

'Here, take this one as well.'

'Are you sure?' Jack looked thrilled at the thought.

'Go on. Worst thing that can happen is we fall into the water. And we have life jackets for that.'

Ninni waited until he had a good grip on both oars before moving away, hoping he didn't see the relief on her face. It was too ... intimate to sit that close.

'Now, don't go too fast. We are just going around the point, then you have to slow down and turn towards land.'

He smiled at her. 'This is not the same as a rowing machine in the gym.'

'I should think not. This is a proper wooden boat,' Ninni huffed.

He looked good rowing, even if he was slightly out of breath.

'How do I stop this thing?' Jack was rowing too fast and he knew it.

'You can lift up the oars; the boat will slow down.'

Jack tested and looked slightly worried when the

boat didn't slow down much. 'I hope there's an easier way,' he said.

The boat glided past the point and a narrow bay without a beach appeared.

Ninni waved her arm. 'Go right. No, I mean your left. Lift up the left oar and gently press against the flow with the other.'

She was secretly impressed when he executed the orders perfectly and the boat turned, but she didn't want him to get all smug again.

'Fine. Do you see the pole closer to land?' She pointed towards a tall pole sticking out of the water.

Jack looked over his shoulder. 'That one?'

'I need you to get as close as you can.' Ninni leaned carefully over the gunwale.

He made a complete mess of it and they missed the pole by metres. Then he laughed as he barely managed to avoid hitting land.

'This is not as easy as it looks,' he said, panting with the effort of stopping the boat.

Ninni was delighted that he laughed. Perhaps he wasn't such a stick-in-the-mud after all. 'Okay. We have to turn the boat around. Sit still for a moment.' Ninni put her hands next to his and pulled the oars towards her. The boat slowed down. Jack let her captain the boat and soon they slid in towards the pole.

'Put one oar in the water and hold it still against the

flow. That's how you brake. It's also how you turn the boat around, so watch it.'

Jack figured out how to do it quickly. Ninni smiled at him. 'You're doing really well.'

'Thank you. What's with the pole?'

Ninni reached out and grabbed it as they glided past. 'You'll see. Could you slow down, so I don't lose my arms?'

Jack did his best and the boat remained still enough for Ninni to find the rope that was wrapped around the pole. She pulled it up and into the boat, and it made a crunching noise as it hit the bottom.

'That's a lot of mussels,' Jack said.

The rope was thick with big oval-shaped blue mussels growing on it, reflecting the light in shades of blue and green. Ninni pulled a face. 'I think this will be enough.'

Jack watched as she plucked the mussels off and dropped them in the bucket one by one, after giving each a quick clean and squeezing them between her fingers.

'How do you know they're safe to eat?'

'You don't know?' Ninni was surprised.

Jack shrugged. 'When I use mussels, they arrive at the kitchen already cleaned and safe. So how do you know?'

'We test them on unsuspecting visitors.' Ninni rubbed the "beard" off a large mussel, discovered a crack in the shell and threw it out into the water again. 'That's not safe.'

Holding the oars with one hand, he picked up one and looked at it. 'Very funny. Is that why you don't eat them yourself? Are you scared of being poisoned?'

'No, I absolutely hate the texture of the things. Jens checks with the food safety authorities every day on mussels so you can be sure they're safe. He also keeps tabs on the weather and water quality by the beaches. Anything you need to know about nature, he'll know about it.'

The bucket filled up quickly and Ninni dropped the rope back into the water.

'We can go back now.'

Jack had more control now. He rowed more gently. 'I thought there would be a farm or something like that,' he said.

'A mussel farm?' Ninni shook her head. 'It's not commercially viable, I think.'

He cocked his head. 'I bet you fish crabs as well out here.'

'Of course we do. The crabs here are fantastic and you can fish for them all year.'

'What sort of crabs do you get?'

'Red crabs and the occasional troll crabs. I usually throw those back in the water.'

Jack turned the boat around the point again and kept looking over his shoulder towards the boathouse. The boat wobbled and it was clear he would miss the mark by a mile if he kept it up.

Ninni stopped him. 'Not like that. Fix on a point over my shoulder and I'll let you know when we're close.'

He got it right almost at once and the boat's course steadied. 'What about lobster? There are lobsters here, aren't there?'

'Yes, especially further south, but it's strictly regulated. You can only fish for lobsters if you have a licence, and only between October 1st and December 31st, and if the lobsters are smaller than twenty-five centimetres you have to throw them back in.'

Jack nodded. 'Sounds reasonable. Am I hitting the pier yet?'

Ninni looked over his shoulder. 'Nope. Just keep going, but not so fast or you won't be able to stop before we hit land.'

'What about cockles?' Jack suddenly asked.

'Aren't they a kind of chestnut?' Ninni had no idea.

'No, that's conkers. I mean white mussels, the ones you dig out of the sand. That beach looks promising.'

'Oh, those. They are called *hjerteskjell* or heart shell. I think the children dig them up and then Sigrid sells them to restaurants in town. I don't think it's very profitable,' Ninni said.

'What about winkles?' he asked.

'Excuse me?' Ninni raised her eyebrows.

'You know, periwinkles. Those little snails that live on the shore.'

Ninni smiled. 'I think you mean beach snails. What about them?'

'You can buy them on beaches in the UK, boiled in seawater. They're a treat. There must be loads of them here.'

'There are, but I wouldn't dream of eating them. That sounds awful. We use them for fishing bait,' she said and laughed.

'You guys could survive for years out here, without ever having to go to town, couldn't you?' The idea seemed to excite him.

Ninni smiled. 'Yes, we could if we had to, but that would mean no chocolate or wine. Sometimes the islanders still have to go without such luxuries in the winter months when the weather gets too bad for the ferry to run. It can get really nasty here.'

He looked at her, suddenly serious. 'Who's Karl?'

It came so out of the blue that Ninni had no idea what to say.

Chapter 12

Jack slowed down the rowing to make sure he wouldn't hit the pier. She looked a bit shocked by his question. Which of course was his intention.

'He's my ex. How do you know about him?' Ninni frowned.

'I was right behind you and Britt down the pathway to the beach and heard you mention the name. I asked her. She doesn't like Karl much, does she?'

Ninni sighed. 'It's not polite to eavesdrop, you know.'

It had to be a recent break, Jack thought. She was flustered and angry. 'Did he treat you that badly?'

Ninni narrowed her eyes. 'You'd better slow down. That pier is getting awfully close.'

Jack looked over his shoulder and realised she was right. Suddenly the boathouse looked huge. 'Shit,' he said.

Ninni leaned forward and put her hands on the oars next to his again. She pushed the oars towards him without lifting them out of the water and the boat

179

slowed down. It wasn't long before Ninni could grab the pier.

She didn't mention the question about Karl while she fastened the boat line, nor when they carried the bucket between them. He didn't repeat it. But he was intrigued.

By now more people had arrived on the beach, making it look like a proper picnic with children and a few more dogs running around. Petter and Tobben sat on a couple of old camping chairs, engrossed in a conversation that included a lot of hand-waving and finger-pointing.

'What are they arguing about?' Jack said, as Ninni handed the bucket to Jens, who looked excited at the sight of it.

'It's about the old harrow. Pappa thinks he knows about farm tools and Tobben tries to convince him he doesn't know a harrow from a ladle. It's an ongoing thing between them.'

'They look like they're having fun,' Jack said.

A slight tone of longing in his voice made her look at him. He smiled. 'My dad is the same. Always bickering about things he doesn't have any idea about. My sister is almost a doctor and he drives her up the wall with what he thinks is medical knowledge.'

'He'd fit right in here,' Ninni said with a wry smile.

Jack wondered for a moment if he should ask her about Karl again, but reckoned she would have said something if she wanted to tell him.

Instead he sat down on the sand and stretched his legs, enjoying the scenery. The children had thin branches in their hands, the old man helping them to stick sausages on them. They held the sausages over the flames, turning them black and sooty. The children had no patience and started munching on sausages black on the outside and pink on the inside.

Ninni got a hot dog from Jens and sat down next to Jack. She offered him the snack. When he shook his head she took a big bite, obviously enjoying it.

'Are you eating those sausages raw?' To Jack, that looked unsafe.

'Don't worry. They're precooked. You'd be hard pressed finding raw sausages in any shops.' She nodded towards the firepit. 'I think Jens wants a word with you.'

Jack turned his head and Jens smiled broadly at him.

'I might have told him that you have never cooked mussels picked directly from the sea,' she said.

Jack laughed. 'I have to see this,' he said.

By the firepit, Jens had put the bucket on top of a makeshift table.

'Is it true?' Jens asked when Jack came over to him. 'You have never cooked mussels like this?'

'Nope. Not many firepits in London, I'm afraid.' Jack felt the heat from the pit against his face. The burning wood smelled sharp and fresh.

'Then you are lucky. I have done this since I was a boy. You'll like this,' Jens said. He folded a couple of foil sheets and added some herb butter. 'You'll like this,' he said again.

'Where's the white wine?' Jack looked for a bottle and didn't see any.

Jens' eyes twinkled. 'This is Agnar's recipe. He loved mussels, but not with wine. It has to be good butter with chives and ramson, and a bit of lemon. If you don't have ramson, you can use a generous amount of garlic. And since I don't have any of the little green weed, take this.'

Jens handed a package of garlic to Jack, together with a small knife. 'I expect you know what to do with those?'

Jack peeled the garlic and dropped it into the foil. Jens added the mussels, carefully arranging them over the top.

Jack picked up one of the mussels and squeezed it gently. It gave slightly. Jens grinned. 'You know your mussels.'

'I'm not completely without knowledge about food, you know,' Jack said. 'And anyway, Ninni showed me.'

Jens added a few slices of lemon, a handful of chives and butter, and then folded the package tightly. He put it carefully on the side of the firepit. 'If you put them on the open fire, they will burn. They just need a few minutes to be done.'

Someone had added sausage rolls to the camping table, someone else a pile of golden buns and his pasties. Jack handed the two packages to Jens.

'There's ten of those in the bigger package. You can put them on the grill. Make sure the smaller ones goes to you. Those two have a special ingredient,' Jack said to the old man with a wide grin.

Jens raised his eyebrows. 'What's in them?'

'Some of your excellent mutton and potatoes, with some herbs and onions. Nothing fancy. Except in the ones for you. I'm not sure anyone else will like those, to be honest.'

Jens opened the smaller packet and sniffed one of the pasties. 'That's interesting,' he said and put it on the firepit next to the mussels.

Olav turned up and handed him a beer. It was nice and cold, and tasted sweet and sharp at the same time. Jack took another sip, enjoying the flavours.

'Thank you,' he said to Olav.

'You're welcome. It's Britt's special island brew. Don't ask me what's in it,' Olav said.

Jens and Olav exchanged a few words Jack didn't understand. It was annoying, not understanding anything anyone said. Fortunately he wouldn't need to worry about it for too long. He'd soon be back in London.

Then his eyes found Ninni and something shifted inside him. She was talking to her father, and Jack watched her. She seemed completely relaxed. He liked that.

'How are you settling in, Jack?' Olav turned towards him.

The kids sat on the sand, happily munching their second hot dogs.

'I might stay for a while longer,' Jack said, keeping an eye on Ninni.

'Good for you,' Olav said. 'I'll talk to you later.'

He walked off and Jack looked at Jens, who smiled broadly.

'Perhaps the island is growing on you. Agnar would like that,' Jens said. 'Now, let's see how you like this, my friend.'

Jack watched with interest while Jens carefully lifted the mussel package over to a paper plate and opened it. The steam filled the air, wafting the smell of herbs and lemon towards him. Jens scooped some onto another plate and handed it to him. 'Enjoy,' he said.

The mussels were steaming hot. They had all opened, and Jack picked one, broke open the shell to fish out the mussel and popped it in his mouth. He tasted the garlic and the herbs, but the butter made all the difference.

'Oh, that's fantastic.'

Jens nodded, pleased with himself. 'Oh, yes. Simple is always best, in my opinion. Now, let's see what you cooked up.'

Jack popped another mussel in his mouth. Amazing, he thought.

Jens bit into the pasty and chewed carefully. He frowned and chewed some more. 'Old Cheese?' he said.

'Yes. I experimented a little.' Jack wasn't sure if he liked it himself. 'You don't have to eat it, you know. It's not a wager.'

Jens ate the whole thing, then started on the second one. 'This is marvellous,' he said.

Jack laughed and shook his head. He felt ridiculously pleased by the praise.

'I think someone is summoning you,' Jens said and nodded towards a group of people on the grass.

Ninni smiled when he caught her eye. 'Yes, I'll think I'll eat this over there,' he said.

Jack walked over to her. She was quite the sight with dark curls falling in her face and a huge smile to everyone who stopped by to exchange a few words. She looked tired, he thought. The dark shadows under her eyes revealed she wasn't sleeping well. Was it because of Karl and whatever it was he had done to her?

Jack balanced another portion of mussels and the beer, and sat down beside her.

Petter leaned over. 'Are you enjoying yourself, Jack?'

'Very much so. Are there always this many people?'

'It's most of the island's population, plus a few visitors like me.'

Jack put down the bottle to be able to eat the mussels.

Ninni frowned. 'How can you eat that?'

'This is the best meal I have eaten in a long time,' Jack assured her.

185

Petter laughed. 'You can't convince my girl of that. She hates mussels.'

Ninni's expression lit up at Jens, who brought over a plate for her. 'I've given you a bit of everything. Enjoy,' he said, before returning to the fire.

Ninni showed Jack her plate. One of his pasties sat next to a pork chop, a baked potato and what looked like a dollop of tartare sauce. 'See? This is proper food.'

'I made that one,' Jack said, and pointed at the pasty. 'It's completely mussel-free, so you're in no danger.'

'What's in it?'

'Taste it. It's good, I promise,' he said.

Ninni took a bite and chewed carefully while at the same time trying to see what was inside. 'Beef,' she said.

'With potatoes and onions. No fancy ingredients,' Jack said.

'You're right. It's good. Here, Pappa. Try this.' She handed the other half of the pasty to Petter.

He ate it quickly, clearly enjoying it. 'Agnar would have loved this. He loved to cook.'

Ninni scooped some of the mayo onto the potato. 'Want to taste this? It's good too.'

She handed him the plastic spoon filled with sauce and potato. Jack tasted it and frowned. 'That's not tartare,' he said after enjoying the taste of slightly sweet and sour cream. 'What is it?'

Petter used his spoon. 'This is Ninni's speciality.

Remoulade made with sour cream and herbs and a dash of fresh cream. Good?'

'Delicious,' Jack said and tried to take another spoonful.

Ninni moved the plate out of his reach. 'Get your own,' she teased.

Petter patted her shoulder. 'Wait. They're playing.'

Jack stretched his neck and spotted Sigrid and Olav sitting close to the water. The music was sweet and filled with longing.

Accordion and flute, for some reason. Jack listened, fascinated by the melody. He leaned over to Ninni. 'What is it?'

'Folk music,' Ninni said. 'I have no clue as to the name of the melody, I'm afraid.'

'I like it,' Jack said.

Ninni just smiled and handed him the rest of her potato.

A few hours later people started leaving. Sigrid took the children back to the house. Jens and Alma returned to their boat and Ninni helped Olav put out the fire with buckets of seawater that they poured over the firewood. The wood hissed and created clouds of smoke.

She looked up when Jack approached. 'Hi. How are you getting on?'

'I'm heading back, I think. Your dad just left.'

'Yeah, I know.' She took the water bucket from Olav

and poured it carefully over the pit. It steamed and hissed, and she waited until it died down.

Jack waited until Olav returned to the water to fill the bucket. 'Would you mind walking me home?'

Ninni smiled. 'Are you afraid of the dark?'

'Not so much afraid of the dark as I am of falling into a ditch on the way back.' He put his hands in his pockets and obviously had no intention of going back alone.

'Okay. I just have to make sure this is out.'

Olav came up from the water with another bucket. This time he poured.

Ninni took a step back. It wasn't steaming much any more.

'One more,' Olav said.

Jack looked at the pit. 'Does this mean you have to make a new pit every time there's a barbecue on the beach?'

'We use the same place, but yes, it's to make sure the fire is out. We don't want embers starting fires further up. There's no fire brigade on the island, you know.'

Jack waited until Olav said it was fine. They were the last ones to leave.

'Where's Frikk?' Jack said.

'Oh, he followed Pappa. He'll come back for me.'

Jack smiled. 'He comes back for you?'

'Always. Buhunds are excellent herders and Frikk likes to keep his flock together. It's a strong instinct.'

'Is that what he is – a buhund?'

'Yes. It's an old Norwegian breed. A Viking dog, if you like,' she said.

Jack raised his eyebrows. 'Shouldn't the breed be called Old Norwegian Dog then?'

'A joke! Finally!' Ninni laughed even more when he looked overly pleased with himself.

Ninni remembered Britt's observation and couldn't help checking out Jack's bottom. Oh, my God, she thought. I'm insane.

At the top of the road, Ninni closed the gate behind them.

'Are there any animals loose now?' Jack looked over the fence.

'No, but it's important to keep up the good habits,' Ninni said.

He smiled. 'Right, I see.'

They walked slowly away from the farm. Ninni put her hands in her pockets and had no idea what to say to him. She only hoped that he wouldn't ask about Karl again.

'It's not very dark, is it?' he said after a while.

'Never is this time of year. Not too long now before there will only be a few hours of night, even here.'

'And the further north you get, the lighter it gets, right?'

Ninni nodded. 'Yes, because the further north you go, the shorter the night.'

'Do you get the Northern Lights down here during the winter?'

Ninni hid a smile. 'I've never seen them. It's either too cloudy or we are not far enough north.'

Jack nodded, looking very serious. 'What about the midnight sun? Will it be twenty-four hours' sunshine here on the island?'

'You obviously haven't been to Scotland, have you? We're roughly on the same latitude as Shetland. No midnight sun. Again, we're not far enough north and even if we did get Northern Lights or the sun, it's raining here more or less constantly.'

'I've been here for some time now, and it hasn't rained yet.'

Ninni looked up. She realised she hadn't thought about it much, but he was right. 'I hadn't noticed,' she said.

'Because of Karl?' he said.

Ninni scowled at him. 'It's not really your concern, is it?'

'No, but I'd like to know. Out here, on the island, I'm guessing weather conditions are seriously important. If you haven't noticed a lack of rain because of him, he must be a right bastard,' he said.

Ninni hunched her shoulders. 'Well, yes, he is.'

There, it was said. It was the first time she had said it out loud. It felt strangely easy.

'What did he do to you?' Jack sounded kind and Ninni fought hard not to show how she felt.

'He broke my heart,' she said in a light tone. 'There's nothing particularly original about it, I'm afraid.'

'There's nothing mundane about getting your heart broken. If someone treats you like shit, that's hard. Did you love him?'

Ninni burrowed her hands deeper into the jacket. 'I thought I did. How do you know if you love someone?'

'Good question. I thought I loved my girlfriend, turned out I loved all the things that came with her. And that turned dull faster than I thought possible.'

Ninni looked at him properly. He smiled and the smile reached his eyes.

'Did she break your heart?'

'No, she didn't and I didn't break hers. I was furious for a short time, but only because I had made such an idiot of myself.'

'How?' Ninni pulled back. 'I'm sorry. Now I'm being nosy.'

'No, it's okay. I don't mind. Roland, Fedra's father, promised me for years that I would become a partner in his restaurant. That's why I worked so hard. So when he gave it to Fedra instead, I finally understood that he never intended to give it to me in the first place. I think the loss of the restaurant hurt more than anything Fedra did. Stupid, isn't it?'

'Only if you stay angry, I think.' Ninni took a deep breath. 'I thought Karl and I would move in together, start a family, all of those things. We were together for almost two years.'

'What did he do?' Jack sounded even kinder.

'Karl is a pilot and travels a lot. It wasn't unusual for me not to see him for weeks on end, and then he would show up and stay with me for a period of time.' Ninni couldn't really believe she was telling him all this.

'He cheated on you, didn't he? He had someone else?'

Ninni smiled quickly. 'Not really. It turns out that Karl is married and I was the someone else he had on the side. He even has children. I had no idea. I didn't even suspect it, you know. After I found out, I couldn't breathe for days. And I felt so stupid. I still do.'

There, she had said it out loud, to another person, instead of Frikk. She held her breath again.

'I'm sorry. You didn't deserve that,' Jack said softly.

Ninni shrugged. 'Neither did his wife. I hate it that I didn't understand anything until she sent me a picture of him and his kids. I would never have started a relationship with him if I had known.'

'What did you do to him?' Jack was suddenly walking so much closer to her.

'I threw him out, of course, and told him to go to hell.'

She remembered Karl looking at her, mouth wide open, eyes wide open, and then actually trying to explain himself. Ninni closed her eyes for a second, sending the memory to the darkest corner where it belonged.

'Good for you. How long ago was this?'

'Last time I talked to Karl was just before you hit me with your car. I was yelling at him,' she said.

Jack smiled. 'See, I told you it was your fault.'

'Yeah, no. You still drove the wrong way through the roundabout,' Ninni said. The lights from the house caught her eye. 'We're here.'

'Are you really going to let me walk down to the farm by myself in the dark?' he said.

'You really are afraid of the dark, aren't you?' She couldn't help smiling at him.

'What if I walk down the path and have a nasty fall? These wellingtons are too big for my feet and I could easily trip. You'll find me there in the morning with a broken leg or a broken neck.'

'But you're not concerned that I have to walk back up again, risking my neck?' Ninni laughed when he was the one to shrug.

'I've seen you running down this hill like a maniac. I think you can manage,' he said.

'Scaredy-cat,' she said.

He held out his hand. 'You have no idea.'

Ninni hesitated for a second before putting her hand in his. He gently folded his fingers around hers. It felt surprisingly good.

'Did you enjoy the beach party?' she said, feeling as stupid as she sounded.

'You didn't notice? I even loved the potato-planting.

More than anything, I enjoyed the mussel-picking with you.'

They walked carefully down the narrow shortcut to Agnar's house. Jack didn't have any problem walking down.

When they came down to the farmyard, Jack stopped. Ninni looked at him. 'Safely delivered. Are you going to be okay now?'

'More than when I came here. I slept in the garden that first night. This isn't very manly to admit, but I was spooked.'

Ninni smiled. 'Scaredy-cat,' she said again.

'I'm afraid so. It's not something I'm proud of.' He was smiling when he said it, not the least embarrassed.

'I would have slept outside too. Probably for longer than the first night,' she said.

'Yeah?' Jack locked eyes with her and pulled her closer.

'Absolutely. Ghosts thrive in a house that has been standing empty for some time.' She didn't pull away when he kissed her.

The kiss turned from light to deep before she could even think. Then she didn't want to think. Jack tasted of smoke and sea, and made her weak at the knees.

'Wow,' Jack said when they broke apart.

Wow indeed, Ninni thought. She took a step away.

'I think you're safe now,' she said, clearing her throat.

He looked confused and she would rather leave it at

that. If they kissed again, it would bring about all sorts of unwanted things. Ninni wasn't ready for anything remotely summer flingy.

'Goodnight, Jack. My dad will be waiting for me,' she said and walked towards the path.

She turned around at the top of the pathway and looked back. He was still there. He lifted a hand, and she did the same.

Damn, she thought. I hoped he'd be a worse kisser than Karl. He wasn't.

Chapter 13

On the following Sunday, Ninni followed Petter to the last ferry. He looked thoughtful and a bit concerned, not his usual happy self. He didn't even throw the usual sticks for Frikk, who looked disappointed at the lack of attention.

'I have to ask you something,' Petter said.

'Okay,' she said, hugging his arm.

'Why didn't you tell me about Karl?' He gave her one of his sharper looks, the one he had used when she was a teenager and tried to argue about curfew.

'I was embarrassed. I still am,' she admitted.

Petter looked horrified. 'Why on earth would you be? That little shit cheated on you. I'd like to throw him overboard on a dark night.'

Ninni couldn't help laughing. 'Please don't. He's not worth it. I'm getting over the whole thing, Pappa.'

He put his arm around her shoulder. 'That's my girl. Don't let that bastard get to you. I would never have survived your mother's departure if I took things too seriously.'

Ninni smiled. It wasn't exactly how she remembered her parents' divorce, but she didn't correct him. He had got over her, but not as lightly as he thought.

'Yes, I know and, as you know, it takes time.'

He nodded several times. 'Of course. But you are okay, aren't you? I don't have to worry about you?'

Ninni leaned towards him. 'Of course not. I'm not that dramatic.'

'No, you're like me. You should be happy about that. Drama is so exhausting.' He hugged her again and laughed.

They passed the road to Agnar's farm and Ninni avoided looking down. Petter, on the other hand, had no such reservations. He pointed at the farm. 'Now, what about your Englishman? He seems like a nice young man.'

'He's not my Englishman, Pappa.' Ninni rolled her eyes.

'You could have fooled me. The way the two of you looked in the boat the other day? He fancies you. Even I could see that.'

'Pappa, there's so many things wrong in those sentences. Please stop. I'm not talking to you about this. And, for your information, Jack has just left a bad relationship. He's not looking for someone else, and neither am I.'

Petter thought about it as they got closer to the quay. 'Then you have something in common, haven't you?'

'I can't believe we're having this conversation.' Ninni

discovered Frikk digging in a flowerbed and called him back.

'Fine, fine. I'm trying to help. I like him.'

'Then you go out with him. I won't.' Ninni smiled to disarm him. 'It's good for me to be alone, Pappa. I need that.'

'That's all fine and dandy, but you were alone for most of the time even when you were with Karl, weren't you? He was always off somewhere, wasn't he?'

Ninni knew he was right. She had been alone a lot more than together with Karl, when she thought about it. But she wouldn't admit it so easily.

'Yes, but that doesn't mean I will throw myself at the first man who comes along.'

'You could have a fling,' Petter said, shaking with laughter when she looked at him in horror.

'Please don't tell me you've been talking to Britt?'

He pulled a face and pretended not to hear. 'Oh, it looks like the ferry is coming in early.'

'You are so sneaky,' she said.

At the harbour they met Alma, waiting for goods from the mainland. Frikk sat down at Petter's feet, placing one paw on his shoes. He didn't approve of his people leaving.

'Are you going back to Bergen so soon?' Alma seemed surprised.

'I have a business to take care of,' Petter said.

While they chatted to each other, Ninni pulled back a little. It had started to rain, a light drizzle at first then a little heavier, and it was obvious that it would get worse. Ninni pulled the hood on her rain jacket over her head.

'I'd better get myself onboard. It's my turn to open the store tomorrow,' Petter said.

'You're the only one who works there,' Ninni said, shaking her head.

He gave Ninni one of his bear hugs and looked at her. 'Look after yourself now. I left some books in the house. And don't become a hermit.'

'No, Pappa, I promise. Drive carefully and call me when you're home.' Ninni hugged him back and stood close to Alma.

Frikk got a quick cuddle, and then Petter walked on board the boat.

Alma frowned. 'Did he talk to you about Agnar and Jack?'

Ninni put her hands in her pockets. 'No, not really. He talked to Jack and he likes him, so I guess it's okay.'

'Hmm,' Alma said.

Ninni looked at her. 'What? You don't like Jack?'

'No, he's fine, but that doesn't change anything, does it? Jack is still going to sell Agnar's farm and we will still be overrun by those kinds of people.' She nodded towards a huge yacht gliding past them with passengers on board, staring towards land. 'Right now we have nothing here that they'll find interesting. That will change if Haldorsen, or someone like him, gets their grubby hands on Agnar's farm.'

'It might not be that bad,' Ninni said, knowing she didn't sound convincing.

Alma suddenly looked tired. 'Things change so fast these days. Even on this island. I can't keep them at bay for much longer, Ninni.'

'Perhaps you should talk to Jack about your concerns. We have no idea what he thinks, do we?'

'All I can do is beg Jack not to sell to the worst developer, people like Haldorsen, but sooner or later it will happen.'

Ninni put her hand on her arm. 'It might not be that bad, Alma,' she said again.

'If it does, I'm sure some bastard would want to buy the *landhandel* from us, tear down the house and build a gourmet supermarket for the yacht people.'

'What will you do if that happens?' Ninni smiled at her now.

Alma shook her head. 'We can move to the mainland or even to Spain, if that happens.'

'Mamma loves Spain,' Ninni said to tease her.

Alma scrunched up her face and for a moment Ninni thought she was crying. It took a second to realise that she was laughing.

'Oh, I can just picture myself in one of those tourist apartment blocks, next to your mum. She'd love that, I'm sure.'

Ninni couldn't help joining in with the laughter. 'She could teach you to play bridge.'

'I'd rather have my teeth pulled out.' Alma lifted her hand and waved at Petter, who stood aft in the ferry.

Ninni waved too. 'I always wondered why he doesn't move back here. He loves this island.'

'You know how it is. Your father went to university. He wasn't meant to be a fisherman or a sailor.' She looked grim. 'And he could never sell enough books here to survive. Not even if it becomes a millionaires' playground. That lot haven't read a book in their lives.'

The ferry disappeared out of sight. Ninni shivered and Alma noticed. 'Come to the shop. You can help me get the last of these things up there.'

"These things" were magazines and books to go on sale the next day. Alma took one package and Ninni the other, trying not to reveal how heavy it was. The plastic wrapping didn't make it easier, only more slippery.

She had time for a coffee. It wasn't as if she was actually busy with anything useful.

Ninni found Frikk outside the shop. He was snoozing under one of Alma's red currant bushes, but jumped up when she called his name.

She gave him a doggy biscuit before they left. It had started to rain again while she was in the shop, but she wasn't worried about that. It was a nice change from all the sunshine.

On top of the hill, she looked down towards Agnar's house. The lights were on in the kitchen. Perhaps Jack was cooking? Those pasties he had brought were really good. For a brief second she considered going down there. They should probably talk about the kiss, but she hesitated.

After all, it was just a kiss.

She turned away and walked towards the house. Better go home and do some work, she thought. There were bills to be paid, dog food to buy and she needed a distraction from good-looking men who could kiss.

From where she stood, she could see darker clouds moving in from the open sea. More rain, she thought. Perhaps a summer storm. Ninni smiled. Storms made for great reading weather. She could cosy up in the big chair, or in bed, with a good book and a steaming mug of hot chocolate.

Frikk ran ahead of her. He loved the rain too, putting his nose to everything he could reach. Once in a while he stopped and looked back at her to make sure she was following. Then he ran ahead until she couldn't see him any more.

Ninni turned from the path to Agnar's house. All she wanted was to get home and lock herself away for a few days. She increased her pace, suddenly eager to get inside. The dog was nowhere to be seen.

'Frikk? Frikk? Come here, boy,' she called, whistling her usual signal for him.

He didn't appear. Ninni frowned. Now what? She started running, calling his name, and when he still didn't show up her heart raced so fast that at first she couldn't breathe.

She found him in the thicket, whimpering.

Jack looked at the translation app on his phone and swore to himself. 'Bloody useless thing,' he grumbled. After the meeting tomorrow, he would find a bookshop and buy the biggest dictionary he could find.

The notebook from his grandmother was difficult to translate. He couldn't find the words on the app. Grandmother, he thought. That was a strange word. He had never called anyone Nana or Granny. Holly and Danny called their grandmother Granny. He never did, despite the fact that she was the nicest of the lot.

Most of Paul's family regarded him as an intruder, and treated him as such. It didn't bother him now, but it had been hard growing up and seeing how differently they'd treated Holly and Danny.

Would Magni have been nice – given him cookies when he came to visit, always remembered his birthday? Perhaps. Petter had said she'd wanted grandchildren and that she'd loved her son. Chances were she would have loved him too.

He smiled, a bit sad at the thought. They'd never got the chance, any of them. It didn't really matter now, did it? They were both dead.

Jack shook his head. Good Lord, if he wasn't sitting there, feeling sorry for himself. He stood up so abruptly that the chair almost tipped over.

Better go outside, clear my head instead of sitting here feeling sorry for myself, he thought.

He grabbed a raincoat from one of the pegs, pulled on the wellingtons and headed out. Before leaving, he hesitated then grabbed the phone as well. Just in case he got in the mood to call someone that mattered.

Outside, he looked up at the grey sky. The rain seemed to come in bursts. Not so pleasant now, he thought, but it was a relief after all the hot weather.

On the field, Olav's *hesjer* looked miserable. It took him a few seconds to see that they were covered in plastic or some kind of tarp. Obviously Jens' weather reports worked. He hadn't even noticed they were there, putting it up.

He closed the door behind him and shoved his hands in his pockets. He looked up towards Ninni's house, and realised she wasn't at home. The windows were dark.

No point in knocking on her door then. He had to admit he was disappointed. That kiss showed promise.

Instead of going up to the road, he decided to go to the beach, to get a proper view of the storm. If that was even what it was. The islanders probably called this a drizzle.

He turned around and started walking towards the

boathouses. When he got closer, he realised someone was there.

The outside light on Ninni's boathouse was on, and he could see her getting ready to get into the boat. The boat jumped and dipped, as if it was trying to get onto dry land.

'What the hell are you doing?' he called out.

Ninni looked at him and he could see the desperation in her eyes. Jack was suddenly worried. 'What's going on?'

'It's Frikk,' she said.

He could see tears running down her face, and the way she was drying them off with an impatient hand. 'Vipers,' she said. 'A bloody nest of bloody vipers. I have to get him to the vet.'

Jack bent over and looked at the dog. Frikk was panting and he didn't look like his normal energetic self. His nose was swollen and bloody. It didn't look good.

'You can't go out there alone. Not in that boat,' he said.

'I don't have time to get any of the others. Frikk needs help now. There's an emergency vet in Haugesund. I've called them, and they will stand by for us.'

Her teeth were chattering. Jack made a quick decision. 'I'll come with you.'

Ninni shook her head. 'No, you can't. You're not *båtvant* – I mean, you're not used to boats. I can't worry about you too.'

Jack picked up the old life jacket from the boathouse and put it on. 'I'll take care of Frikk while you drive. Get in the boat. There's no time to waste.'

She didn't argue, but got into the boat. Jack lifted Frikk carefully and handed him to her, then got into the boat himself.

'Sit down in the middle,' Ninni said. 'That way there's not that much water on you and it's a bit easier to travel.'

She didn't wait for him to do as she instructed; instead she got the engine started and the boat headed out to sea.

Jack tried not to think about the movement of the waves, or the wind pulling at the hood of his raincoat. He focused on the dog, holding him tight to his chest and trying to shield him from the rain as best he could.

Ninni held onto the engine handle and steered them out of the bay and into the open sea. Jack had no idea if she was going in the right direction.

'You know where it is, right?'

She nodded, grim-faced. 'I've been sailing this way since I was eight, Jack. We'll be fine. It's just rain.'

It didn't feel like "just rain" to him. There were no bursts any more, just a solid wall of rain. His trousers were soaked. I have a soggy bottom, he thought, and didn't find it remotely funny.

'Hang on, Jack. I'll try to get in as fast as I can, and it will be a bit bumpy. How is he?'

She had to bellow over the wind. Jack looked at the dog. He was breathing, but it was shallow. 'Just get us there.'

The blanket she had wrapped around Frikk was wet too. Jack knew that if the dog went into shock they would have a bigger problem than getting to shore. He fiddled with his raincoat and managed to slip Frikk inside. His shirt got as wet as the rest of him, but at least it gave Frikk some shelter.

He watched Ninni. She looked like a Fury with her hair flying in the wind, whipping her face while she paid no attention to any of it. She had to be as drenched as he was, possibly more, as she was sitting on the stern, more open to the elements than he was. And yet she didn't seem to notice anything.

Vikings, he thought. That would be what they'd looked like in their longboats, fighting for their family. Did female Vikings fight? He had no idea, but it wouldn't surprise him.

'We're getting closer. Do you see the lights?' Ninni had to yell to be heard.

Jack turned his head. He spotted a few lights, blinking through the rain. 'That's Haugesund? Are you sure?'

'That's the town, yes.'

Jack checked on the dog again. He was listless. 'You'd better hurry up then,' he said.

Ninni didn't say anything. The boat seemed to fly across the water.

Chapter 14

It took them another half an hour before the boat glided close to the harbour. They were below the edge and the concrete was lined with old tyres to protect the heavier boats when they moored.

Ninni grabbed hold of a metal ring hanging from the concrete.

Jack sat still, cradling the dog. He had no intention of standing up and falling into the black water. There were other boats close by, some tied directly to the concrete, others to each other. There were lights from houses on both the mainland and the two islands.

Over their heads was the bridge to Risøy Island.

Ninni secured the line and jumped off the boat. Jack discovered she stood on a narrow step. She pointed up.

'The steps are slippery. Be careful when you climb out of the boat. I'll go get a taxi.'

Jack held onto the dog for dear life and managed to get himself onto land. He stood for a second and looked around. There was no one in sight. Everyone was inside because of the rain, he figured. Now he also realised there were people in the boats. None of them paid any attention to him.

There had to be an anti-seasickness gene in these people, he thought.

He pulled back the hood of the raincoat and tried to see where Ninni had gone. There was no sign of her. Then he checked on Frikk. He was still breathing, but it was shallow and the wounds looked even more swollen.

'She'd better get here soon, Frikk,' he muttered.

When he turned around a car came down the road. It stopped next to him and Ninni threw open the door to the back seat.

'Get in!' she yelled.

The car sped off and Jack fell back against the seat. 'Oof,' he said.

Ninni looked at the bundle. 'Is Frikk okay?'

Jack pulled down the corner of the blanket. 'He's not in great shape, but he's still here.'

Ninni was fighting back tears. 'I can't believe he got into that thicket. I was just behind him. Damn curious idiot.'

'How long until we get there?'

The driver answered. 'A few minutes,' he said.

He drove fast, so they were there in even less time. The veterinary surgery was fully lit.

Ninni opened the door and held it open for him.

Jack realised she'd made no attempt to take Frikk from him.

Inside the surgery, it was nice and warm. A smiling woman dressed in surgical clothes came towards them and took a quick look at Frikk. The smile disappeared. 'Follow me.'

Jack did as he was told. He wouldn't have dared to let the dog out of his sight, anyhow. Inside the examination room, she pointed at a bench. 'Put him down there.'

Jack carefully put Frikk down on the bench and stepped back. Ninni leaned against him. The vet turned on the big overhead lamp, peeled away the soggy blanket and looked at Frikk. 'And what have you done to your lovely self?'

'It's vipers,' Ninni said. 'He's fascinated by them, and he got bitten.'

The vet pulled the lamp down more closely over the table. 'More than once by the look of it. He's got at least three bites in the face.'

She looked at Ninni with concern in her eyes. 'There's only so much I can do. The rest depends on his strength and how much poison he got. I can't promise anything right now. You do know that, right?'

Ninni swallowed. 'Please, do what you can.'

The vet got out a couple of syringes. 'I'll give him the antiserum, take some blood tests and give him something for the pain. Then we'll have to keep him calm for a few days. Do you have anywhere to stay for the night? I'm guessing you're not going to be able to return to the island now. The wind is getting stronger.'

'No, there's no point in that now. We'll find somewhere.'

The vet smiled. 'There's a sofa in the office and there's coffee. Also, there are some blankets in the hallway cupboard. They smell of dog, but I hope they'll do.'

'We'll be fine,' Ninni said.

The vet fastened an IV needle to one of Frikk's paws and secured it with a piece of tape. 'Frikk is the only overnight guest at the moment. I'm sorry, Ninni, but I have to go back home to my baby. I'll come by in a couple of hours to see how he's doing. If you notice any deterioration, call me and I'll come right away.'

'You're going to leave everything here with us?' Jack couldn't help himself.

The vet smiled. 'Well, Ninni's Frikk is here. I doubt you're going to leave him. Don't have any wild parties and all the drugs are locked up. Get those blankets. You guys look drenched.'

Ninni stood up. 'Yes, thank you.'

'There's also some overalls and sweaters there, if you want to dry your own clothes. And if you take a look in one of the drawers I'm pretty sure there's a bottle of Scotch somewhere. For emergencies,' she said, before carefully lifting Frikk off the table and setting him down on a comfortable doggy bed in the corner. 'Keep an eye on him and let him know you're here,' she said to Ninni.

Ninni nodded. 'I will. Thank you for coming.'

'That's what we're here for.'

With a last look at the dog to see he was breathing properly, she left. They heard the main door slamming after her.

Jack realised he was cold to the marrow and he was dripping on the floor. He took Ninni's hand. It was ice-cold and he could feel her shaking.

'Your teeth are chattering,' she said.

'So are yours.' He found the blankets in the hall and handed one to her.

She pulled it around herself and sat down on the sofa. 'God, I'm so cold. I never freeze.' Ninni was shaking, and Jack sat down next to her. At first he thought it was the chill, but he suddenly realised she was crying.

Jack didn't say anything. He put his arm around her and held her close. It seemed the best thing to do. She was a silent crier and it didn't take long before she stopped. 'Oh, this isn't helping at all.'

'I would have found you a handkerchief, but it would probably be wet already,' Jack said.

Ninni looked at him and smiled through her tears. 'Another joke. I'm impressed.'

'I aim to please,' he said. 'And on that note ... Wait here while I find the clothes she talked about.'

He came back with a few odds and ends and handed her one of the sweatshirts. 'Put this on before you get pneumonia. And try one of the overalls. They look like they would fit you.'

Ninni pulled off her clothes, totally ignoring him. Jack got a glimpse of soft curves and white underwear, and forced himself to breathe slowly. Wow, he thought.

To hide his embarrassment, he pulled off his own shirt and changed into one of the sweatshirts. It was bliss.

'You should try these trousers. I think they will fit you,' she said, holding the item out to him.

Jack lifted them up and made a little show by measuring them and looking at himself in the mirror on the wall. Ninni laughed, which was exactly what he was hoping for.

'I would rather have a pair of socks,' he said.

'Don't think they stock anything but bandages, I'm afraid. I'll just see to Frikk.' Ninni stood up from the sofa. Trailing the blanket after her, she went out to check on the dog.

Jack tried the overalls. Not a perfect fit, too wide and too short, but it was better than the other way around, he thought.

I'm bonkers, he thought. This is bonkers.

He looked up when Ninni came back. 'He's sleeping and he's breathing better. I think the serum is working.'

'Good. I'm starving – is there anything to eat here, apart from dog food?'

Ninni smiled. She was more composed now. 'Let's see what's in the kitchen.'

'They have a kitchen?' Jack followed.

'Where do you think they keep the coffee? Also, it's a lunchroom,' Ninni said.

It was more of a mini version of a kitchenette – an electric kettle, a small fridge, a table and four chairs and, most importantly, a stove.

'I'm not touching anything in there,' Ninni declared and shut the refrigerator door.

'Where's the nearest shop?' Jack could see she was at the end of her tether.

'Oh, there's one by Hotel Saga, I think.' Ninni sank down on one of the chairs. 'You don't have to go. It's still raining.'

'You're not the only one starving.' Jack inspected the cupboards to see what kind of pots or pans, if any, were available to him. Not very impressive, he thought. But not unexpected. It was a vet's surgery, not a culinary school.

'You know, we can just order something. There are fast food places in this town, most of them quite decent.' Ninni nodded towards the wall where different menus were tacked to a cork board.

'No, I think we need proper food to cheer us up. Especially as we're going to be here all night.'

He put on his rain jacket again. Ninni looked at him, a small smile showing on her face. 'Are you really going out like that?'

Jack looked down at the short trousers and wet socks. 'I have wellingtons. Would anyone care about my fashion choices, do you think?'

'In this weather? Probably not.' Ninni looked at him. 'Thank you for coming. I don't think I would have managed alone.'

'I'm glad to be of help,' Jack said.

For a moment their eyes locked and then she looked away. Jack cleared his throat. 'Well, is there anything you prefer? Of food, I mean.'

Ninni shook her head. 'Anything will be fine. I'll go and sit with Frikk while you're gone.'

Jack got the keys to the surgery from the desk and walked outside. It was still pouring down so he pulled his hood up. There was hardly anyone outside.

Sensible people, he thought.

He quickly found the shop and felt a lot better when he discovered they also sold socks and underwear. After a moment of hesitation, he bought some for Ninni as well, in two different sizes to be on the safe side.

A quick tour through the supermarket left him wondering. Why did they have such a limited variety of produce? The prices were a good indication. He shook his head. Some of the basic greens were double the price they were in the UK. No wonder Norwegians ate minimalistic.

In the end, he settled for eggs and flour for the pasta and some tomatoes and basil for the tomato sauce. Onions looked nice, as did the garlic he found in a corner. That should work well, he thought. Easy and quick to make.

He looked for wine, and didn't find any. Asking one of the assistants granted him raised eyebrows. 'You have to buy that in *Vinmonopolet*, but they're closed now. We don't even sell beer now. It's after eight.'

'What's *Vinmonopolet*?' Jack was sure he hadn't heard that before.

'They are the only shops where you can buy alcohol. Unless you go to a bar or a pub, but you can't buy any bottles from there and take them with you.' The shop assistant grinned, obviously pleased by the confused foreigner. 'A bit different from where you live, I guess.'

'Yes, I would say so.'

Jack wondered how people lived without the basics. He refused to make tomato sauce without a drop of red wine. So carbonara it was, he thought. 'I'll be right back.'

After putting the tomatoes and basil back where he'd found them, he returned with bacon, more eggs and a carton of heavy cream. The shop assistant smiled at him. 'Did you find everything you wanted? Apart from the wine, of course.'

'We'll soldier on,' Jack said.

'*Hæ?*'

'It's fine. Thank you for your help.' Jack waited while his purchases were added up.

Armed with two bags filled with groceries and a few other things, he headed back to the surgery. It was time to cook.

Ninni was waiting in the reception when he arrived. She looked at the heavy bags. 'What did you do – buy the whole shop?'

'They don't really have anything here, so we have to make do the best we can.'

Jack put the bags on the counter and rummaged through one. 'Here. I hope this helps.'

He handed her a large bar of chocolate and smiled when her eyes lit up. Ninni opened the chocolate and broke off a piece. She handed it to him. 'Better than almost anything,' she said.

He put the piece in his mouth. It melted on his tongue. 'Almost,' he said.

Ninni peered into one of the bags. 'Why would you buy a frying pan?'

Jack frowned. 'I had to. All they have here is a saucepan. You need proper tools to do a proper job, you know.'

Ninni munched on another piece of the chocolate. 'What are you cooking?'

'It's a surprise. In the meantime, I bought these for

you. As I'm not sure about your size, I bought two different ones. I hope it's okay.'

Ninni took the packages and looked at them. She laughed. 'Did you really buy knickers and socks for me?'

'You're as soaked as I am, and dry underwear and socks always help,' he said, grinning back at her.

Ninni looked at him. It was that moment again. Something unspoken. She lifted her hand and put it to his cheek, just for a moment. 'You are quite unexpected,' she said.

Jack frowned. 'I have no idea what that means,' he said.

'It's a compliment.' Ninni clutched her gifts. 'I'm going to change into this and you should do the same. You're right. Dry underwear is one of the keys to happiness.'

'And I thought it was all about the cooking,' Jack said.

Ninni smiled. 'Another joke. You're improving.'

Jack picked up the bags. 'I do my best. Dinner should be ready in about an hour.'

'Thank you.' Ninni smiled. 'You are a really nice man.'

He shrugged. 'Not too nice, I hope.'

Nice man, he thought. The death of everything. He knew he shouldn't have bought the knickers.

Ninni took a deep breath. She clutched the socks and the knickers to her chest. Wow, she thought. He can't be for real. She paid a quick visit to the bathroom and changed out of the last wet items of clothing.

And he cooks, she thought when she came back out. He might be close to perfect. Even when he was wearing trousers that were too short and he looked ridiculous.

She went back in to check on Frikk. He was breathing more easily, she thought. She hoped. He didn't react much when she spoke to him, but that didn't stop her. She scratched his ears and he blinked at her. He tried to wag his tail, but didn't have the energy for it.

'Keep breathing, Frikk. That's all you have to do,' she said. With one hand on his chest, she was relieved to feel the dog's heart beating strongly. That was surely a good sign, she thought. 'I hope you have learned your lesson now. No more vipers, all right?'

Frikk kicked one of his legs and Ninni breathed a bit more easily. She kept a hand on his fur until he settled again. This was going to be okay, she thought. He was going to be okay.

Ninni didn't know how long she had been sitting there, when Jack put his head in. 'If you're still hungry, the food is ready.'

'I'm starving.' She almost jumped onto her feet.

'How is he doing?' Jack dried his hands on a tea towel.

Ninni looked back at the dog. 'I think the antiserum is doing its job.'

'That's good. I can bring the food out here, if you want.'

Ninni shook her head. 'No, I don't think we should eat food on the floor of a vet's surgery.'

She followed behind him. He still looked silly in those trousers. Silly, but good.

'It smells amazing. What did you make?'

Jack looked over his shoulder. 'Pasta carbonara. Best I could do under the circumstances.'

Ninni went quiet when she sat down. Somewhere he had found plates and cutlery, even paper napkins and a candle. It was bright red, so probably a leftover from Christmas, but even so. The effort was impressive and that was even before she had tasted the food. He had bought fizzy drinks to go with the food and she smiled at the sight of the bright yellow bottles.

'It smells wonderful,' she said.

Jack put the pot on the table. 'I hope you like Italian food.'

The pot was steaming and promising all sorts of deliciousness. 'I love Italian food.'

Jack filled her plate with a generous portion, then grabbed a grater and a piece of hard cheese. 'Parmesan.'

Ninni looked at him. 'This is proper Parmesan? Are you serious?'

'I'm always serious about food.' Jack sat down opposite her.

The food looked too good to eat. 'Do you cook like this every day?' she asked.

'I don't have time to cook for myself. I usually eat at the restaurant.' Jack filled his own bowl.

'So, you eat the food that you make at the restaurant. Isn't that cooking for yourself?'

'Not really, no. I would be happy with a cheese sandwich if I only cooked for myself.' Jack lit the candle with a lighter he told her he'd found in the same drawer as the Scotch the vet had mentioned.

Ninni chewed the pasta and swallowed. 'Did you make this pasta?'

'Of course I did.' He frowned. 'Why? Don't you like it?'

'I can honestly say this is the best pasta I have ever tasted. I can't believe you made this here. Why didn't you just get us a pizza?'

Jack looked as if he was considering it, then shook his head. 'They don't have an oven here.'

'Otherwise you would have made a pizza from scratch, right?' Ninni took another bite. There were hints of onion, pepper, mushroom and those little green peas, and a lot of bacon, in a rich creamy sauce. It was to die for.

'Yes, I would.' He finished his food. 'Do you know they don't sell any wine or booze in the shops here? Like, not at all?'

'I have noticed, yes. You can buy beer and cider in

the shop, though,' Ninni said, shaking with laughter now.

'No, you can't. Not after eight o'clock. That's not normal.'

Ninni laughed out loud. 'I guess that depends on your point of view. Buying whisky or a bottle of red wine in Waitrose or Sainsbury's on a Sunday morning isn't normal.'

'It ruins the possibilities for a proper red wine sauce,' Jack said. 'Otherwise we would have been eating a nice tomato sauce right now.'

'Most of us adapt to the opening hours of *Vinmonopolet* and we prefer it like that,' Ninni said, a bit defensive.

Jack frowned. 'I guess it means I have to plan my sauces a day in advance then.'

'Or always keep a couple of bottles in your cupboard,' Ninni said, grinning at him.

'Which a good chef does, anyway. But on an island, that has to be a problem.'

'No, not really, we shop what we need when *Vinmonopolet* is open. Agnar used to make his own brew, like Tobben does now,' Ninni said.

'Alma said he drank too much at times.' Jack smiled. 'I learn all these bits and pieces about him, but I can't get a whole picture, you know?'

Ninni took a sip from the bottle of fizzy drink. 'It must be difficult for you. I can't even imagine.'

Jack put the plate aside. 'It's not difficult in a sense; it's more ... surprising. I never expected this connection.'

Ninni smiled. 'You're obviously discovering your roots. I can't imagine what that feels like.'

'A bit overwhelming, but not bad,' Jack said.

'How did you get into your type of cooking? I mean, it's one thing to cook at home, but this food is far beyond anything anyone could throw together.'

'I was lucky. I studied cooking in college and then had some work training in a really good restaurant. Roland took a liking to me and asked if I wanted a job at the weekends. He encouraged me to experiment, gave me all the training I could dream of, even sent me to Le Cordon Bleu in Paris, and he promised me the management of the restaurant if I got him a Michelin star.'

There was a hint of bitterness in his voice. Ninni took a sip of her soda. 'You were about to get a Michelin star; I read that online. He didn't follow up on his promise, did he?'

Jack shook his head. 'No, of course he didn't. I should have known better, of course. But I trusted him.'

'What did you do?' Ninni watched him.

Jack waved his hand. 'I told him to go to hell, then I came here.'

'Oh, I see. That must have been quite an upheaval. You seem to be handling it all very well.' Ninni smiled at him.

'Not really. I'm a bit of a mess, but I'm getting there,' Jack said.

She finished off the rest of her food and leaned back. 'I'm so full.'

'I don't have any dessert, I'm afraid. Unless you have more of that chocolate left.'

'There's half a bar in the reception, if you want it.' Ninni stood up and started to clear the table.

Jack moved the pot to the oven. 'Breakfast,' he said.

'Britt told me that the restaurant, your restaurant, could lose the opportunity to get that Michelin star. Is that because you're here?'

Jack nodded. 'That, and the fact that I took the book with me when I left.'

'The book? What book?' Ninni turned towards him.

'Every chef has one. It contains all the recipes I have developed and used in the restaurant,' Jack said.

Ninni lifted her hand. 'I bet they didn't like you taking it, did they? There was a woman in the article online – I can't remember her name – she's the new owner, isn't she?'

'Fedra. She's his daughter, and she's furious that I took the book with me.'

'And you like that, don't you?'

Jack looked slightly embarrassed. 'I can't deny that I enjoyed messing with them, no. When I confronted Roland with his promise, she stood next to him and I

225

could see the smug triumph in her face. So I walked away.'

'With your book.' Ninni smiled. 'Good for you.'

'It wasn't my finest hour, I'm afraid. I actually considered hitting a seventy-five-year-old man. And his daughter.'

'But you didn't, did you? I think you should get some credit for your self-control. I'm impressed.'

He smiled and Ninni's heart jumped at least three beats.

'Impressed, ha? First my food, then my ability not to hit people. That's not bad.'

'I was impressed long before that,' Ninni said.

'You were?' Jack's smile deepened.

Ninni took a step closer. 'Absolutely.'

He kissed her then, and Ninni sank into him and into the kiss. It was even better than the first time.

Chapter 15

Jack leaned back in the boat. He felt infinitely better in his own clothes now that they'd dried, the weather was nice again and Frikk, resting his chin on his leg, was alert, although a bit knackered.

'The swelling has gone down,' he said.

Ninni smiled at him. She seemed relaxed and happy. He wondered how much of it had to do with the dog and how much with what had happened between them.

It had heated up rather nicely, he thought. But there was no way they were going to have sex for the first time on a smelly sofa in a vet's surgery.

'You look funny,' Ninni said, stretching her legs in front of her. Next to her was a bucket with a few paper bags. She hadn't told him what it was, and he didn't ask. It didn't mean he wasn't curious.

'I do? Even in my normal trousers?' He smiled.

'Not that kind of funny. Your expression,' she said.

Jack raised his eyebrows. 'Funny, how?'

'I don't know. Like you regret we didn't sleep together

last night. Do you regret it?' The question was hesitant and direct at the same time.

Jack smiled. 'No, I don't. Do you?'

Ninni smiled with a shadow of relief. 'Not even a little bit. It wasn't the right setting – or time.'

That's good, Jack thought. 'So, there's a right time? Okay, I can live with that.'

Ninni laughed and Frikk lifted his head. 'Well, how about I invite you for dinner tonight? Since you made dinner for me last night, it's only fair that I cook for you.'

Jack decided to tease her. 'You can cook? What kind of food?'

'Nothing fancy, if that's what you were hoping for.' She looked a bit annoyed, which made him smile.

'Okay. I'll be delighted with whatever you serve. What can I bring?'

Ninni cocked her head. 'Are you any good at baking bread?'

'I make fantastic bread, actually. People cry when I make them bread. In fact, people have named their children after me, that's how good I am,' Jack said.

Ninni narrowed her eyes. 'Then fine. Bring bread, but it has to be white bread.'

'I thought you guys were fanatical about brown bread.'

'It depends on what you're eating with it. What I'm cooking is absolutely white bread food,' she said.

They fell silent. Jack studied the calm water, so

different from the night before. The sun was shining, making the surface sparkle.

'It changes so fast,' Ninni said and looked over his shoulder. 'Sometimes you turn around and there's a storm coming. It takes some time getting used to.'

Jack turned around and looked behind him. The sky was clear blue as far as he could see. 'Not now, right?'

Ninni laughed. 'Not now. You're safe.'

Jack scratched Frikk on his head. The dog looked mournful, but his tail flapped a few times.

'What are you going to cook for me?'

'Oh, I don't know. Something, I guess. Are you allergic to anything? I don't want to accidentally kill you; that would be bad for my plans.'

'I'm not allergic to anything. I hate runner beans, though. Please don't cook them.'

'And there goes my runner bean mousse,' she said.

Jack smirked. 'Thank you. It's awful.'

'There's your islet.' Ninni pointed suddenly.

Jack caught sight of it immediately. There were no sheep to see today. 'Where are they?'

'Most likely on the other side, or in the middle, I'm guessing. It's their islet. They roam freely.'

'I'll never get used to owning goats,' Jack said.

'They are still sheep.' Ninni laughed.

Jack liked seeing her laugh. The first time they met, she had been so furious with him, but right now she was happy.

'You look beautiful,' he said.

Ninni frowned. 'No, I don't.'

'Yes, you do. You are beautiful.'

'No need to flatter me. I won't throw you overboard.'

She was teasing him and he enjoyed it. 'Doesn't change anything.'

'Okay. We're here.' Ninni nodded towards a point behind him.

Jack turned again. The two boathouses were clearly visible now, and behind them he spotted the roof of his house. Agnar's house, he corrected himself.

'Good. I could do with a shower, right about now,' he said.

Ninni grinned. 'Yes, you could.'

'You're cheeky,' he said.

And beautiful and funny, and so different from everyone he'd ever met.

Ninni made sure Frikk was comfortable in his bed before having a shower. When she came back into the kitchen she checked on him again. His tail wagged against the floor, but he stayed where he was.

She sat down next to him and gently pulled his ear. 'You're fine, aren't you? Stupid dog. Will you ever hunt vipers again?'

Frikk licked her nose as if to say he promised to be good.

'Good. I have work to do in the kitchen today. I'm

almost as stupid as you are, volunteering to cook for an almost Michelin chef. He's going to hate it, isn't he?'

She talked while looking through the contents of the fridge and pulled out different items. She found a tub of sour cream and some herbs – that looked promising.

It took less than ten minutes to make a decent remoulade, then she mixed some whipped cream into it, adding dill and chives. She looked at Frikk. 'What about garlic?'

Frikk sighed and rested his head on his paws. Ninni laughed. 'Perhaps not.'

She took the paper bags from the bucket and put them in the fridge. The dessert didn't need to be made until they were ready to eat it, so she left the rest of Britt's eggs on the counter. Then she took a small bag of frozen redcurrants out of the fridge. They'd been picked from the garden the year before but they were still good. She poured them in a bowl and sprinkled some sugar on them.

'Now, if this doesn't impress him, I don't know what will, Frikk.'

She kept talking and smiled every time the dog responded.

In her head she ran through everything she needed to do. Her hands were shaking. What am I doing? she thought. Her next thought was that the bed needed new sheets.

'Here, sweetie.' She gave Frikk a treat, then ran upstairs.

Changing her bed took about five minutes. She looked around. Perhaps not the most seductive room, she thought, glancing at the toy planes hanging from the ceiling and the Barbies on the shelves.

'Bugger this,' she muttered.

She headed back downstairs and opened the door to the lounge. Her father had bought a huge couch a few years ago, American style, so that he would have the perfect place to read and relax. That will do, she thought.

Ninni looked at the time. Only ten hours until dinnertime.

I need a nap, she thought. She flopped down on the couch and fell asleep, and didn't notice Frikk coming in from the kitchen and climbing onto the couch and settling in the crook of her knees.

Jack hummed. Bread, he thought. That would be easy, but perhaps also an ice cream? It was warm outside and ice cream would do nicely. She would like that, he was sure of it.

A quick rummage through Agnar's kitchen cupboards and shelves revealed treasures he hadn't discovered before, like a bottle of decent red wine and half a bottle of Amaretti liqueur.

He hurried off to the shop and bought everything he could possibly imagine he would need. Jens didn't comment on anything, just sorted out which cream was the equivalent to double cream. It turned out there was only one option.

There was no ice cream machine in Agnar's kitchen, so he had to go old school, whipping everything together, putting the ice cream in the freezer and then resigning himself to stirring through it every second hour. She liked chocolate, so he opted for a chocolate chip. With a twist, always a twist. He hummed again.

It paid off to be sneaky, he thought. Then he made the dough for the bread and left it to prove.

A shower, he thought. I need a shower and a nap. The vet's office couch was not sleep-friendly at all.

His mobile buzzed when he came out of the shower. It had buzzed more than once, by the look of it. One text from Holly, one from his dad and three from Fedra. He texted the first two and said he would call them later. He ignored Fedra's texts.

Six hours to go, he thought. Plenty of time to get the ice cream perfected and the bread ready.

Plenty of time.

He put the alarm on, closed his eyes and fell asleep in a second.

A few hours later Jack rang her doorbell. He heard Frikk barking a few times, then he stopped.

'Come in,' Ninni yelled.

It wasn't that easy, Jack thought. His arms were full,

but he managed to push the door open and step into the hallway.

Ninni came down the stairs as he stepped out of his shoes.

'I asked you to bring bread and you've brought everything in your kitchen! Are you that scared of my cooking?'

She smiled while she talked and Jack handed her the bread. 'I always try to be on the safe side.'

Ninni put the bread to her nose and sniffed. 'Oh, that's good.'

'I made ice cream too.'

Ninnis eyes lit up when she took it from him. 'Lovely. That will go perfectly with my dessert. Thank you. Are you hungry?'

'Getting there,' Jack said. 'What are you serving?'

Ninni put the ice cream in the freezer. 'It's a surprise. Go into the lounge, please. I'll be right with you.'

'One more thing. I found this in one of Agnar's cupboards.' Jack pulled the red wine from his pocket. 'It's not half bad.'

'Thank you. You'll find a bottle-opener in the lounge. My dad has a drinks cabinet in there.'

She disappeared into the kitchen and closed the door behind her. Jack was confused. There were no delicious smells coming from there. What on earth was she doing?

He walked into the lounge and looked around. A huge sofa in one corner, books everywhere, including the floor, and an old-fashioned cabinet with an array of bottles on top. He found the corkscrew easily enough. While he pulled up the cork, he looked around. Pictures on the wall showed Ninni and her parents – the nice-looking woman had to be her mother; the curls were the same. Most pictures were of Ninni and a variety of dogs.

He didn't notice that she had come in until she spoke to him.

'Here.' She handed him a glass.

Jack filled up their glasses and put down the bottle. He smiled. 'You look nice. I haven't seen you in a dress before.'

Ninni frowned. 'Well, I thought I'd make an effort for a change.'

The dress suited her. She eyed him a bit suspiciously. 'What?'

Jack shook his head. 'Nothing. I'm just happy to be here.'

Ninni sipped the wine and frowned. 'So, this is not quite half decent? Are you sure this isn't one of Agnar's homemade brews?'

'It has a proper label, from a vineyard in France.' But it was far from great. 'Maybe I will use it for sauce next time.'

'Good thing I didn't invite you for the wine,' Ninni said. She put down her glass and looked at him.

Jack did the same. He smiled. 'So, why did you invite me?'

She had a determined look on her face when she got closer.

Ninni figured the best way to approach the evening was to get the whole thing over and done with before dinner. That way, they would quickly find out if it was worth the effort.

'Stand still,' she said.

Jack grinned. 'What are you up to?'

She put her hands on his waist and slid them under his T-shirt. 'I'm seducing you. You can say stop, if you want to.'

Jack had no such ideas.

Ninni picked his T-shirt up off the floor and pulled it on. 'I'm starving,' she said.

Jack admired her shape. 'And what am I supposed to wear?'

'I don't know. You look good naked, by the way.' Ninni smiled.

'Ah, so do you.' He leaned over the couch and picked up his shorts. 'Do you know that nobody on this island knocks on doors before entering?'

'Yes, I suppose they don't.'

Ninni disappeared into the kitchen and Jack followed.

'What's for supper?' he asked, looking around the kitchen and not seeing any evidence of food.

'I hope you weren't expecting too much,' she said and handed him a bowl of remoulade.

'I'm not sure what to expect, to be honest. I didn't expect to end up on your couch, for starters,' Jack said.

She brought out a huge bowl of pink shrimps, kissed him quickly and pointed at the table. 'I hope you didn't mind.'

'Not at all,' Jack said.

He followed her to the table and inspected the shrimps. 'They still have their shells on and their heads,' he said.

'They're supposed to. This is a Norwegian summer treat. I got them from a fishing boat this morning. They boil them before they come in to land. Don't touch them yet. Could you cut up your lovely bread, please?'

Jack was intrigued. He dutifully cut the bread and put it on the table.

Ninni handed him a plate with butter. 'Do you want to stick with the wine? I have a few bottles of Britt's beer,' she said.

Jack couldn't care less what they were drinking. 'Beer will do fine.'

He sat down and watched her bring the beer bottles from the fridge. She spotted him watching her and blushed a little.

'What? You're not getting the T-shirt back,' she said, laughing.

'I've never eaten shrimps this way,' he confessed.

'And you call yourself a chef.' Ninni picked a shrimp out of the bowl and held it up. 'Twist the head and break it off. Then pull the rest of the shell apart and take out the meat. See?'

She showed him and Jack snapped the shrimp from her, putting it in his mouth. It was salty and chewy, and tasted like the sea. 'I like this.'

Ninni buttered a piece of bread and handed it to him. 'It's even better if you put a pile of shrimps on buttered bread and eat it with some of the remoulade.'

Jack followed her example and heaped shelled shrimps onto the bread, followed by a generous amount of the remoulade. 'This doesn't count as actual cooking, you know,' he said before biting into the bread.

It was delicious, he had to admit that.

'I'm not a fancy chef,' Ninni said, unbothered.

Jack realised he was being watched. Frikk was staring at him with a mournful look. 'Do dogs eat shrimps?'

'You can give him a few, but not too many,' Ninni said.

Jack flipped a shrimp and the dog caught it in the air.

'I think he swallowed it whole.' Jack flipped him another one. 'Yes, definitely whole.'

Ninni laughed. Jack smiled. For the first time since he had met her, she didn't look haunted or tired.

Ninni woke up, feeling slightly off. She looked at Jack, sleeping soundly next to her. He obviously felt comfortable. She enjoyed watching him sleep for a few seconds before realising how creepy it was, and had to stifle a laugh.

She swung her feet over the edge of the bed and almost passed out. 'Whoa,' she said quietly.

For a second she sat still and waited for the room to stop spinning. Must be the wine and the beer, she thought. I can't remember the last time I drank. But it was lovely, and worth every minute, both him and the meal. Except that now the idea of food made her queasy.

'Whoa,' she muttered again.

She stood up as quietly as she could and tiptoed across the hall to the bathroom. She barely made it to the toilet before throwing up.

Afterwards she flushed the toilet and then washed her face with cold water from the tap. When she looked at her face, she looked ghostly with dark circles under her eyes and paler than a hermit crab's belly.

'No one should look this bad after a wonderful night,' she said to her reflection.

She brushed her teeth before returning to the bedroom. Jack still slept. He was smiling in his sleep, which made her smile too.

Instead of waking him up, she walked downstairs and put on the coffee machine. Frikk lifted his head and wagged his tail. He slowly got out of bed and came over to her.

Ninni sat down and took his face between her hands.

She checked his eyes. 'You're all bright-eyed and bushy-tailed, aren't you? You're lucky you don't drink, my boy.'

Luckily there was a pack of paracetamol in the kitchen drawer. She popped a couple in her mouth and swallowed them with some water from the tap.

From the kitchen window she could see that it was early morning. No rush then.

There was nothing left of Jack's lovely bread. He'd turned out to be a brilliant baker too, she thought, and broke off a piece of the normal wholegrain bread. It took away the bitterness from the paracetamol and settled her stomach.

She considered making breakfast. What did someone like Jack eat in the morning? There was no way she was cooking him an English breakfast with eggs and beans and whatnot. If that what he wanted, he would have to cook it himself. The idea made her head spin again. Better not, she thought.

She sighed with relief when the coffee machine gurgled a few times, then stopped. A cup of coffee would make her feel as right as rain.

It did. That first sip of morning coffee made life seem manageable. She drank one cup, then another, and finished the dry piece of bread. By the time Jack came down she was on her third cup.

He leaned against the doorpost and folded his arms. He was smiling. Ninni's stomach did another jolt, but this time of pleasure. 'Good morning.'

'Good morning to you too. I missed you when I woke up.' He came into the room and held out his hand. Ninni let him pull her up.

'You will learn soon enough that I'm not a morning person. I need coffee to be cute.'

Jack brushed her hair away from her face. 'I think you'd look cute no matter what,' he said.

'Not with a hangover, I don't. How much did we drink last night?'

Jack's hands did something interesting to her back. Ninni leaned into him.

'I don't think a few bottles of beer gives much of a hangover. Perhaps it's because of sleep deprivation.'

He kissed her and Ninni could feel her knees weaken. Oh, my God, she thought. I'm so done for.

She wanted it to last forever. Jack smiled. 'Do you have any coffee left?'

Ninni sat down again and pulled her feet up on the seat. 'I have tea if you want it,' she said.

'Tea is good, but not first thing in the morning. I need something to wake me up.'

He filled a cup and sat down beside her on the bench. 'Good coffee.'

Ninni looked at him. 'Are we crazy?'

Jack frowned. 'You mean to go to bed together? Why do you think that? We're both free and can do whatever we want, right?'

'Yes, of course. No, it has happened so quickly. I will

241

return to Bergen in the fall, and you're going home to London at any moment, aren't you?'

'Sooner or later, yes.' Jack became serious. 'I hope you don't regret it.'

Ninni shook her head. 'To say that would be silly. It was rather … enjoyable, wasn't it?'

Jack smiled slowly and Ninni felt dizzy again, but this time in a wonderful way. 'It certainly was,' he said.

'Then let's keep it like that. A summer fling, if you like. Just for fun.' Ninni watched him while she spoke.

He thought about it. 'Okay. I can definitely do that. Summer has barely started, so that should give us plenty of time to fling.'

Ninni laughed. 'That's a verb? To fling?'

'English is a rich language.' Jack rubbed her feet. 'If our fling is going to be half as energetic as last night, I'm going to need sustenance. What do you normally eat for breakfast?'

Ninni shrugged her shoulders. 'Sandwiches, mostly, but I'm not hungry yet.'

'I'm starving. Do we have any of those shrimps left?'

'There's loads of *pålegg* in the fridge.'

'What's *pålegg*?' he asked.

'It's a word for everything you can put on a sandwich. There's all sorts of stuff in the fridge. Pappa is always worried I'll starve when I'm here alone. Help yourself. I'm just going to sit here and watch you.'

And he was a delight to watch.

He opened the fridge and started pulling out things, holding them up for her to see. 'What is this?'

He held up a flat yellow can with a picture of a fish on the front.

'It's mackerel in tomato sauce. You would put it on a piece of bread. Please don't open it now; I'm not in the mood for boiled fish,' Ninni said.

'Me neither. And this?' He showed her a red square.

'It's called Brown Cheese. It's a sweet cheese made with some goats' milk. It's a staple food for Norwegians.' Ninni hid a smile behind her cup when he opened the package and sniffed suspiciously.

'There's a cheese slicer in the drawer if you want to taste it,' she said.

Jack found the slicer and inspected it carefully before cutting a thin slice. 'To sum up, you have Old Cheese and Brown Cheese and Jarlsberg.'

'Yes, but Jarlsberg is actually a white cheese. White cheese is also called yellow cheese and, of course, there's Christmas Cheese. That's an Edam with red wax wrapping, in case you're wondering.' Ninni laughed at his expression.

'You're messing with me now, right?' He didn't wait for an answer, but put the slice of cheese in his mouth. 'It sticks to the roof of my mouth, it's too sweet and it has a weird texture.'

'It's no worse than your Marmite or mint sauce.' Ninni felt a need to defend her favourite cheese.

Jack grinned. 'Touché. Is it only used for sandwiches?'

'No, some people actually use it in venison sauce, or in ice cream or on waffles. But mostly we eat it as it is.'

Jack tasted another slice. 'It's ... interesting.'

Ninni giggled. 'You don't have to eat it. There's salami and quite a selection of jam to choose from. We finished off your bread last night, so I only have brown bread, I'm afraid.'

'Yes, I noticed the lack of white bread everywhere. It's edible, you know.' He sliced two pieces of bread and stuffed them in the toaster.

'Yeah, but it doesn't taste of anything, not like the one you made. Bread should have proper flavour.'

He smiled then. 'What about eggs? You want some eggs?'

Ninni stomach churned at the thought. 'No, thank you, but I'd love a piece of toast.'

'With cheese?'

'No, just the bread.' She sipped more coffee, savouring the sharp, bitter taste.

He put a plate with her toast on in front of her and filled up her cup. Then he put a selection of all the *pålegg* he'd found in the fridge on the table and sat down.

Ninni chewed on the toast, finally feeling better. 'Are you a waiter as well?'

'Chefs are not born chefs; we work at it, starting at

the bottom of the food chain, and if chef Roland needed help with service, I did it. I would have done anything to stay in that kitchen.'

He buttered the toast, then opened the lid of one of the jars in front of him and read the label. 'What is *stikkelsbær*?'

He made a complete mess of the word, and grinned at her.

Ninni laughed. 'Good effort. It's gooseberries. Alma makes it every autumn. It's good.'

'I love jam,' Jack said, heaping the sticky golden jam on the toast and taking a big bite. 'That's really good. Not too sweet, a bit tart and chewy too.'

Ninni watched him. He was a funny one. She had noticed that he ate all his food this way, with all of his attention on the flavours in his mouth. She sipped her coffee and enjoyed the feeling of her feet against his thigh.

'It must be strange for you to come here from London. Nothing happens here on the island,' Ninni said. 'Do you miss your job?'

'This has been the longest I have gone without working in years. I've always worked six, sometimes seven days a week. I arrive at the restaurant early to check deliveries, start prepping, put people to work and go home and sleep a few hours, then come back for service. It's what I do. What I love.'

Ninni smiled. 'It sounds exhausting. No holidays?'

'Only if this trip counts as one.' Jack took another

bite of the sandwich. 'Does Alma buy these berries somewhere?'

'They grow in her garden. You should taste her goose-berry trifle. It's to die for.'

'Then I have to taste that. Did you always want to be a translator?'

'I studied literature and languages at university, and sort of fell into it. It pays well and I can decide my own hours. That's more important to me than anything else. But it's not as if I knew from the time I was five that I wanted to translate legal documents. It's not a lifelong dream,' she said with a small laugh.

Jack turned to look at her. 'What is your dream?'

The question took her by surprise. 'What do you mean?'

'You must have a dream. Everybody does.'

'I want a family and I want to live here.' Ninni avoided looking at him. 'There should be laughter and ... and children, and books and dogs, you know.'

'And good food,' Jack said.

'Yes, that too. And there should be a sense of peace, I think. You should be able to enjoy your own company and the company of someone else. I don't think that's too much to ask for.'

Jack smiled then. 'No,' he said softly. 'I don't think so at all.'

'Are you laughing at me?' Ninni shoved her foot gently towards him.

'Not even a little bit,' he promised.

He leaned over and kissed her, tasting of bread and berries and coffee. 'I wonder what we can do today,' he said, grinning.

Ninni smiled. 'I thought we'd have an outing today. You haven't really seen the island yet, have you? Not properly, anyway.'

Jack pulled away. 'Go outside, you mean?'

'We could take lunch. And a blanket. I know all the best places,' she said.

'Or we could go upstairs again. Get some rest.'

Ninni considered it and shook her head. 'No, outside it is.' She smiled when she saw how disappointed he looked. 'But not right now.'

Jack took her hand, then stopped. 'I would love nothing more than to ramble around the island with you today, but I have to go to town. To Agnar's bank, actually.'

'Then we'll go when you come back.' Ninni smiled. 'I'll teach you how to fish.'

Jack raised his eyebrows. 'Yes, well, there are still better things to do, I think.'

He pulled her up the stairs, a man on a mission.

Chapter 16

Jack looked at the fancy office and caught a glimpse of his reflection in the window. He was wearing his power suit and felt a bit awkward. He straightened his tie. At least he was dressed for the occasion. They wanted something from him, not the other way around. Bugger them, he thought.

He pushed open the door and went inside. It was clearly an office designed to impress. The reception desk took up half the length of the room. Leather sofas in a designated waiting area. Oak panels on the walls.

Jack smiled at the receptionist. She gave him a haughty look that would have been right at home in London.

'I have an appointment to see Erik Haldorsen,' he said.

'Oh, yes, you're the Englishman from the island. I'll go and check to see if Erik is available.' She stood up and walked over to a glass door. Two seconds later she returned and almost smiled. 'You can wait there. Erik will be with you soon.'

'Thank you.' Instead of sitting down, he went for a stroll around the room. The receptionist kept an eye on him and smiled whenever he met her eyes.

The view from the windows faced Haraldsgaten. It didn't look very busy, even though it was midday. Perhaps it was a slow day, he thought. He hoped it wouldn't take too long. He was eager to return to Ninni.

'Mr Greene?'

Jack turned around to see a man in the first suit he had seen in the town since he'd arrived. The man looked more like an estate agent than Mats did.

'And you are Mr Haldorsen, I presume?' Jack couldn't help himself.

Haldorsen smiled so the caps on his teeth reflected in the fluorescent light. 'Indeed I am. I am so thrilled that you have come.' He shook Jack's hand. 'But please call me Erik. Follow me.'

Jack restrained himself from pulling a face at the receptionist. She ignored him.

Haldorsen let him pass first into an impossibly huge office. 'Make yourself at home. I understand that you're a chef?'

Jack nodded. 'You've checked up on me.'

'Of course I have. You were a chef at a Michelin-star level restaurant. That's pretty impressive for someone so young, I think. I'm guessing you're eager to return to London, get rid of the old homestead,' Haldorsen said, grinning like a wolf.

Homestead, Jack thought. Okay.

'For the right price, of course,' Haldorsen continued.

Jack smiled. 'That's why I'm here. I understand you have an offer for me.'

Haldorsen's smile reached his hairline. 'Straight to the point. Good, good. Now, as you have probably realised, properties like yours are not something that come along every day. And by that I mean they're not easy to get rid of. Fortunately for you, I'm interested.'

He looks even less of a farmer than me, Jack thought. He didn't interrupt the man.

'I've had a proposal prepared for you. Do you want me to read it to you?'

'Is it in Norwegian?' Jack smiled.

Haldorsen laughed. 'Ah, the wonderful British sense of humour, I think. No, of course not. It's all in English. You can take a look at it, and then tell me what you think.'

Jack leafed through the papers and tried to look as if the figure on the last page didn't impress him. That was a lot of money, he thought. Enough to get a restaurant started and then some.

'What do you think?' Haldorsen looked excited.

'I'm interested, of course, but I need some time to consider my options,' Jack said.

Haldorsen smiled. 'Smart man.'

'Why are you interested in the farm?' Jack said.

'What do you mean?' Haldorsen gave him a blank stare.

'You're obviously not a farmer and, as such, probably don't want to farm the land. You're a developer of some sort, are you?'

Haldorsen nodded, looking pleased with himself. 'Yes, I am. I find interesting properties for investors, and the island is such a property. My investors have plans for the place, of course, and unfortunately I can't disclose them. Mostly because I'm not privy to such information,' Haldorsen said with forced laughter.

Everything about him made Jack feel bad. He certainly didn't come across as someone he wanted to do business with. On the other hand, the money was good. It was worth some thought.

He nodded. 'I see. Well, I'll get back to you, Mr Haldorsen.'

Haldorsen shook his hand again, then proceeded to follow him out into the reception, where he leaned over to the receptionist and grinned from ear to ear. 'Whenever Mr Greene calls us, put him through to me at once.'

The last thing Jack saw through the glass doors was Haldorsen waving cheerfully at him.

Jack stopped at a coffee shop and sat down. He'd had no idea the farm would be so valuable to Haldorsen. This would take some getting used to.

Jack finished the coffee and stood up. He still had to go to the bank.

Ninni petted Frikk, who was watching the fish in the clear water with his full attention. 'Fish are a lot safer than vipers. Remember that next time, silly dog.'

Frikk lay down with a sigh, his paws hanging off the edge of the pier. She didn't want to take him out in the boat yet. He was almost back to his old self, but not fully.

'Jack is a strange one, isn't he, Frikk? All warm and lovely. It's hard to picture him as this ambitious man who wants to impress everyone with his ability.'

Frikk barked and lifted his head.

Ninni didn't pay attention. 'Good thing he's leaving soon, I think. Better sooner, before I get too attached and miss him when he goes.'

He'd been gone for over two hours and she was already missing him. Damn it, she thought.

Frikk barked again, but friendlier this time. Ninni turned her head and smiled when she saw Britt. 'Hi.'

'Hi, Ninni. I haven't seen you in a few days. I guess you have a new deadline. My house is full of wine if you're still up for it.' Britt sat down next to her, feet dangling. 'You don't look well. Are you okay?'

Ninni was taken by surprise. 'I must have eaten something that doesn't agree with me,' she said.

Britt put a hand to her forehead before Ninni managed to pull away.

She laughed. 'I don't have a fever, silly.'

'No, you don't, but you are pale. Do you sleep well?'

Ninni leaned her shoulder against Britt's for a second. 'I'm fine.'

She wasn't but she didn't want Britt to make a fuss.

'Nonetheless, I think you should go and see a doctor. No point in waiting. When did you eat this thing you think you have reacted to?'

'Not sure ... At the party, I think. I thought I had a hangover, but it isn't going away.'

'That's was days ago. There is not a hangover in the world that lasts that long. And you only had a beer or two,' Britt said.

And a few beers and some red wine with Jack, Ninni thought, but didn't tell Britt that.

Britt continued. 'You were a bit green when you came to my house for eggs. I don't really think it's a hangover. Unless you're secretly drinking vodka every day, which I doubt. It could be a stomach flu or something, or perhaps some of those sausages were off. Always better to check it out than ignore things for too long. Trust me, I know.'

Ninni smiled. 'Thank you.'

'For what?' Britt looked surprised.

'For looking after me. How's school?'

'Thankfully over in a few days. We're all ready for

254

summer now, I think. Basically, we haven't done anything except swimming for the last few days. As soon as the kids are off on their holidays, I'm opening the B&B. I already have bookings, so it's looking good. If Jack decides to stay, perhaps I can get him to cook for the guests once in a while. That would be fantastic. What do you think?'

Ninni put a hand to her stomach, feeling queasy again. 'Bah,' she muttered.

Britt watched her. 'Perhaps you're pregnant,' she said with a concerned look on her face.

'God, no, I'm not pregnant. That's not possible,' Ninni said, waving her hand.

'Are you sure about that?'

Ninni nodded. 'Yes, I'm absolutely sure. That's the last thing I am.'

Pregnant. There's a laugh, she thought. Not even a little bit funny.

Britt patted her on the knee. 'Go and see the doctor, please. I'll come with you if you want. You look like shit.'

'Oh, thank you. That's a nice thing to say to a person,' Ninni said.

'I aim to please. How's your Englishman?'

'He's not my Englishman,' Ninni said, but remembered that he sort of was now, wasn't he? She couldn't help smiling.

'Oh, my God,' Britt exclaimed. 'You've slept with him.'

Ninni gaped. 'How did you know?'

'I didn't until now.' Britt laughed. 'How was it? All and any details, if you please.'

'Not on your life.' Ninni shook her head.

'You're such a prude. At least tell me if he was better than Karl.'

Ninni felt the heat just by remembering Jack. 'Oh, so much better,' she admitted with a sigh.

Britt giggled. 'I knew it. Damn, I should have snapped him up before, when I had a chance. He looks like he knows what he's doing, you know. Must be all that cooking.'

'Why? What does cooking have to do with how good he is in bed?' Ninni was laughing so hard now, she had a problem talking.

'You know, all that hands-on stuff, kneading and touching, tasting. Cooking is sensual. I wonder if all chefs are good in bed.'

'Only if their massive egos don't get in the way,' Ninni said.

'I'll just have to check it out then, wont I?' Britt laughed again.

Ninni scratched Frikk on the head. She listened to Britt's chatter with one ear. Her stomach was still acting up. Perhaps it *was* time to see a doctor.

The trip to the bank didn't take long. As instructed, Jack had brought with him both Agnar's will and his own passport, and everything was on the up. With a signature and a beaming smile from the bank assistant, he was a lot richer than before he had gone in there, even before Haldorsen's offer.

Jack leaned against the railing on the ferry. Not in a million years would he understand why Agnar had given him everything without ever wanting to meet him. He wasn't sure what to think about it. He didn't believe in "blood is thicker than water", but perhaps Agnar had. He wondered if Magni's books could have answers for him, and decided to ask Ninni to look at the rest of them for him.

Thinking about Ninni made him smile. She was an unexpected surprise in all of this. A good surprise.

His mobile buzzed and he looked at the screen. Fedra. But this message was different. After a moment's hesitation, Jack called her back.

'Oh,' she said. 'I thought you'd stopped talking to me.'

He didn't bother with niceties. 'Is this true, or is it just a ruse to get me to call you back?' he said.

'No, it's not. Daddy wants to talk to you. He's sorry about the whole debacle. Will you come and talk to him?'

Jack watched a pair of seagulls chasing each other. He smiled to himself. 'Why can't he just call me?'

Fedra was silent for a second. 'He's not well, Jack. All I'm asking is that you talk to him.'

'Will it change anything?' Jack wasn't about to show his cards to her that easily.

'I really don't know. But please don't be a bastard simply because you can.'

She ended the call before Jack had a chance to respond. He put the mobile in his pocket again. Roland wanted to talk. Of course he would talk to him. It was time to clear up this mess once and for all.

By the time the ferry docked on the island, he had already ordered plane tickets home to London for the following day.

Ninni felt silly, standing on the harbour waiting for Jack. But she still waited with Frikk next to her, his tongue lolling and tail wagging whenever she looked down at him.

She grabbed the mooring rope that the deckhand threw at her with a wide grin on his face. 'Evening,' he yelled.

'Same to you,' Ninni said and tied the thick hemp rope to the pole.

Jack stood by the gangway, smiling at her.

He looked different, Ninni thought. Her stomach did somersaults at the sight of him.

When he stepped off the boat she waited until he reached her.

'Hi,' he said with a smile.

Frikk sniffed at Jack and let him pet him. 'And hi to you too.'

'Hi. Did it go all right?' She had no idea what it was he had to do in the bank, but it must have been important. He was wearing a suit. 'You look elegant. Tie and everything.' The same suit he had worn when he'd hit her with his car in Bergen.

Jack touched the tie. 'Well, yes, it was just a visit to the bank, for the last of the formalities with Agnar's estate,' he said. 'I'm now officially in charge of everything, including the house, the farm, the meat business and the sheep.'

Ninni nodded. 'Does it feel strange?'

Jack put his hands in his pockets, creasing the jacket. 'Of course it does. I still don't understand why he left it all to me, and I never will now.'

Ninni took his hand. 'You're his son, no matter what the circumstances are. Agnar left it to you because of that. It mattered to him.'

'Yes, but I didn't matter enough for him to contact me,' Jack said.

'I'm sorry,' Ninni said.

'Enough of this. It doesn't matter any more. I can't change the past, anyway.' He smiled and pointed at the large building on the end of the harbour. 'Why don't you tell me about this place instead?'

Ninni looked towards the building Jack was indicating. 'That one?'

'Yes, start with that.'

Ninni smiled. 'It's a *sjøhus,* a "sea house". It was built

during the time of the big herring fisheries, so it's more a place for business than anything else.'

The old building was huge, with a sliding door on the side and what looked like a bay window jutting out from the top floor. Except it didn't have a window but another pair of sliding doors and a crane sticking out in front instead. He frowned.

'It looks as if it's about to fall apart. Why is it still standing?'

'It's not falling apart. All it needs is a coat of paint. According to Jens, it has good bones. Whatever that means. We use it for celebrations – we had a wedding once, even a few christenings, and every Christmas it's used for the island market and other festivities,' she explained.

'Can we take a look?' Jack seemed interested.

Ninni pushed open the door and they went inside. Jack looked around and Ninni smiled. 'Not so bad from in here, is it?'

'It's like finding a treasure right in front of your eyes.' Jack said.

There were a few windows high up. Ninni took a few steps further in and started pointing. 'Downstairs used to be the sales floor. Agents from the mainland would come and buy the herring from here. Upstairs, they would keep crates for the herring and salt to preserve it, and then they would haul up the fish from the fishing boats. There's also an office up there, for the shipping office. A lot of the herring from here ended up in Hull or Newcastle.'

'This is amazing. I love the history of the place,' he said.

He suddenly turned to her and kissed her. Ninni was taken by surprise but kissed him back.

'I have to go to London tomorrow,' he said, still holding his arms around her.

Ninni frowned again. 'Is that why you're acting weird?'

That made him smile. 'I guess so. I talked to Fedra. She told me her father wants to talk to me, but not on the phone. I have to go to London to see him.'

'Of course you do. He was your friend, wasn't he?'

Jack shrugged. 'I thought so. Perhaps I can put this behind me,' he said.

'Or get your job back and perhaps that Michelin star. If that's what you want,' Ninni said. 'Is it?'

'I love what I do, and I've worked for years to get to that level. Of course I want my job back.'

He looked a bit lost. Ninni smiled at him. 'Well, since you're not going until tomorrow, how about a swim?'

Jack took a last look at the "sea house" and followed her. 'I have my swimming trunks at home,' he said.

Did he even realise he had called the farm home? Ninni didn't ask.

The beach was crowded when they came down, but no one was using the pier in front of their boathouses. Jack smiled at her. 'You know, I'm not sure this would work back in the UK.'

'What do you mean?' Ninni had already stripped out of her clothes and stood in her bikini. Frikk was sprawling on a beach towel, looking as if he too was sunbathing.

'I mean, ignoring the best sunspots on the beach. Look at them, so careful not to come too close. Brits would never do that.'

Ninni smiled. 'Of course they would. Haven't you seen that at the airport when you fly to Norway? You guys rule the whole queuing thing; I've never seen anything like it. We, however, clump together and use our elbows to get in first. No matter what seat numbers we have.'

'I think I remember that, now that you mention it. Now, that was scary.' Jack looked at the water and the rather DIY-looking diving board. 'Is it deep enough to dive from here?'

'Yes. That's what it's there for. My mother hates the seaweed and the potential creepy-crawlies hiding in it. My father made the board. It's been there for thirty years, so it's safe.'

She laughed at him now. Jack knew why. 'I don't want to whack my skull on the bottom, if you don't mind.'

'Oh, go on, before I push you in.' Ninni came towards him and Jack walked out on the board.

He stopped on the edge and looked down. The water

was crystal-clear and inviting. Without hesitating, he dived in. Ninni dived in right behind him and broke the surface with a wide smile on her face.

'Isn't it wonderful?' she said, treading water.

Jack swam over to her and kissed her. She tasted of saltwater and something that was just her. 'You are wonderful.'

She put her hands over his head and ducked him under. Jack grabbed her waist and pulled her with him. She wriggled loose and swam away. Jack had no problem keeping up the pace.

'Did I ever tell you I was in the swimming team at school?' he said.

Ninni splashed a hand at him. 'No, I don't think you did. I bet I can beat you out to the raft.'

He looked where she was pointing. The raft was perhaps twenty metres away, filled with kids.

She almost beat him, but he managed to pull her back at the last inch, to the great delight of the kids cheering them on.

'You cheated!' she shouted.

'Well, of course I did,' Jack said.

She hauled herself on top of the raft and talked to the kids. Jack held onto the ropes. The water was cool and refreshing, and the sun was burning. He sank under the surface for a second.

Ninni jumped over him with a huge splash. 'I'll let you win on the way back,' she teased.

'That's decent of you,' he said.

He enjoyed watching her, taking long strokes and splashing her feet. She looked over her shoulder at him. 'You're so slow!'

'I'm enjoying the view,' he said.

There was a small ladder on the side of the pier. Ninni climbed up like she must have done since she was old enough to do it on her own. Jack swam over to the pier and held onto the ladder. All this, he thought – all this was so normal to her. As it would have been for him if he had grown up with Agnar.

It was a strange thought.

They sat outside in the sun. Ninni pulled a large bath towel over them.

'For protection against the sun,' Ninni said. She liked the feeling of having him so close.

'You know, if you sold ice cream on this beach you'd make a fortune,' Jack said, watching the busy beach.

'I know, but I don't want anything to do with something like that.'

'Because you don't like ice cream?' Jack looked confused.

'No, because I couldn't imagine standing out here, selling ice cream in the hot sun. I'd die of boredom. I leave that to Alma. She usually pays one of the kids to come out here and sell cold stuff. Including fizzy drinks and ice cream.'

Jack nuzzled her neck. 'She has a hand in almost everything out here, doesn't she?'

'Yes, she told me once it was her duty to keep the island alive, and that to do that she needed to encourage people to come and live here.'

'I see.' Jack looked at her. 'Now, how big is this towel?'

'What do you mean?' Ninni grinned at him.

'Is it big enough to fool around in? Without anyone noticing?' Jack pulled her closer. The towel was absolutely not big enough for what he had in mind.

Ninni jumped up. 'Come with me,' she said.

Jack followed her into the boathouse. It was a lot more messy than his – loads of rope and the walls packed with fishing gear. A huge rowboat made from wood, placed on rafters in the middle, caught his attention.

'I hope you don't mean in the boat? It looks damn uncomfortable,' he said to make her laugh.

Ninni took his hand and pulled him with her. 'Up here.' She climbed a small ladder, disappearing through a door. 'Watch your head.'

He followed her up, curious as to what was up there. He stopped on top of the ladder and looked in. 'What is this? A guest house?'

'No, this is my place. Sort of a tree house, if you know what I mean.'

Ninni sat on a narrow bed with her legs stretched out. She cocked her head. 'Are you coming?'

Jack climbed up the rest of the ladder and joined her on the bed. 'This is very practical,' he said, letting his fingers run over her warm skin.

'We are a practical people,' Ninni said, laughing softly.

'You know, I thought you were going to teach me fishing today,' he said.

'There's plenty of time for that when you come back,' Ninni said.

She pushed away all thoughts of doctors and every word Britt had said. It wasn't true, anyway.

Chapter 17

Ninni stared at the doctor, wondering who the crazy one was, herself or the doctor. 'Sorry?'

'You're pregnant,' the doctor said.

Ninni had no idea how to respond. For some reason she was angry with Britt for sending her to the surgery. Which was absurd.

'Erm ... I wasn't really expecting it to be true,' she finally said.

The doctor looked sympathetic. 'Oh, I see. You're not happy. Well, you have options, you know. It's not too late to terminate if that's what you want to do. When was your last period?'

Ninni tried to think, but her brain didn't function. 'I've always been irregular, so I don't have an exact date. Sometimes it jumps a month or two. I never gave it a second thought, to be honest.' She felt like a complete idiot and, from the look on the doctor's face, she thought so too.

'Oh, I see. In that case, I should think you're about eight to nine weeks in. That gives you, at the most, two to three weeks to make up your mind.'

Ninni thought about Karl, trying to count back to when this could have happened. She had received the photograph from his wife an hour before he'd arrived, and hadn't even let him into the flat.

It made her sick thinking about it.

Ninni cleared her throat. 'I'm on the pill, for God's sake. Doesn't that make this almost impossible?'

The doctor smiled. She had a kind face. 'I think the magic word here is *almost*. Even the pill isn't one hundred per cent, I'm afraid. I think it's about one in one hundred, if I remember correctly. Which is good, unless you're the one, then of course it's not.'

Ninni felt sick again. The doctor handed her a few leaflets to take home and gave her a friendly pat on the hand. 'Don't worry; it's not the end of the world, whatever you choose. Although I should tell you that getting pregnant doesn't get easier as you get older.'

It was such an absurd statement that Ninni burst into tears.

The doctor patted her on the hand again. 'I'm sorry. I shouldn't have said that. Tell you what, go home, sleep on it, then come back in a few days and we'll talk it over when you're a bit more used to the idea. By then you will have loads of questions. For the morning sickness, get some fresh ginger and make a brew. It will help. I'm also going to give you a list of things you should do, in case you decide to keep it.'

'I drank half a glass of really horrible red wine a few days ago, and at least two or three beers. Will that ... could that do any damage to ...?' Ninni bit her lip. She couldn't get her mouth to say *baby*.

'I doubt it. The risk is higher the more you drink. Do you smoke?'

Ninni shook her head. 'No, never have.'

'Good. Listen, you're young and healthy. There's no reason why you shouldn't have a good pregnancy and a healthy baby at the end of it. Promise me that you'll consider all your options.'

She followed Ninni out and gave her a quick hug. 'Good luck, and please come back in a day or two.'

Ninni stood still outside the doctor's surgery for a few minutes, more dizzy than ever. This is beyond horrible, she thought.

She found her way to Haraldsgaten and sank down on one of the benches in the small park in front of Hotel Saga. Her knees felt impossibly weak and her head was spinning out of control.

Now what? She didn't want to tell Jack about this. It was obviously not his baby. Then there was Karl. She didn't want to tell him either. Oh, God, she thought. Do I have to tell him if I decide to keep it? That will tie me to him for ever.

The ramifications made her nauseous and dizzy. She pushed Karl out of her mind as much as possible.

Thank God Jack is in London. It will give me a few days to figure out what to do. Until then, perhaps I can sit here and not move, Ninni thought. Until it passes. Until I'm not pregnant any more or until I wake up from this nightmare.

Jack paused outside the restaurant where he had worked for the last decade. He had been gone for a few weeks and it felt as if he had been gone for years.

London was so hot, he felt as if the air was sticking to him. And yet he stood still, staring at the restaurant front with its exclusive look. The only guests who could afford to eat in there were people who didn't care what the bill said at the end of a meal.

He caught a glimpse of himself in the door glass. He was dressed in a T-shirt and jeans. Coming in a suit would have made it all so formal. And it was also a statement, even if it was a childish one.

His mind filled with memories of the time he had spent in there, first on work experience, then as an apprentice, until he'd left for three years at Le Cordon Bleu in France. But he'd returned as head chef because Roland had promised he would eventually become a partner. It was a place he'd thought he would be for the rest of his career. And now it would finally happen.

He would get what he was owed.

For a second Jack considered not going inside – leave it all behind. Return to Ninni and enjoy life as an island farmer. All of a sudden London felt noisy and so full of people he could barely breathe.

He decided against it immediately. They owe me an explanation and the damn partnership, he thought. I want what I've always wanted, what I was promised. I've earned it.

Still feeling angry, he pushed open the door and went inside. This early, the restaurant was quiet. The dinner rush was still a couple of hours away. From the kitchen came the smells of delicious cooking and the sounds of food prepping. Jack couldn't help smiling. People talking and laughing, pots and pans clanking, cupboards slamming and hissing from the cooking on the hob. It was all so familiar.

The restaurant was empty. Jack stood for a moment and looked around. It was ridiculous to expect things to have changed. After all, he had only been gone for a few weeks. And yet he felt different.

'Jack, there you are, darling. It's so wonderful to see you.'

Jack turned around. Fedra looked the same as always. Hair coiffed, perfect make-up and those big brown eyes he had drowned in once. Well, more than once, if he was honest. Now they seemed calculating and cold, despite the huge smile.

It wasn't fair, he knew that. Their affair hadn't lasted

271

very long, and there had been no hard feelings between them when it had ended. At least not from his side.

'You look nice,' he said, putting on his best smile.

Fedra looked him over. 'I can't say the same about you. What happened? Have you gone native on your little Viking island?'

Jack smiled. 'Perhaps. Now, what is so important that you had to summon me to London?'

'I told you. Daddy wants to talk. He's in the kitchen. He told me to bring you to him when you arrived.'

Jack shrugged. 'I'm here.'

She walked in front of him and he knew what she was doing. Her insane high heels made her walk with a swing in her hips that he knew was supposed to be sexy. It didn't work on him any more.

The three cooks working in the kitchen stopped what they were doing when they entered. Roland held a spoon in his hand, obviously in the process of tasting the contents of the pot. His face lit up when he saw Jack.

'There you are, my boy. How are you, Jack?'

Jack narrowed his eyes. 'I'm fine. I see you're feeling better.' He kept his voice neutral. The kitchen brought back a lot of good memories, and a few not so good ones. He knew every pot and pan in there, every plate on the hob, every grill, every dish. It felt so ... comfortable.

Roland tasted whatever was in the pot. 'More salt,'

he said to one of the chefs. 'And a pinch of pepper, please. How can you cook if you can't season the food?'

Jack waited and watched. Roland talked to the new chef in the same way he had talked to him. Patronising and charming. Still so French after fifty years in London, he seemed like he'd arrived the day before.

Roland put the spoon in the sink and came over to him with outstretched arms. 'It's so good to see you again, *mon cher garçon*.' He hugged Jack and kissed him on both cheeks.

'Why am I here, Roland?' Jack pulled away, annoyed with the niceties.

Roland stepped back with an expression of mock surprise. 'Straight to the point, I see. You haven't changed a bit.'

'I left a few weeks ago, Roland. That's not much time to change,' Jack said.

'No, no, I detect a difference in you. I told you, years ago, that you should always make sure you have a holiday every year. The time in Norway seems to have done wonders for you. That's good. It means that you are rested and eager to come back to work, *oui?*'

Jack smiled slowly. 'Are you offering me my job back? You're going to have to do a lot better than that.'

Roland pulled a face. 'I'm sorry we parted on such angry terms, but all this bitterness will do you more harm than good, I'm afraid. We can do better than that,

I'm sure. I have a proposal for you. Will you hear me out?'

Jack looked at the other two chefs in the kitchen. They were staring at them, curious and quiet. Fedra leaned her hip against the counter, watching him with a small smile.

'Let's talk in the restaurant,' Roland said.

Jack realised they had wanted him to see the kitchen, to become nostalgic about it. Were they always this transparent? Probably. He decided to let them play it out.

Roland chose a table by the window. He was dressed in his usual handmade suit, a little scarf perfectly folded in the front pocket and his hair as perfect as his daughter's. As always.

'Can you bring us coffee, Fedra? Jack looks like he could do with a cup, and so do I.'

'You're not allowed to drink coffee, Daddy. I'll bring you tea.'

Roland frowned. 'It's a terrible day when your children start bossing you around.'

Fedra scoffed. 'Get used to it, Daddy. Don't upset him, Jack. He's still not well. Even if he pretends he is.'

Jack waited until she left before turning to Roland. 'Is it true? You're ill?'

Roland shrugged. 'I have a little trouble with the old ticker. It's not something to worry about.'

'Fedra is worried,' Jack said.

'She's my daughter and a woman,' Roland said, dismissing the whole thing. 'Now, let's talk about you.'

'Let's. Why don't you start with why I'm here? I hope I haven't wasted my time. It's a bloody complicated trip from the island to get here.'

Roland folded his hands on the table in front of him. He looked at Jack. 'I rarely admit my mistakes, Jack. I don't see the point in regret. But I made a mistake when I didn't offer you the partnership. You deserved it, and I failed you. I'm sorry, my boy.' Roland looked serious, but Jack found himself wondering what the old bastard was up to.

'When you decided not to keep your word, you mean?' Jack had no intention of making it easy for him.

'That's a bit harsh, don't you think?' Roland looked offended.

'We had an agreement, you and I. I think you called it a gentleman's agreement at one point. Which is also why we don't have a proper contract, because you made me believe we didn't need one, and I was stupid enough to trust you,' Jack said, watching him closely. 'Of course, now I'm happy we never had a contract.'

Roland's face darkened for a second, before he put on the smile again. 'Well, yes, in hindsight everything is easy, isn't it?'

'Why am I here, Roland?' Jack was getting fed up with the whole thing.

'I have an offer that will make you happy,' Roland said.

He was interrupted by Fedra coming back with tea and some biscuits. She put the tray on the table and handed them their cups. 'Have you told him yet?' she asked her father.

Jack looked at her. She seemed annoyed and frayed, and didn't return the look.

'No, I was getting to it when you came, my darling. What is this?' Roland looked at the teacup with disdain.

'Herbal tea. No caffeine, remember? That also means no black tea. I shouldn't have to explain this every time you want a cup of tea, Daddy.'

'I'm hoping that one day you will show mercy and give me a proper espresso,' he said with a wicked smile.

Fedra sat down next to her father. 'Go on then, tell him.'

Jack kept still. Let them talk, he thought.

'We want you to come back, to come home, Jack. I propose that you and Fedra share the restaurant,' Roland said, looking as if he were giving him the world. 'Of course Fedra would run the place, but you would be running the kitchen as you see fit.'

Jack looked at them. They seemed so pleased with themselves. Something fell into place in his head. 'In other words, we keep it the way it was. Except that this time you'll have me and my recipes.'

Roland frowned. 'Yes, like before. We realise that we acted too harshly.'

Jack smiled. 'You're not getting the Michelin star, are you? Because of me? Or, rather, because I'm not here.'

He knew he was right when he saw their expressions. He leaned forward. 'How stupid do you think I am, Roland? Do you really think I'll just come back like some kind of obedient servant because you decided you need me after all?'

Roland narrowed his eyes. 'You ungrateful little shit,' he said. 'I trained you. I taught you everything you know. And this is how you thank me? By abandoning us now?'

Fedra put her hand over her father's. 'Calm down. He wants something, Daddy. What do you want, Jack?'

He smiled then. 'I want what I was promised. Full partnership, my name on the restaurant front, and I want to run it – without Fedra looking over my shoulder. And I want a huge bonus when I get you that Michelin star.'

'That's outrageous. You were perfectly fine with me running it before,' Fedra said sharply.

'Yes, but that was before I knew you would screw me over. Now I know that you can't be trusted. Either of you,' Jack said. He pushed the chair away from the table. 'I'm going home to my dad, and in a couple of days I'm going back to Norway. You have until then to think about it.'

Before either of them managed to react, he was outside, breathing in fresh air. Or as fresh as it could be in the middle of a London heatwave.

He called Ninni.

Ninni looked at the phone display and hesitated. She didn't want to talk to Jack, not now. She was still in shock.

So she ignored the call and put the phone back into her pocket. The ferry docked at the island and she hurried onto land, pulled the hood of her rain jacket down over her face and almost ran up the road towards the house.

Right now, she couldn't talk to anyone, especially anyone sympathetic. She relaxed when she'd put the houses behind her, relieved that the rain was keeping everyone indoors.

She opened the door and Frikk threw himself at her.

'Take it easy, you silly dog. I've just been gone for a few hours.'

He jumped around her, as he always did when she left him alone. And, as always, he made her feel better.

'I'm happy to see you're feeling better,' she said.

Ninni took off her wet clothes and went into the kitchen.

'What do you think, Frikk? Think we should have a baby? Would you like that? Someone who would pull your ears and tail, throw up on you and jump on you with a full nappy?'

The dog perked his ears, listening to her voice. Ninni smiled. 'I bet you would, you goofy doggo.'

She threw him a dog biscuit and made a cup of coffee. With the mug in one hand and a sweet bun in the other, she made herself comfortable on the sofa in the lounge. Frikk jumped up and rested his chin on her leg.

'You are lucky, sweetie. You don't have to make decisions like this.'

Ninni pulled out the mobile and looked at it. Two messages from Jack. *Please call.*

She couldn't postpone it for much longer, and decided to call him.

'Hi,' he said, answering at once. 'How are you doing?'

'I'm fine. I'm actually on the sofa with a blanket and Frikk. How did it go?'

He laughed, sounding so happy and carefree. 'They offered me the same conditions as before. I told them it's a full partnership or nothing, and said I'm returning to Norway the day after tomorrow.'

'That's good. Are they going to give it to you, do you think?' Ninni wasn't sure what to think of it. It was obvious that he wanted to go home to London, of course he did.

'We'll see. I'm not taking anything for granted. I'm

heading out to my dad's house now. I'll talk to you later, okay?'

'Sure. Later.'

Ninni put down the mobile. Perhaps that was the solution, she thought. Jack returned to London, none the wiser, and she did whatever she decided to do. Which she had no idea about yet.

She lay down on the sofa and closed her eyes. A bleep from the mobile made her look at it. From Karl. She almost dropped the mobile on the floor.

'Just what I needed. Not,' she muttered. 'If you wanted me to call back, you shouldn't have left your name, you twat.'

She read the text. He wanted to talk to her. *Please.*

'Please my arse,' she said, wondering if she should respond or not. In the end she texted back. *Don't ever contact me again.* Then she blocked his new number too.

That would show him, she thought. She put the phone on silent and closed her eyes.

She was exhausted. All she wanted now was a long nap.

Chapter 18

Ninni spent the next day in her boat, pretending to fish but mostly staring into the distance. Frikk kept close, much closer than normal, and she knew he felt something was wrong.

The sun was glaring from an intense blue sky and she could hear people laughing and shouting on the beach. There were plenty of other boats moored on the water, and the beach was full of people in holiday mood. She could smell the smoke from disposable barbecues. She wasn't on "beach duty" – Tobben was in charge this week.

She spotted him walking towards the barbecues, talking to people. She knew exactly what he was telling them. Mostly people were good about it. This was the hottest summer anyone could remember. Olav and Sigrid were happy for the hay, but worried about the potatoes.

Ninni considered having a bath, but she wasn't in the mood. Her thoughts kept churning over and over.

She knew that keeping the baby meant she couldn't involve Jack. It wasn't his baby and whatever the relationship was, it wasn't ready for a situation like this. But that was hardly a reason to abort a baby, she thought.

It was just a summer fling, she thought. Nothing to take too seriously, nothing to get attached to or be sentimental about, and certainly nobody's heart would break. Except she felt miserable at the thought of not seeing Jack again.

You can't have everything, she thought. No matter what they said. Sometimes you had to make impossible choices. Realising that was the easy part. No matter how panicky she felt, it was up to her, and her alone. It was her decision.

She decided to call it a day. Jack had sent a text earlier, telling her he had arrived at his dad's house. She knew he was busy catching up with his family, and that would give her some extra time to figure things out.

Frikk jumped out of the boat the second she steered it alongside the pier. He sat there, panting, while she secured the boat and unlocked the engine.

'You could help, you know,' she said, heaving the engine onto the pier.

Frikk licked her face. 'Silly dog,' she said, patting his head.

The sun chased them inside the boathouse. Ninni put the engine in the box her dad had made for it, then locked the doors and walked towards the house, leaving the beach to the summer guests.

She didn't see him until she came up the hill. For a moment she thought it was Jack, and smiled. The smile faded quickly when she realised who the visitor was.

'What do you want?' she said, grabbing hold of Frikk, who growled next to her.

Karl smiled his most charming smile, the one that always got to her. Now she couldn't care less.

'I came to talk to you. I feel I owe you an explanation.'

'Well, I have no interest in your explanation, Karl. Leave.'

Karl tried to look sorry. 'I can't. The last ferry has gone to town. I have no choice now but to stay here. Are you going to make me sleep outside?'

'The weather is warm. You'll be fine.' Ninni unlocked the front door and let Frikk inside.

'Please, Ninni. Just give me a few minutes. I feel horrible because of what happened.'

Ninni narrowed her eyes. She was boiling. 'I have nothing to say to you.'

'No, but perhaps you can let me talk to you? Please. I have come all this way.'

'You being an idiot isn't my problem. Perhaps Britt has a place for you in the barn. If you're lucky.'

Karl didn't give up so easily. 'I really need to talk to you. Please, Ninni. I want to explain.'

Ninni turned her back on him and walked inside, shutting the door in his face. Suddenly the idea of having a child with him made her sick. She ran to the bathroom and threw up.

When she came out, Frikk was waiting in front of the door. She looked at him. His tail slapped the floor.

'Oh, for God's sake.' She opened the door. Karl was sitting on the step, looking pathetic. 'Fine, but this doesn't mean I'm talking to you.'

Karl followed her inside, not saying a word. Ninni nodded towards the kitchen table. 'Sit down.'

'Thank you,' he said.

Ninni put on a pot of soup from the fridge. All the hurt and the anger welled up inside her.

'I can't believe you have the nerve to come here after what you did. You know what I've been wondering about? How many other women you've used for bed and board? You're such a bastard,' she said.

She grabbed a bread knife from the drawer and had the satisfaction of seeing him shudder. The bread was fresh, and she cut a few slices.

'I know I've behaved like a shit,' Karl said. He took a piece of bread and shredded it between his fingers. 'And I'm more sorry than I could ever express.'

Ninni barely listened to him. She found a bowl in the cupboard and put it on the table. 'I'm going upstairs. You can sleep on the sofa.'

'But don't you want to talk? I've come all this way. I'm begging you.' He was serious.

Ninni looked at him properly. He looked sad and pathetic, and he still believed he could fool her.

She realised she wasn't angry with him any more. She was tired of his games and had wasted enough time and energy on him. 'You used me for two years while your wife and kids lived in Oslo. You're a sad little shit and I don't want to see or hear from you again in my life. My guess is that you're here now because your wife threw you out and you think I'll be stupid enough to take you back.'

The surprised and annoyed expression on his face told her she was right.

Ninni pointed at him. 'If you are still here when I wake up I'll have the police wait for you on the harbour in Haugesund. The first ferry leaves at six. Turn off the lights when you go to sleep.'

She whistled and Frikk came to her side at once. Without looking at Karl again, she went upstairs. He didn't come after her.

Ninni closed the bedroom door and sat down on the bed. Now what? she thought. The idea that she was having a baby with that idiot downstairs made her clench her teeth to avoid screaming.

She curled up on the bedsheet and closed her eyes. Frikk jumped up behind her. What was she going to do? What would she say to Jack? She had to make him see that whatever it was they had between them was over. Whatever it took, he needed to believe this was the end.

Jack walked up the path, exhausted from the trip. He had spent most of the night at the airport in Oslo because of a cancelled flight to Haugesund. Then, when he arrived in Haugesund, it was too early for the ferry. Someone with a boat took pity on him.

He was close to Ninni's house when he saw a man leaving. He closed the door behind him and started walking along the road. At some point he spotted Jack and nodded at him.

'*God morgen*,' he said, passing him.

Jack nodded back. '*God morgen*,' pleased with himself for saying it in Norwegian.

The man kept walking, with his hands burrowed in his pockets. He looked like he had all the burdens of the world on his shoulders.

Jack wondered who he could be. He obviously knew Ninni, otherwise he wouldn't have come out of her house. Not an islander, though. He knew all of them by now.

He knocked on the front door. Frikk barked and he could hear Ninni shushing him. Jack smiled. He had great news, and he was eager to share it with her.

Ninni opened the door with a cross expression on her face. For a second her face lit up when she saw him, then it darkened again. He leaned forward to kiss her and she pulled away.

'I'm sorry, I'm not feeling too well. Better stay away for a while,' she said.

'You look a bit worse for wear. Can I make you some tea or toast?' Jack said, hiding his disappointment.

Ninni smiled slightly. 'That would be nice. I didn't expect you until tonight,' she said when he entered the house.

'I was planning to come yesterday, but they cancelled the plane and I ended up staying at the airport in Oslo,' he said quickly.

'Sorry, that must have been uncomfortable for you,' she said.

She looked awful, he thought. Something was wrong. Jack lifted his hand to stroke her hair and she flinched. Something was definitely wrong.

'Yes, it was, but it wasn't a problem. I slept a few hours on a bench in one of the lounges.'

'And then you came here. It's nice to see you, Jack.'

She grabbed a blanket from the sofa in the living room and went into the kitchen.

Jack pointed at a chair. 'Sit down, Ninni. I'll get you some tea to settle your stomach. You should consider going to a doctor if this continues.'

'I don't like doctors,' Ninni said, pulling the blanket tighter around herself. 'All they do is give you bad news you don't want to hear.'

'Nobody like doctors, but if you're sick you go. Who was that guy leaving your house?' Jack watched her to see her reaction.

Ninni looked at him, a bit startled. 'You saw him?'

'Walked right past him. He said good morning. I said good morning. Was that Karl? It was, wasn't it? He looked miserable, by the way.'

Ninni nodded. 'He came by last night. To talk. You know, about what happened between us and all that. He wanted to explain himself and ... and the last ferry had left.'

She didn't look at him when she said it. Instead she picked at her fingernails.

Jack put the tea mug on the table in front of her. She made no attempt to take it.

'And did you talk?' Jack realised he was holding his breath.

'Yes, we did.' Ninni lifted her head. She smiled, but it was a shaky smile. Jack frowned. Something was going on, and he could clearly see that she wasn't happy about it.

'And you let him?' Jack chose his words carefully, but he also remembered how she had talked about Karl before. It had seemed like she wouldn't give the man the time of day.

'He has ... changed,' she said.

Jack felt a stab in the pit of his stomach. He suddenly knew what was coming next. He leaned against the kitchen counter, bracing himself. 'And did you believe him?'

She took a long breath. 'Yes, I did. I have known him for a long time, Jack. I know when he's sincere,' she said in a strained voice, avoiding looking at him.

Jack wanted to shake her. How the hell could she be so stupid? He didn't say it though. She looked awful enough.

Ninni finally pulled the mug of tea closer to her and folded her hands around it. 'I needed to talk to him, you see. About ... about something else.'

Jack had no idea what was going on with her, but something wasn't right. Was she lying? And if she was, why would she?

'After what he put you through I would think you'd kick him out of here,' he said.

'I ... I decided to give him a chance to explain himself. He showed up last night, and I couldn't let him spend the night in the field, now could I?' She narrowed her eyes.

Jack folded his arms across his chest. 'I'm not trying to tell you what do to, Ninni. I'm just surprised. When you told me about Karl, I got the impression you didn't want to talk to him ever again.'

Ninni sipped the tea. Jack waited. It wasn't his place to say anything. If she wanted to talk to her old boyfriend, she had every right to do so.

Finally he broke the silence. 'I'm here, Ninni. Talk to me. Tell me what's going on.'

'Maybe later,' she said.

Jack made a decision before he said something he would regret. 'Then I think I should go back to my house and get some sleep. Airports are not comfortable. See you later?' She nodded again, not saying anything. Jack looked at her. 'Are you sure nothing else happened?'

'Like what?' She looked at him then, a quick glance up.

'I don't know. You don't look well and there's something bothering you. I can stay, if you want.'

Ninni shook her head. 'That's not necessary. It's best if you go and get some rest. I'm going to do the same. Just as soon as I have thrown up again. Excuse me.'

She pushed the chair away and disappeared upstairs, her hand to her mouth. Jack looked at Frikk, who perked his ears and gave him a puzzled look.

'You and me both, Frikk.'

She had left the blanket on the floor. Jack picked it up, folded it and dropped it on the bench before he sat down at the table. He had no intention of leaving her alone when she was sick – no matter how hard she tried to push him away.

After a while he could hear her moving about on the first floor. It didn't sound as if she was going to bed. Frikk decided to show his affection and put his head on Jack's knee.

Jack stroked the soft ears. 'You probably know what's going on, don't you?' He sighed. 'And I had such good news too. But you don't care about that, do you?' he said to the dog.

Ninni suddenly appeared in the doorway. She looked even paler than before. 'I'm sorry, Jack, I should have told you right away, but I didn't know how to.'

So she had been lying. Jack waited for the explanation with a bad feeling in his stomach.

Ninni hesitated for a second, then talked so fast he almost didn't understand what she was saying. 'I'm going back to Bergen. To move in with Karl.'

That was the last thing he had expected her to say. 'I'm sorry?'

'I've made up my mind. Our summer fling is over, Jack. It's time to return to real life.' Ninni looked down and he knew she was lying.

'That's rubbish,' he said.

She smiled then – a sad smile that didn't reach her eyes. 'No, it's not. It's my decision. I hope you can respect that.'

Jack stayed seated. 'I don't believe you,' he said and didn't take his eyes off her. 'For some reason you don't want to tell me whatever is going on, and you're feeding me this bullshit. I'm a big boy, Ninni. Don't lie to me to spare my feelings. Tell me the truth. I deserve that much, don't I?'

She folded her arms over her chest with an angry look on her face. 'Fine,' she snapped. 'I'm pregnant and Karl is the father. That's why he was here. Are you happy now?'

Jack felt as if someone had punched him hard in the stomach. He forced himself to talk slowly. 'You're pregnant? How do you know?'

Ninni shook her head. 'I went to the doctor and got a test. That's why I've been ill.'

He believed her. She wouldn't lie about something like that. At least the truth was out. Jack frowned. 'So you're keeping the baby, right?'

'Yes, I am. I had an abortion when I was seventeen, Jack. It was the right decision at that point; I had no business being anyone's mum back then. And this time it's the right decision to keep the baby. I called Karl, he came here and we talked.'

'You called him? Asked him to come here?' Jack tried to wrap his head around it, but it seemed too much.

'Yes, I did. I want to do this right, Jack.'

Jack lifted a hand. 'Let me get this straight. You're pregnant with Karl's child, and you're going back to a man who cheated on both you and his wife? A man who has no moral qualms about lying to his wife and children. Why on earth would you do something so stupid?'

Ninni narrowed her eyes. 'The baby needs a father too, you know, and I don't want to do this on my own. And don't call me stupid, you idiot.'

'Well, you are beyond stupid, actually. No child deserves a bastard for a dad. I think Karl has proven beyond any doubt what kind of father he is.' Jack started pacing the floor, then stopped in front of her. 'How does Karl feel about this?'

'He was shocked at first, of course, but now he's happy about it.'

Jack thought about Karl's face. That was not the face of a happy man. 'Are you sure about that? He looked pretty depressed when I saw him.'

Ninni closed her eyes for a moment, then took a deep breath. 'Listen, Jack, this doesn't concern you. I have to do what's right for me and for the baby.'

'How can raising a child with a man like Karl be the right choice? He will be bloody useless, Ninni. Why don't you give me a chance?' Jack threw it out there before he had a chance to think about it.

Her eyes widened. 'It's not your child, Jack. What if you decide further down the road that this isn't for you anyway? And I have to explain to a child that you're not his or her real father, and that's why you're leaving?'

It stung, and it made him even more mad. 'In what universe do you believe that Karl will stay with you and the baby? You don't love him, you don't even respect him. There's nothing there to build anything on.'

Ninni rubbed her forehead. 'Karl promised to be there for us,' she said quietly.

'I bet he promised his wife and kids the same at some point,' Jack said, unable to hide the bitterness in his voice.

'There's no need to be nasty,' Ninni said.

'I'm sorry, but it doesn't make it less true. Why don't you give us a chance, Ninni?'

She looked at him now. 'I know you think you can do what your dad did. He raised you like his own child and he did a great job. But that was a different situation. You knew from the beginning he wasn't your real dad. This baby has a right to know his or her real father.'

He smiled slightly. 'Do you want me to come back in five years' time? I might, you know.'

Ninni didn't smile back. 'You're not your dad and this baby is not yours. I can't risk it.' She stepped back. 'Please, Jack. Let's end it here. I have made my decision. What you and I had was lovely, but everything has changed now.'

Jack realised he couldn't change her mind. He wasn't even sure if he wanted to. What if she was right? What if he couldn't do it? She was right on another count too. He wasn't his dad.

She moved away from the doorway and he passed without looking at her.

He could hear her locking the door behind him. She never locked the door. That was what she had said.

He pushed his hands into his pockets and walked down to the farm. When he reached the house, he stopped and looked up at Ninni's house.

Damn, he thought. He'd never got to tell her his good news. Now he had to rethink everything.

Ninni stared at the door, not quite believing what she had done – that she had lied to Jack. She bit her lower lip. Frikk came up to her, whining and trying to push his nose into her hand.

She sank down and put her arms around his neck. 'I'm not going to cry. I did this to myself, and I'm the one who can fix it. Let's go home, Frikk. I can't stay here now.'

She looked at the time. The next ferry would leave in half an hour. Plenty of time. Karl would have taken the previous one, and she wouldn't risk meeting him on board.

She would ask Olav to put the boat back into the boathouse, but not until she was back on the mainland. She didn't want anyone coming to the house when she was in this state. She would cry her eyes out, and probably beg Jack to stay.

'Let's pack,' she said.

She ran upstairs and packed her backpack in five minutes. Then she walked through the house and pulled down the blinds. Her father would come at the weekends; he would look after everything.

The pile of Magni's books on the table in the lounge stopped her. She had worked so hard to get them translated for him. Jack needed to see them.

With half an eye on the time, she sat down at the laptop and quickly wrote him a short letter. Then she copied everything over to a USB stick.

She put all of Magni's books in a carrier bag before leaving, together with the stick. Then she locked the door and hurried towards the harbour, all the while not looking at Jack's house. Just as the ferry docked, she popped into the shop and handed a surprised Alma the carrier bag.

'Give this to Jack when you see him. I have to run. Something has happened and I have to go home. I'll talk to you later,' she said to Alma before she ran out again.

Once on board the ferry, she relaxed. She could see Alma coming out of the shop and waved at her. Alma waved back. I'll call her tonight, she thought. As soon as I'm in control of myself again. I don't want her to tell Jack anything.

Hopefully he would sell up and leave for London again.

Chapter 19

Ninni opened the door to the balcony. It was small, with barely enough space for a chair and a tiny table. The summer heat had dried out the lawn in front of the apartment building. No one in Bergen could remember the last time there had been sunshine almost every day for weeks.

The small apartment felt suffocating in the heat and she longed for the cool air on the island. And, if she was honest with herself, she also longed for Jack.

Ridiculous, she thought. She put a hand on her stomach. There was barely a bump yet, but it was there. She hadn't told her father yet. It wasn't really something she could do over the phone or by text. She hadn't even told him she was back in Bergen. And then there was her mother. She would have to know as well.

Ninni smiled at the thought. Her mother wouldn't mind becoming a grandmother. Hopefully. She might even come home for a visit. Stranger things had happened.

Frikk put his nose in her hand. Ninni patted him. 'How do you think Jack is doing?'

The dog licked her hand. Ninni sighed. Two break-ups in one month and a baby on the way. That was a new record. She could only hope Jack wasn't as miserable as she was.

The summer fling with Jack had helped her get over Karl's betrayal. And, as it was just a fling, it should be easy to get over. She hoped.

She stood in the doorway for a long time, until Frikk barked.

'Yes, yes, I know. Food. I should cook something for myself too.' She chatted to the dog while she filled his bowl with dry food. In the few seconds it took him to hoover up the food, she made herself a half decent omelette.

I'll call Pappa after dinner and ask him to come over, she thought.

No time to mope over Jack; she had other matters to concern herself with now. Like buying a crib, and working out how to keep a baby alive. There were plenty of books on the subject, apparently.

She looked at Frikk. 'It's not as easy as taking care of a puppy, you know.'

Frikk barked again.

A few days after Ninni had disappeared as quickly as she had come into his life, Jack decided to return to

London. There wasn't anything keeping him on the island, and he decided a clean break would be best.

It had been a nice dream, but that was all. For a moment there, he had contemplated settling on the island – he could become a farmer and perhaps build something with Ninni. And now that was all gone.

Good thing too, he thought. He had a job back in London, a life and his family. What did he need a farm in Norway for?

He popped inside Alma's shop to say goodbye, and found Jens looking at a crate of tangerines with a puzzled expression on his face.

'Oh, *hei*, Jack.' Jens held up a peeled fruit, missing a few wedges. 'There's something wrong with these oranges.'

'They're tangerines,' Jack said.

'Tangerines? Oh, you mean clementines. But they can't be. They're so tart it burns the roof of your mouth,' Jens said.

He spotted Jack's suitcase. 'Are you leaving?'

Jack smiled. 'Yes, I'm going home. I just wanted to say goodbye.'

'But you're coming back, of course? We have got used to having you at the farm, you know,' Jens said.

'We'll see,' Jack said, trying to be diplomatic.

'Oh, I understand. Well, it's a good thing you came by. Ninni left something for you.' Jens shuffled over to the post office desk and pulled out a carrier bag. 'I don't know why she left it with us when she could have given it to you herself, but here it is.'

'What's this?' Jack couldn't think of anything Ninni might leave behind for him.

Jens smiled. 'I don't know. We're not allowed to open other people's mail. It's against the law.'

'Thank you.' Despite Jens' obvious curiosity, Jack stuffed the bag in his suitcase.

'Have you had any breakfast?' Jens didn't wait for a reply. He went over to the baked goods section and put two school buns in a small paper bag. 'Here. Alma would have my head if I sent you on your way without anything to eat.'

Jack smiled. 'Thanks. Give her my love, will you?'

'Of course. She's over at Britt's, helping with the B&B. She'll be sorry to have missed you.'

The arrival of the ferry ended the conversation, and Jack sighed with relief. Obviously Norwegians were as awkward at saying goodbye as the British, he thought.

Even so, Jens followed him out, gave him a pat on the back before he walked up the gangway and even waved when the ferry left.

Jack stayed on deck, watching as the ferry moved away. His eyes fell on the community building. It would have made a great restaurant, he thought.

And then his thoughts returned to Ninni. He didn't like that.

Chapter 20

Jack came in the door of his apartment with one carrier bag too many. He almost fell over his own suitcase, blocking the hallway.

'Watch out for the suitcase,' Holly yelled from the kitchen.

'Why is the bloody thing standing in the hallway?' Jack shook the rain off his hair.

His sister was sitting at the table with a stack of books in front of her. 'Can I borrow your suitcase?' she said, barely looking up at him.

'Why do you bother to ask me when you've already taken it?' Jack stretched his neck to see what she was looking at. It looked ... medical. 'What is that?'

Holly rubbed her eyes. 'Exams,' she said.

'Is that why you need the suitcase?' He failed to see the connection.

'Yes. I have to study this weekend, and I've rented a cottage in the Cotswolds with some friends.'

Jack put the bags on the counter. 'That sounds more like a party than a study group.'

Holly laughed. It was more of a snort. 'We all have the same exams, Jack. It will make revision easier. We help each other stay awake, for one thing.'

'Is that why you're here so early? Where's Dad?'

'He's coming later. He and Danny are fixing the roof of the shed. There's a lot of hammering and swearing. It's insane. I had to get out of there,' she said.

'I see.' He placed an apple next to her. 'Eat something. You look like a ghost.'

'Right, and you don't? At least I'm not miserable,' she said.

Jack ignored that. But she took a bite of the apple and kept reading. He smiled and started taking things out of the bags. He was cooking for the family today, and they had high expectations.

Holly leaned over and grabbed a plastic bag from the table. It was vaguely familiar. Jack looked at the carrier bag and frowned. 'Where did that come from?'

'I found it in the suitcase. How have you not cleared it out since you returned from your little island?'

'There was nothing in there that I needed,' Jack said.

Truth was, he had taken out toiletries and clothes, then shoved the whole thing in the closet when he'd come home, too depressed to look at it. But he would never admit that to his baby sister.

'I forgot about this,' he said.

'Liar.' Holly tapped at it with her pencil. 'What is it?'

'I don't know. I never looked inside,' he said slowly.

Holly smiled. 'Aren't you curious? Don't be such a chicken, Jack. Open it.'

'Stop your nagging.' He wasn't sure what to expect when he saw Magni's exercise books in there. In the bottom of the bag he discovered an envelope with a USB stick.

'Hand me my computer, Holly,' he said and pointed at the end of the table.

Holly grabbed it and handed it to him. She looked worried now. 'Is it something bad?'

Jack shook his head. 'I doubt it,' he said and put in the stick.

A row of documents popped up on the screen. Eleven in all – one for each of the exercise books he had asked Ninni to translate. The last document was simply called *Letter*. He hesitated a moment before curiosity won and he opened the document.

Dear Jack, I'm sorry it had to end like this. I hope it doesn't ruin the island for you. I finished translating Magni's books. I'm sure she would have loved for you to read them. Love, Ninni

No, not love, Jack thought while he opened the first document. He tried not to think about her too much.

'I'll be damned,' he muttered, reading the text.

'What is it?' Holly tried to look over his shoulder.

Jack smiled. The contents were a curious mixture of a diary, recipes and descriptions of both the farm and Agnar. 'These are one of the diaries my grandmother wrote. Ninni translated them for me.'

Holly smiled. 'That's nice,' she said and went back to her books.

Jack sank down on one of the chairs and started reading. He had no idea what to expect.

In the older books, from when Agnar was a boy, every year, on Agnar's birthday, Magni described how much he had grown, how he was getting on at school and the work he did on the farm. Small things, daily chores, but important to her.

And then there were the other things. Recipes for meals she made. So many different ways of preparing fish. Christmas dishes. No wonder Agnar made "*fenalår*" and cured ham; his mother taught him how.

The recipe for Magni's venison sauce made his mouth water. He remembered that Tobben told him they hunted deer and elk in the mountains every autumn. Perhaps he could introduce venison at the restaurant. Now that he was a full partner, he had a lot more influence in the running of the kitchen.

In the last diary Magni wrote about her husband's passing: Agnar was heartbroken, but refused to talk to her about it. Instead he left on a ship. To meet my mum, Jack thought.

Ninni had also translated letters from Agnar to his mother.

'Wow,' he said.

Holly looked up. 'What?'

Jack waved his hand and frowned as he read on. Agnar had stayed away from the island for a few years, leaving his mother to tend to the farm. Apparently she had managed fine without him. In one letter he told her she didn't have to thank him for sending his wages to help with expenses.

'It's letters from ... from Agnar to his mother,' he said when Holly poked him.

'From your father to your grandmother,' she said.

'I don't know what Agnar was, but he was never my father,' Jack said.

'So, he was more like a sperm donor?' Holly laughed when he scowled at her.

'Let me finish reading, please,' he said.

'Sure, but you have to let me read it too,' Holly said.

'Uh,' Jack said.

Magni had lived for Agnar's letters. He'd responded kindly when she'd told him he needed to get married, have children who could one day take over the farm. She was sad he seemed unable to settle down. She must have told him her worries because Agnar had responded in a letter, saying perhaps it would happen one day.

Magni would take walks on the island and picture

herself watching Agnar's children play on the beach. It was heartbreaking. Jack was moved and angry with Agnar at the same time.

This is stupid, he thought. These people mean nothing to me. They are strangers. They are both gone. Magni never knew about me, and Agnar never wanted to know me.

Mental, he thought.

'Are you crying?' Holly interrupted his thoughts.

Jack frowned. 'No, of course not. Don't be daft.'

'Well, something is affecting you.' Holly took one of the original notebooks and opened it. She let her finger follow the spiky letters. 'It's a diary, right?'

'Sort of. More like a farmer's log book that she wrote in occasionally. There are so many recipes in there. And then there's the letters Agnar wrote to his mother. He was her only son and she loved him. She wanted him to have a family and to be happy.' He smiled. 'It's weird, isn't it?'

'A bit,' Holly admitted. She handed the book back to him. 'But mostly it's nice and sad. I'm sorry you found out about them too late. I'm sure they would have been nicer to you than our lot.'

Jack closed the computer. Magni's books brought back his fascination with the island. He realised he missed the place.

'You have a funny look on your face,' Holly said.

Jack shrugged. 'It brings back memories of the island.'

'Why did you leave? You never really told us about it,' Holly said.

'It's not important.'

Holly looked at him with a serious light in her eyes. 'I think it is. What about Ninni? You never speak about her either.'

'You know why. She's back with the father of her baby,' Jack said.

'Are you sure?' Holly raised her eyebrows.

'What do you mean?' Jack stood up from the table, not really wanting to talk about Ninni. 'Of course I'm sure.'

Holly didn't give up so easy. 'Well, you told us she had left that guy because he cheated on her, and that he was a proper bastard. Why would she go back to him? I don't understand.'

'Neither do I. But she did, and that was it.'

Holly turned around in her chair and studied him while he shuffled vegetables around on the counter.

'Why are you here, Jack?'

'I've invited you and Danny and Dad for dinner, haven't I?' He took one of the chef's knives from the rack and started cutting tomatoes.

'No, that's not what I mean. You so miss this strange little island of yours. Do you remember how miserable you were with Roland and Fedra before you left? Before you knew about the farm and the island? You were so fed up with the place, with everything, really.'

Jack remembered the relief when he'd left the restaurant behind. And after he came back things hadn't changed much. He didn't feel any triumph over becoming a partner either.

'Yeah, I remember,' he said.

Holly pointed at her books. 'Do you know why I do this?'

'If you're going to preach to me or share snippets of your great wisdom, I'm not interested.' Jack smiled at her.

'My point is that I work this hard because all I ever wanted was to be a doctor. You always wanted your own restaurant, and you're not getting it here in London. Roland may have made you a partner, but you're not feeling like one, are you? I can see it. Why can't you?'

'It doesn't matter any more,' he said.

'Then why haven't you sold the farm?' Holly wagged her finger at him. 'You know I'm right.'

'I don't want to talk about it, Holly. Now, let me cook in peace.' Jack shoved Magni's books back in the bag and put it on one of the bookshelves.

Holly shook her head then returned to her books. 'Men,' she muttered.

Jack ignored her and started preparing for dinner. He didn't want her to be right, but she was. He knew she was.

Not that it was Holly's business, but he hadn't gone

for Haldorsen's offer and had asked Mats to look for a better buyer, someone who would look after the farm.

Perhaps it was time to rethink that.

Ninni rubbed her lower back and pulled a face. The shop overwhelmed her. It was filled with everything a baby could possibly need, and then a lot more she was convinced it didn't need. There seemed to be millions of stuffed animals and cute accessories.

She could see her father checking out prams. He had the same expression of amazement he had when he looked at new cars.

'Pappa, what are you doing?'

Petter beamed at her. 'We want the type of pram that grows with the baby. So that you don't have to buy a new one every time she hits a new milestone. Look how practical they are.'

Ninni looked at the pram he was pointing at. 'Why do they all look like they are made for Formula One drivers? Do they expect the baby to drive on the motorway?'

Petter chuckled. 'You should have seen the pram we had for you. It was chunky and smelled of mould. Your grandmother had it in the garage for twenty years. I want you to have a good pram, a nice one for when you take her outside. Like this one, I think.' He pointed at a pink pram amongst the gleaming wonders.

Ninni checked the price tag. 'Pappa, are you insane? For one thing it's insanely expensive.'

He looked insulted. 'But it's my gift to you. My granddaughter will be safe and look stylish.'

'Yeah, well, I'm not getting a pink pram. You can forget about that.'

Now he was disappointed. 'But we're having a girl!'

'Still, no.' Ninni shook her head.

Petter wasn't ready to give up. 'But it's lovely. It will stand out amongst all the other boring prams.'

Ninni rolled her eyes at him. 'We live in Bergen, not in Spain. And in case you haven't noticed, we're back to normal weather conditions. Summer is over. It's September, Pappa.' Ninni waved her arm towards the window. The rain was pouring down outside.

Petter looked disappointed. 'Ah, well. A navy one will have to do then.'

They chose a more sensible one that, according to Petter, she would be able to take apart and turn it into a car seat. Or a backpack. Ninni wasn't sure. But it would have to do.

'Now, let's get the rest of everything.' Petter looked around with a greedy glint in his eyes. 'Where do you want to start?'

A couple came in from the rain, laughing and shaking water off their raincoats. The woman smiled at Ninni, a shared feeling of anticipation, perhaps. She held hands with her partner, who fixed his eyes on the super prams. Obviously having a flashy pram was a man thing, Ninni thought.

The partner looked a bit like Jack and her heart jumped.

Petter seemed to sense her moment of sadness. 'You okay, sweetie?'

Ninni turned away from the couple and smiled at him. 'I'm tired. Can we do the rest another day?'

'Not a chance. We're here, let's get it done. You've postponed it too many times already, my girl. It's now or the baby will end up sleeping in a cardboard box.' He pointed at a chair. 'Sit down and relax. Hold onto the pram. Leave this to me. I have done this before, you know.'

Within a matter of minutes, he had placed two wire baskets filled with colourful toys, bedclothes, pacifiers and a lot of things she had no idea what they were next to the chair. She was exhausted just looking at him.

The baby suddenly kicked and the surprise made her laugh. She put her hand on her stomach again, and another little kick hit her. It was such a strange sensation.

'What's wrong?' Petter appeared in front of her with a fluffy yellow duck in his hand, for some reason.

'Nothing. Active baby, that's all.'

He beamed at her. 'That's what we want. She's getting a lot more active now.'

Ninni nodded. 'Two more months until she's here.'

'And that's why we are here, in this store. Here, take this.' He handed her the duck. 'What else do we need?'

'A crib,' Ninni said. 'And please, let's not get one that's too complicated to put together. You know how you get.'

He pretended to look insulted. 'I have no idea what you're talking about.'

'I've seen you with bookshelves,' Ninni said.

At the sales desk the woman smiled at Petter, then let her eyes move over Ninni with a tiny glint of judgement, obviously making a creepy assumption.

Ninni smiled sweetly. 'My father is helping me shop for baby equipment,' she said. 'We are looking for a crib that's not too complicated to put together.'

'But safe. I don't want my granddaughter to fall out of it,' Petter said with a huge smile.

The woman's face lit up. 'I can help you with that.'

Ninni let Petter do the talking. He seemed to enjoy it a lot more than she did and, besides, her back ached again.

The couple walked past her again. She was holding the same duck and waved it at Ninni.

Ninni almost burst into tears, then scolded herself for being stupid. Hormones, she thought. It had nothing to do with shopping for baby supplies with her father.

She wondered how Jack was getting on. Was he doing better? It seemed like it; she had seen online that he was back at the restaurant in London.

She put a hand on her stomach again. It was better this way, she thought. They would be fine, the two of them.

Paul was telling a long-winded story about a woman who came into the garage. 'I was impressed, actually. She knew the difference between ABS brakes and hand-brakes.'

Holly rolled her eyes and made Jack laugh. He leaned back in his chair. The food went down faster than Frikk's dinner, and he felt good watching them.

'You're quiet,' Paul said suddenly.

Holly shook her head. 'He's pining for his island, Dad. Did you know that he has a bunch of exercise books – log books, he calls them – written by his grandmother? They were in his suitcase.'

'You never mentioned that,' Paul said to Jack.

'I ... forgot about them,' he said.

'I see. That's easily done, I guess.' Paul gave him one of his looks.

Jack smiled. 'It's not a big deal, Dad. I was tired from the trip.'

'Is that why you have barely mentioned why you left the island since you returned?' Paul put his elbows on the table and looked at him.

Holly chimed in. 'Ask him about *her*, Dad. He never talks about Ninni either.'

'I'm not a talker,' Jack said.

That made Paul roll his eyes. 'Tell us. We're your family. We all thought that you had found someone far better suited for you than that snooty Fedra.'

Jack sighed. 'You know what happened, Dad. Ninni is having a baby with her partner. We decided it was a summer fling. There's really nothing to talk about.'

Holly did. 'I bet he hasn't told you that the baby daddy is a bastard. I bet she's not even with him any more.'

'Holly, please stop. You sound like a five-year-old telling on me.' Jack started to clear the table. 'It doesn't matter now, does it?'

Paul looked at him with a strange smile. 'Did I ever tell you how I met your mum?'

'Yes, it was love at first sight,' Jack and Holly said at the same time.

'Well, but did I also tell you that the first time Rosie brought Jack to meet me, he asked me if I was his new daddy?'

'The first time he met you? That's cheeky.' Holly laughed at Jack.

'Oh, yes, I think it was his way of asking me what my intentions were.' Paul shook his head. 'Problem was, it scared Rosie. She pulled away. She said she couldn't involve me in Jack's life in case it didn't work out.'

'What did you say?' Holly was mesmerised.

'I said, what if it did? What if I really was Jack's new

dad? And I also told her she was an idiot if she didn't give us a chance. She told me not to call her an idiot.' Paul grinned. 'And, just like that, I was a dad.'

Jack started loading the dishwasher.

Later, after dinner, after they had left, full of food and beer and wine, Jack went for a walk.

He entered the big park behind the apartment complex and walked among the trees. It was September warm, a touch of Indian summer, and he hoped it would clear his thoughts.

There were plenty of people walking their dogs, even this late. Quite a few of the pups came over to greet him, to sniff his hand and wag their tails and demand belly rubs. None of them looked like Frikk. Mostly lapdogs or retrievers, from what he could see.

Eventually he sat down on a bench close to a small duck pond. He missed the view of the ocean from the cairn on the island. Ninni had called it a mountain, but it wasn't, not really. But from the cairn he had been able to see all the way out to the little islet where his sheep grazed.

There were possibilities out there, he thought. The community building could be turned into an excellent bistro. The produce of the island, the things that grew out there, the things that people made – if he put all those together he could create great food.

Wow, he thought. That's mad. That's really, really mad.

For the longest time he sat there, staring at the duck pond.

He wondered how the sheep were doing, and if Olav took good care of them. He wondered if Tobben and Britt managed the meat production on their own. And, more than anything, he wondered how Ninni was doing. If she was with Karl. He didn't want to believe that any more. Holly was right. She would never go back to Karl.

When he finally stood up and walked back down to the apartment he felt calm for the first time in months. All the stress melted away.

Suddenly everything seemed obvious. He found himself smiling.

Damn, it felt good.

Chapter 21

J ack looked around the block of flats. It was modern and concrete. Not at all like the wooden houses he had seen everywhere else driving up the hill, although Bergen was a proper city, with lots of concrete buildings, cars and people. No wonder Ninni wanted to stay on the island, he thought.

He rubbed his hands together. It was bloody cold. The wind howled around the corner of the building and he pulled the woollen hat down over his ears. There were already quite a few Christmas lights in the windows, which was strangely comforting.

Jack read the names on the door tags until he found hers. Then he rang the bell. The buzzer opened the door almost immediately and he slipped in. Inside, he shook his head, happy to be away from the wind.

Ninni lived on the third floor, and Jack took the steps two at a time.

Outside her door, he hesitated. What if he was wrong? What if she still didn't want anything to do with him?

What if Karl opened the door? He frowned. No, he knew better than that. Alma had told him.

Besides, it would be worth the risk, no matter what happened. Not doing anything wasn't really an option. He lifted his hand to knock when he heard screaming through the door. That did not sound good.

Before he managed to knock again, however, the door opened and Ninni stood there, holding a howling baby. She looked a total mess. Her hair was plastered to her face, there were stains on the T-shirt and she had dark circles under her eyes.

'You,' she said. 'What are you doing here?'

Jack didn't have chance to say anything before she burst into tears. Without hesitating, he entered the flat and closed the door behind him. He held out his arms.

Ninni shook her head. 'I'm revolting. Please go away.'

'True, but you are also lovely. Hand me the baby.'

For a second he thought she would refuse, but then she put the bundle in his arms. He felt the weight of the tiny girl and rocked her a little. She kept howling, but Jack tickled her chin and the action seemed to surprise her. She hiccupped and stopped.

'How did you do that?' Ninni stared at him.

'I speak baby,' he said, attempting a joke.

Ninni shook her head. 'What?'

'You're not a *Doctor Who* fan then. Well, we'll work around that. Now, you don't look like you have slept in weeks. Have a shower, get some sleep. We'll be fine.'

318

Jack kept rocking the baby, who stared at him with those blue eyes all new babies seemed to have.

'What are you doing here, Jack?' Ninni looked like she was about to cry again.

'What's her name? Alma didn't tell me.'

'I can't make up my mind. My mother thinks I should name her after her, which I refuse to do.' Ninni rubbed her head. 'There are so many names to choose from, it makes my head hurt.'

'That's not a problem. We'll think of one together. She's absolutely perfect, by the way. Well done.'

Ninni looked at the baby, then at him. 'Why are you here?' she asked again.

Jack put a hand on her cheek. 'Because I love you and if you weren't so revolting right now I'd kiss you. Go on, have a shower. I bet you haven't had one in days.'

The baby cooed. Jack smiled. 'See? We'll be fine.'

Ninni rubbed her eyes. 'You're mad, and you're right. I do need to get clean.'

She shuffled into the bathroom and Jack smiled at the baby.

'What are you fretting about? You should be asleep, giving your poor mum a much-needed rest.'

He walked with her, listening to the shower running. The baby kept looking at him. He knew she wasn't really wondering who he was; she was just a couple of weeks old.

'I wonder what you're thinking,' he said.

He put his finger close to her hand and she gripped it with those tiny fingers, surprisingly hard. 'I think we'll get along just fine.'

'Where did you learn how to do that?' Ninni came out of the bathroom wearing a bathrobe and towelling her hair.

'Learn what?'

'She's settled. She has been crying for hours, and I had no idea what to do with her. When you rang the doorbell, I was sure it was my neighbour coming to complain.'

'When Danny was born, my mum became ill shortly afterwards. She was in and out of the hospital and she didn't have the strength to care for him as much as she wanted to. Dad and I took over. I didn't mind. Danny was easy. Holly was the tough one. She was four and so jealous of the baby she would spit at him.'

Ninni laughed. 'I like her already.'

She came over to him and put a hand on the baby's head. 'I had no idea a baby would be so much work. I had convinced myself it would be like having another puppy. Boy, was I wrong.'

She looked at him, properly this time, and asked him yet again, 'Why are you here, Jack? And I want a straight answer, if you don't mind.'

'I came to bring you both back to the island. Back home,' he added to make sure she understood him.

She didn't appear to understand anything he said. 'I'm too tired for this. I haven't had more than a couple of hours' sleep since she was born.'

Jack watched her while she flopped down on the sofa and pulled a blanket over herself. He guessed he had to wait until she woke up again.

'I love you too, you idiot,' she muttered.

'Good. Then I guess we return to the island. It's all ready for both of you. I found an old cot in the attic and repainted it. You wouldn't believe what I found on the back of it. The names of all the babies who have slept in it. Agnar was the last one. So, when you decide on the name of this one, we'll put her name on there as well. She'll like that when she gets older.'

He was talking to himself. The baby slept, and so did Ninni. Jack sat down at the end of the sofa. It was fine. The important thing was that they were going home together. He fished out his phone, took a picture of the baby and sent it to his dad. It was time he knew he was a grandad.

Ninni woke up with a jolt. For the smallest of moments she had no idea what she was doing on the sofa.

She sat up. The baby. Where was the baby? She looked at the sofa with her body frozen in fear. Had she fallen asleep on top of her? Relief rushed through her. No, Jack had her. Jack was here and he had the baby.

She stood up and tied the belt around the bathrobe. Rolling her head, she heard popping in her neck. That had been the best sleep in a month, she thought.

Ninni stopped in the kitchen doorway. It smelled divine in there. Jack had the baby sitting in her carry cot while he was cooking something. He talked to her, telling her what he was doing. The baby followed every word he said.

'She's a bit young for cooking lessons,' Ninni said.

Jack looked over his shoulder. His face lit up. 'No, she's not. I'm making an imprint on her brain. This way, she'll connect me with good food.'

Ninni came closer. She couldn't believe he was here, in her kitchen, taking care of the baby. And, by the look of it, taking care of her far better than she'd managed.

'What are you making?'

'You didn't have much in here, apart from eggs and cheese, and some questionable milk.'

'Whatever it is, it smells good.' Ninni drew her breath in. 'Jack, I don't understand. Why did you come?'

'I told you. I have come to take you home.'

'I don't need you to rescue me, and I am home.'

Jack pointed at the table. 'Yes, I know that, but you are only really at home on the island. And also I came to apologise,' he said.

'No, you didn't do anything wrong. That's all on me. I should have told you the truth, but I chickened out.

I didn't really know how to.' Ninni talked so fast, her words jumbled.

'Yes, you should, but I should never have believed you would go back with what's-his-face. That was my mistake. I should have been here, with you.' Jack pointed at one of the kitchen chairs. 'Sit down, please.'

She was too overwhelmed to protest. He put a plate in front of her. 'Eat. You need sustenance.'

'What does this mean? Are you staying on the island now? Have you given up London?'

Jack smiled. 'Yes, I have. I'm opening a restaurant on the island, in the old "sea house". I have investors and everything. We are going to serve local produce. Good food all through summer.'

'And the farm? Are you a farmer now?' Ninni couldn't help smiling at his plans.

'Not really. Olav is taking over the fields, but I'm keeping the sheep. I like them.'

The baby made noises and Ninni looked over at her. She was playing with her fingers.

'I can't get over how tiny she is,' she said and took a bite of the omelette. 'She's a couple of weeks premature, but she's doing so well. It's hard to believe.'

'I know. Barely a handful of a human. She likes me, you know. We had a great time while you were snoring on the sofa.'

'Yes, I remember. You speak baby.' She looked at him.

'You talk as if this is going to be easy, Jack. It's not something you can do on a whim.'

Jack shrugged. 'I'm not. I have thought about nothing since I left.'

'Listen, the plan was always to take care of her by myself. Karl doesn't even know about her, and that's how I want it. But you don't have to do this, Jack.'

Jack looked at her. 'I'm not an impulsive person, Ninni. Not at all, and you and her are a package deal. My dad did it with me, and he had a much more difficult time since I was five years old when my mother married him. He taught me that it makes no difference. That the dad is the one who is there. It's not a big deal. Adoptive parents do it all the time, and they love their kids the same.'

Jack moved the baby's chair closer to himself and sat down. 'Ninni, eat.'

Ninni took a bite. She swallowed and nodded. 'Good. I'm not getting in a car with you, you know, and certainly not with the baby. You're not safe.'

Before she finished the sentence, he leaned over and kissed her. 'Your dad will be here in an hour. I promised him we would be ready. Baby and all.'

Ninni started to laugh. She was shaking with laughter. The baby looked at her, startled by the sound. Jack raised his eyebrows.

'I'm glad you came,' she said finally.

'So am I.' Jack smiled. 'Did you know that there's no

salt and vinegar crisps in this country? Like in the entire country?'

'You're mad. You know that, right?'

Jack grinned 'Whatever it takes.'

THE END

Acknowledgements

When I was five, I wanted to be an artist. I had no idea what that was, but that was my answer whenever someone asked me what I wanted to be. By the time I was 14 I had read my way through my local library and written a novel – and put it in a closet somewhere. I lived in a small west-coast town and publishers existed in a place far away from my life. Probably on Mount Olympus or Asgard or some other strange place.

After 25 years as a writer, I know a bit more. I know that it's not possible even for the most solitary writer to work in a vacuum. You need help to get your manuscript, your *baby*, out in the world. The generosity I have met on this journey has been overwhelming and I have so many to thank.

First, I want to thank Charlotte Ledger and her magnificent team at One More Chapter. I'm forever grateful to Charlotte for not liking anything I sent her, and for asking me if I wanted to write a contemporary romance set in Norway instead.

I want to thank editor and writer Julia Williams for putting me in contact with Charlotte and as such getting the snowball rolling.

Thanks goes to my lovely proofreader/editor Sue Davison, who helped me weed out all the things I thought were proper English, but weren't. Thank you to Clare Abbott who also proofread the manuscript – it's scary writing in a foreign language! Most of this book was written in her lovely apartment in London. I had a wonderful time there.

One of the first things I did when I moved to Wales for two years, was join the Romantic Novelists' Association. The writers in the Association, and the brilliant and talented writers in my South and West Wales chapter, made me feel welcome from the first moment. Probably the best writers association there is.

Thank you also to my Aunt Berit who reads everything I write, even in English, and thinks it's *quite good*, so there you go.

And last – with all my love and gratitude to Maria and Anan who has supported me all these years, never giving up on me even when I was whining the most and pushing me to be the best I can be.

Dear reader, I hope you enjoy my attempt at making Nordic less noir and to show you how romantic my country actually can be.